XPERTS:

The Paranet

Hermann Maurer

Translated from the German by
Wolfgang Wendligner and Douglas Balog

BookLocker.com, Inc.

Booklocker.com, Inc.
2004

Visit the Website www.iicm.edu/Xperts for the latest on new books in the XPERTS collection!

Preface to "Xperts: The Paranet"

This is one of the novels in the XPERTS Collection, a collection of novels that I am coordinating. I am also author of this particular book, "The Paranet". However, other writers from all over the world contribute books to the XPERTS Collection, following an outline agreed upon between the authors and me, thus making sure that the books fit into a general 'master plan'. I am reading and editing each of the books as they progress.

Each novel is completely self-contained, yet there is some coherence due to a set of persons that appear in each of the novels at some stage, usually playing a pivotal role. The books in the collection are an unusual mixture of adventure, human emotions, supernatural powers ('parabilities'), science fiction with glimpses into the future, and all this interwoven with often detailed descriptions of interesting places from across the world, be it USA, Canada, the Arctic, Europe with its many different environments, Brazil, Pacific Islands, Australia, New Zealand, Africa, India, Bali, La Reunion, Borneo... you name it!

Some of the books have been written originally in English, others in German, but they are generally available in at least those two languages. I want to thank all my friends for their continuing support, the Austrian publisher Freya and the US Publisher Booklocker for excellent cooperation, and my US agent Dr. Andrew Burt for his endless patience.

An early version of this book has been read by a number of friends, providing invaluable feedback. I am sorry that I have not been able to take up all suggestions, but this book would not be what it is without (in alphabetic order) 'strategic' suggestions from Lisa Maurer, Helmut Pauer for his supportive research, Thorsten Ries for many corrections and Guenter Schreier for numerous improvements. Remaining mistakes and inconsistencies are my fault. And let me also state very explicitly that all persons are fictional and have no counterpart in real life.

However, most of the geographical descriptions are true to reality, or at least were true, when I was there.

Send me some feedback, positive or negative, to hmaurer@iicm.edu, will you!

Enjoy the book!

Hermann Maurer, Graz / Austria, June 2004

1 Breakdown in Graz

Graz, Austria
Sunday June 9, 2080, 5:00 a.m.

Karl tosses restlessly in his bed. A strange feeling is growing inside him that something is amiss; finally, this uneasiness breaks through the wall of his sleep.

When he opens his eyes, Karl can just make out the edges and corners of his room by the glow of his dim night-light. The timer-activated world-windows are still dark. The air is thick and warmer than usual. Surprised, Karl puts on his XP[1]. The glasses automatically turn on their infrared lamp, which allows Karl to view everything around him clearly, albeit only in shades of gray. Nothing seems to be unusual: Christina, his young wife, lies sleeping beside him. She has shed the blanket that covered her earlier. He can see her beautiful, gently bent, naked back and how it continues into her hips and the round cheeks of her buttocks, which in turn give way to her long thighs and calves. Karl feels a wave of affection. He still loves his lively, temperamental wife, not only because of her looks, which have not changed much since he first met her at the annual ball of the Graz University of Technology, but more for her elegance. For example, how she knows how to dress and make herself up for a big night or how interesting she looks in her doctor's scrubs when she rushes out of the OP after some difficult surgery. And even when she jumps into her beloved Greek sea with the light-heartedness of a young girl, all these qualities combine to deepen the mutual affection they share. For one moment Karl considers snuggling up to her, but he is kept back by the XP's impatience and his own uneasiness.

---

[1] XP (computer expert) is a further developed e-helper (see "Xperts: The Paradoppelganger"). XP is a combination of a highly developed computer and a communication device, which contains a huge library, and an array of sensors, including a camera and a microphone. It allows for almost perfect telepathic communication with its wearer.

'What's the matter, XP?' asks Karl wordlessly.

'As far as I can tell, all computer network and electrical devices in and outside the house have collapsed.'

Karl is irritated. 'So how come the night light is still on?'

'That's only the emergency power from the fuel cell. The situation is rather unusual indeed. The ventilation system should also be working, but apparently some of the regulatory systems must've shut down as well. I myself have also been affected; I can no longer communicate with other XPs. I should still be able to contact XPs and electronic devices nearby, but even such rudimentary and antiquated technologies[2] are nonfunctional at the moment.

'How is that possible? How can such technology just suddenly fail?'

'Of course, it's not the physical fundamentals that have failed. Somehow, the programs that allow for wireless communication have been destroyed, together with many controlling devices. So let me warn you, I cannot even open the doors for you in the usual manner.'

'Why didn't you wake me earlier?' Karl asks accusingly.

'The network collapsed at 4:34. I was also very confused, at first, having been suddenly cut off from the entire world. My sensors even stopped providing me with data and it took me a while to start the necessary programs. Additionally, I would probably have woken up Christina as well. In fact, I have experienced short-lived network collapses before, but I have to admit that this is by far the most dramatic and extensive in the past several decades. When I finally decided to wake you, I realized that you were already on the verge anyway.'

'It must be daytime already. I think I'll have a look outside.'

'Yes, that sounds like a good idea, but I'm afraid you'll have to take the emergency exit. By the way, the elevator doesn't work either.'

Quietly, Karl exits the bedroom into the hallway, which, like the living rooms, is only illuminated by the sparse emergency lighting. None of the automatic lights turn on, as they should.

---

[2] 'Blue Tooth' technology was already in use by the late 1990s.

2

When Karl approaches the door to the foyer, the XP shouts out a warning. But it comes too late. With considerable impact, Karl collides with the door that normally opens automatically.

'I guess I'll have to lose some old habits,' Karl realizes, feeling his forehead for the inevitable bump.

Karl has no difficulties ascending through the emergency exit. The hatch gives him no trouble either. He soon stands in the middle of the field under which the house lies.

Over the last forty years, houses have mostly been built underground for several reasons[3]. Both the heating and cooling have proven to be more energy efficient that way. In addition, the near nuclear war between India and Pakistan, which was somehow miraculously avoided, could not prevent more and more countries from acquiring atomic weapons. Since then, people have had to learn to live with this threat.

For several decades, "world windows", screens that look like windows but are actually connected to cameras viewing the outside world, have become affordable. They alleviate the feeling of living in a bunker. In the beginning, it was considered tacky to have a living room with one window showing live images from a beach in Hawaii, another with a Himalayan mountain, and a third showing an Austrian waterfall, but this eventually became more and more fashionable. After all, it is possible to change these views whenever you prefer to experience a different setting.

Around 2040, underground houses were also constructed for those people who suffered badly from the increasing air pollution. Only years later did new methods of energy production ease this problem.

Karl now stands in the middle of his 800 square meter garden, which would otherwise be mostly taken up by a house and garage. It has been normal for many decades to build underground garages for Mollers[4] as well. The XP soon informs

---

[3] See " Xperts: The Beginning"; Chapter: The Underground House
[4] Flying cars that have been universal as a primary form of transportation since 2030 (See "Xperts: The Paradoppelganger" and www.moller.com.)

Karl that none of the Mollers, which usually provide automatic point-to-point transportation via satellite control, are currently functioning.

Karl enjoys his view from the Rosenhain over his hometown of Graz. It almost looks like one of those nineteenth century engravings: all the beautiful houses and the old city are unchanged. Many of the newer buildings that were considered eyesores have been lowered underground. In addition to this familiar sight, there is another factor that Karl especially relishes: no Mollers spoil the morning calm. Normally, there would be thousands of them buzzing around, but today the early summer morning feels fresh, the birds are singing, and everything seems to be peaceful; but somehow Karl cannot help feeling that this is just the proverbial calm before the storm.

He rushes back down the emergency passage into his apartment. He dresses quickly but quietly, being careful not to wake Christina.

'XP, leave a message on Christina's XP. Tell it that I had to go see my friend Johann about the collapse of the network.'

'Sorry, Karl, but as I mentioned earlier, I'm not able to communicate with any other XPs at the moment.'

More and more, it begins to dawn on Karl how unusual this situation really is: if this goes on for a long period, then there will be a massive and possibly worldwide problem. He grabs a piece of paper and writes a note to Christina. Finally it pays off that both Christina and he picked "Reading and Writing" as an elective back at school. Otherwise, it would be really difficult to leave her a message without a computer.

On his bicycle, Karl rides down into the city to see his friend. Johann lives in one of the old aboveground houses not far from the center of the city. Apparently, no one around here has yet noticed the collapse of the network. Both Johann and his wife are very surprised that someone awakens them at such an early hour. But once they see Karl's worried face, they realize that something serious is afoot. Karl soon tells them everything he knows.

Johann tries the light switch, the XPs, the 3-D entertainment system, and the microwave oven. Nothing works. The refrigerator has almost defrosted, and only hot water, not cold, is coming through the pipes.

Karl explains. "The cold water is pumped here and the pump doesn't work either. However, there is still some hot water in the boiler under the roof, and it's flowing because a valve is letting the air in. But the water is slowly cooling."

Johann becomes very thoughtful. "So you're saying that the whole net has been down since 4:34, for over an hour, and that our XPs can't receive any GPS[5] info? And you're saying that it's not the fault of the XPs, but that the entire electromagnetic spectrum is no more than static? I can't believe this! What really gets me is that I seriously can't see that such a massive breakdown will be repaired in a snap. Optimistically speaking, it'll take at least several days until the whole thing is back to anything resembling normality."

This vexes Karl. After all, Johann is a highly acclaimed computer scientist at the Graz University of Technology and knows what he is talking about. But Johann is also a caffeine addict and has not yet had his first cup of coffee. "How about this: We'll all sit down and discuss the situation over a nice pitcher of coffee," Karl suggests.

Johann's wife disappears into the kitchen only to return several minutes later with bread, butter, marmalade, wurst, cheese, cakes and orange juice. "Sorry guys, no electricity, no coffee".

While the three of them nod understandingly, the doorbell rings. Johann opens the door. It is Christina holding two thermos pitchers in her hands. "I thought you might need some help with the coffee."

"Did you wake up right after I left?" asks Karl.

"Well, my sixth sense told me that something must be wrong when my husband leaves the bed at 5 a.m. without even kissing me good-bye."

---

[5] GPS stands for global positioning system. In 2080, every point on the Earth can be located to the centimeter via parallel and independent systems.

"But how did you make that coffee without any electricity?" Johann wants to know.

"I guess workaholics like you guys have never heard of camping stoves." Suddenly Christina becomes serious. "Do you know any more now?"

The other three shake their heads. During breakfast Johann elaborates. "We can be pretty certain that, without a net for several days, we'll soon have to face serious problems here in Graz and in the other larger cities."

Karl interrupts him. "But why are you so pessimistic? Maybe everything will be just fine in a couple of hours."

"Trust me, I really hope it'll be like that. But the longer I think about it, the more serious this situation seems to me to be. I just had a look at my old laptop, which for sentimental reasons I still use once in a while. It has a fuel cell and should be able to work for at least a month without an external power source. But for some reason, it stopped working at exactly 4:43, even though it wasn't even on line at that time. This means that some kind of virus must've been activated at this time; you could say a virus with a time switch. I must've imported this virus a long time ago because I haven't been on line with this laptop for months. We also know that someone tried to destroy all the XPs' programs. I really doubt this was caused by a freak accident. A powerful group is behind this, but as to why, I don't know. Just thank God it only partially succeeded. So we're facing a really serious problem. All the power plants and power distribution devices, which are controlled by computers, have shut down. In order to get those working again, we need computers. But computers need electricity too, and those that can be equipped with batteries or fuel cells seem to have been infected with special viruses. It's the old chicken-or-the-egg problem: to supply power we need computers, but computers require electricity. And on top of this, we're facing a new and very dangerous virus. You know, our XPs are generally considered to be completely virus proof, and that's why I think that we'll be without a net, maybe for weeks to come. This will definitely lead to serious problems, especially in the bigger cities."

"Just imagine: most families will be without water. In the long run, there will be no way to keep the sewage system operating, we'll only be able to cook over open fire or with camping equipment, so how many people will be able to cook for long? Most of the stored food, especially the meat and frozen vegetables, will go bad, in our homes as well as the restaurants. Shopping will be very difficult: all the Mollers, and Moller-busses will be standing still. And don't forget, it's usually the XPs that pay for our shopping, but they're no longer able to function in the way they were developed. They can no longer communicate with any other XPs or electronic devices. Even when food can be delivered, we'll face enormous difficulties when it comes to paying.[6] Even if we had cash, it wouldn't help us much because we wouldn't be able to withdraw anything from cash machines."

"And let's say the government comes up with a good idea for a change. Then how would they communicate it to us? Are we supposed to rely on a couple of old trucks like the ones they still use at Kastner and Oehler[7]? Drive them through town over the few navigable streets[8] we still have and announce all the important news over megaphones? I don't think that'll do when it comes to avoiding panic and chaos. We can only hope that the net is back up before trouble reaches a critical mass. But whatever happens, there is an uneasy time approaching, and we should definitely not be around to see it happen. Thanks to Karl, we have a bit of a head start. Let's get out of the city. But where can we go?"

Karl answers without hesitation. "I think you're right there Johann. You know what? My sister and I inherited a farm near Wildon, but at the moment she's living with her family in Vienna. I've been trying to take care of it with the help of some of the locals there. It's not really luxurious, but at least we're growing potatoes and other vegetables, and pumpkins, of course. We make some wine and raise chickens and cattle. The place has its

---

[6] Stamps were eliminated in 2018; cash in 2065.
[7] The Macy's of Graz.
[8] Road maintenance was abandoned in 2072.

own well, and a forest that could come in handy when we run out of wood. The two of you and your sons are more than welcome to move down there with us. We'll need your help, actually. And by the way, didn't your oldest just finish his studies as computer scientist? And the younger one is still studying computer science, isn't he? From what you've just told us, I think we could definitely make use of your family's knowledge."

Johann pats Karl on the shoulder. "You're a good friend. I'm very grateful for your offer. In fact, we visited the farm once, remember?"

A frown wrinkles Karl's forehead but Christina reminds him, "Don't you remember, Karl? The two of you went out to collect chestnuts and you came back with two huge bags of them. And then for weeks you made me cook meals involving chestnuts because you didn't want to waste them."

Karl slaps himself on the forehead. "Of course I remember that. We used to call it the Chestnut Era."

This makes Christina laugh but she soon becomes serious again. "But how are we going to get to Wildon without the Moller?"

"That shouldn't be a problem," Johann's wife interjects. "Since I'm a manager at Kastner and Oehler, it won't be a problem getting one of those old trucks you were talking about."

"You would steal a truck from your own company?" Christina asks.

I'm not going to *steal* it; I'll leave them a note with all the details about what we're taking with us along with a direct debit slip. If they want to, they can transfer the money for it right out of my account."

"So we're set," observes Karl. "It's 6:15 now. When can we go? How shall we meet and how much can each of us bring?"

But Johann interrupts, "Wait a minute. This is going too fast. I agree that the farm in Wildon is a better option than staying here in the city, but I still have serious concerns. It's just too close to Graz."

"What do you mean by that?" Karl asks, irritated.

Johann looks down at the ground. "Call me a pessimist or even a weirdo for having read too many books about computer catastrophes like the ones that never occurred in 2000. But if my worst fears are realized, this breakdown will continue for a longer period of time and the entire society will run out of control. People will ride down there on bikes or with whatever other vehicles they can find. Then they'll plunder the potato fields and they won't think twice about slaughtering the cattle and chickens. What do we do in that case? Should we stand guard with our hunting rifles and shoot the hungry thieves? There's no way we can keep watch over the entire property and the forest. I would feel much better if we could get out into a more remote area, maybe a place where people could only approach you from one side. That way we wouldn't have to use guns right away. We could build barriers and maybe keep a watchdog or something. Maybe you should leave the farm to your sister and her husband. He's in the army, right? I'm sure he could protect that place better than we would ever be able to. I don't think there would be enough space for six extra people, but maybe..."

Christina interrupts him. "Whatever you just wanted to say, I think I have the solution. I suggest we try to make our way down to my father's property in northern Greece. It's North of Ioannina, in the mountains northeast of Monodendrion. The property's huge. It's protected by a steep gorge to the north and can only be reached on one side by a dirt road. My father's name is Paul Kalkias. He's a retired general. He's got a lot of clout locally and he's practically built a castle up there. He always keeps a big stock of non-perishable food. I know he's there now, too, because I talked to him last night. My XP must've saved the call. XP, can you play the segment from my father last night?"

So far, the XPs have not taken part in the conversation, even though their programming allows them to understand conversations and give their opinions. Christina's XP repeats in German what her father said yesterday in Greek[9]:

"It's soooo good to hear that you're well, my dear daughter. But maybe the times are less peaceful than you think. There are strange rumors going around, rumors about a coming cataclysm.

---

[9] See "Xperts: The Beginning"; Chapter: Do You Need Language Training?

9

Let us hope they are rumors and nothing more. But I want you to know that there was a reason why I have withdrawn into my bastion here in the mountains. I will stay here at least through the summer. You, your husband, and your friends are always welcome here. Trust me, if trouble strikes, it would not be a problem to put you up, even for several months. You know how to contact me, right?"

"Why didn't I think of this right away?" she stammers. "But it's so far away. How will we get there?"

The other three can't believe what they are hearing. Did the General know something about the breakdown of the network? Was this the cataclysm he had heard rumors about? There is no doubt about the sincerity of the invitation. The venue and the preparations seem ideal, but what did he mean by knowing how to contact him?

After an encouraging nod by her husband, Christina confesses, "It's actually such a big secret that we couldn't even tell you. You have to promise not to tell anyone else."

The friends nod.

"A couple of years ago, my father managed to buy two pieces of the mysterious "Mindcaller". They cost him a fortune."

Johann interrupts her excitedly. "So those things really exist? There have been so many legends about them, almost like UFOs. I always thought they were myths. What can they do? Do you know how many of them are out there?"

"I'll tell you more about this when we have more time. I don't even know how many of them are around. I heard something about eleven. But lets stick to the basics now. My father gave one of the Mindcallers to my brother Alex, who runs a ranch in Alberta, Canada. That's how they can communicate telepathically, without having to use any technical devices. The communication transcends the use of words. It can also contain pictures, sounds, symbols, etc. If the network collapsed at the same time in Canada, my father may be the only person in Europe who knows whether or not North America's net is still functioning. It's most important use for us is that my father can "hear" when someone he knows really well, like Karl and me, has a particularly strong thought about him. But this only works in one direction. He can hear what we think but not vice versa. So if we decide to set out for his "castle," I'll be able to keep him informed of our progress. Basically, messages like this will always keep him informed on the latest developments of the current crisis."

After a moment of silence, Karl speaks up, "I think all of us want to set out for the castle, don't we?"

Johann answers, "It would be great if we could come. We'd be greatly indebted to you."

"Oh, shut up," Christina admonishes him. "We're friends. And practically speaking, we really need your help if we want to get the truck. And that's the only way we can get there. If it's possible at all..."

Now they all begin to speak at once, but Karl finally takes charge of the situation. "In the meantime, my XP has been able to analyze yesterday's satellite images of southeast Europe. The Berlin-Athens motorway, which was quickly finished after Serbia and Macedonia joined the EU, is still mostly intact. We would have to leave the autobahn several times for a couple of kilometers before we reach Belgrade. In Belgrade, large parts of the autobahn have been turned into an amusement park, so we'll have to make a big detour there. It really looks bad south of Skopje. We'll have to drive on rural country roads towards the west. We cannot reach our goal from the south via Ioannina, but only from the north, through Kosani and Konitsa. In the worst case, we'll have to leave the truck behind and walk the last part, so all of us must bring the necessary equipment for a strenuous hike."

"I'll go wake the kids and start packing," says Johann's wife. "You two go back and get your things. You can leave them all here and we'll meet on level two of the underground garage at Kastner. From there we can find everything else we might need for the journey. Then we'll go into the storerooms, take everything we need, load the truck and off we go."

"I suggest we meet at 8:00 a.m. in the garage," Johann adds.

They all look at their watches. It's already 6:30. How are they supposed to do this?

"Johann, why the hurry?" Karl asks.

11

Johann looks at them, one after the other. "It'll all be just a matter of time. Once the people start forming gangs or the police gets coordinated, the first thing they'll do is confiscate all vehicles, at least that's what I'd do, because those are the only reliable means of supply and distribution or escape."

But Karl starts worrying about something else. "We won't be able to get gas anywhere. Do Kastner and Oehler have fuel depots, and will we be able to access them? We'll need at least 350 liters of diesel for those 1300 km."

"Yes, they do. I know where we can find some forty-liter canisters. We can fill them up and take them with us."

Karl stands up thoughtfully. "Christina, why don't you start packing? I'll be back soon. Right now, I think it's time to use our friendship with the governor, warn him, and ask if he wants to come along. He can probably help us somehow." The two women and Johann look at him questioningly but Karl is dismissive. "Come on, Johann, we have no time to lose. We have to talk to this guy."

Governor Heinz Stoeger, robust for his sixty years, has been a father figure for all of Styria for ten years. Since his wife died three years ago, he has lived only for his work and lives next door to his office. He is known to work late but get up late as well. Johann rings the doorbell and wakes him up. When Stoeger opens the door, he is more than a little surprised to see Johann so early in the morning. After Johann introduces Karl as his best friend, the governor asks them inside.

Johann tells him about the breakdown and the governor listens quietly before he speaks. "Let me check first to see if the secure connections to the other governors and the federal government are down too."

The result is sobering: all of those "super safe" connections are dead as well. Johann tells the governor his prognosis, but Stoeger does not want to believe those worst-case scenarios. Johann gets more adamant. "Heinz, you also didn't believe me when I told you that the lines to the federal government were not safe. And who was right? This may be the biggest crisis of your life. Don't you want to come with us? You met the General in person when he was here in Graz, remember?"

"Of course I remember. We had an interesting conversation. Don't get me wrong, Johann. I really understand why you're doing what you're doing. I know you have to think about your kids but you have to understand that I have to stay here. Thanks for the warning, and thanks for the offer. I hope to be able to prevent the worst from happening, but I agree with you: in the event that this collapse lasts longer than a week, it could really get out of hand. But as long as I can, I'll try to stay in control. If we keep up the discipline and tighten our belts, this summer can be overcome. But if we don't have a solution before winter, then God help us. Maybe we'll have to reintroduce the old Euro banknotes and stamps in order to allow people to buy things and prevent looting. Now, what does your friend Karl want from me?"

Karl smiles. "I have both a gift and a favor to ask. Here are the keys to my farm in Wildon. Actually, it belongs to my sister and me. She lives in Vienna but I assume that she'll turn up there sooner of later. Until then, the farm is yours. There's a lot of food down there so you might want to send someone trustworthy over to collect it. But please be sure to let my sister take the place over when she's ready. And one other thing: try to think about the General regularly. He has told me that you know about his Mindcaller. By thinking about the General and my sister, we'll be able to know about your situation in Graz and Wildon. I honestly think that we are better prepared for worst-case scenarios in Greece. There might be a slim chance that we can help you from there. I know there are many boats at Igumenitsa, the port nearest to Ioannina, and where we will be. From there we might be able to transport food or medicine all the way up to Trieste. You might also be able to reactivate one of the old steam engines with the help of the engineers at the University of Technology. The rails are still intact so you could have an ancient but very useful connection to the nearest harbor. Who knows, maybe there'll be thousands of tons of goods you can use there just because there are no longer Mollers or computer operated trains running, and the local population is not large enough to loot all of it."

Both the governor and Johann are impressed with Karl's ideas. The three men shake hands in a bond of trust. "Should this world end, at least it should end with dignity."

When Johann and Karl are already on their way, the governor shouts after them, "Wait! Stop! There's one more thing I can do for you! Does one of you have a holograph of yourself?"

Karl hesitates for a moment. "If it's important, we can use the one from my driver's license."

"Judge for yourself," says the governor, presenting them with an authorized certificate. In all twenty-three official languages of the EU it reads:

'The bearer of this certificate (see holo) is on a special mission for the Austrian government in the name of the European Union. All officials of all member states are required to provide him with all possible help.'

Karl rips the hologram out of his driver's license and hands it to the governor with a shrug of his shoulders. "I never really understood why we would need a driver's license in the first place when you can get all the important data on the security personnel on an XP. I'll probably never need this license again and if I do for some reason, I can always claim I lost it."

The governor carefully glues the hologram on the certificate, adds a digital signature and hands it to Karl. "Maybe this'll help you in the event you are stopped. By the way, at what time do you plan to start loading the truck?"

"Around 8:30," Johann answers, without understanding the meaning of the question. Perhaps he doesn't know his friend Heinz as well as he thought he did.

As arranged, the two families meet at 8:00 in the garage of the department store. They first choose a truck. According to Johann, it would be best to take the smallest one, but Karl insists on taking a larger model, one that is able to pull a fully loaded trailer. He plans to bring along the larger of the two tractors from the farm in Wildon. "If we get stuck, the tractor might be able to pull the truck out. It could also come in handy if we have to build a barrier. And if we actually manage to get it to the castle, it could be useful for farming purposes on the steep fields. If we have to leave the truck behind, the tractor could still be an important means of transport for us. Honestly, I don't find the prospect of having to walk hundreds of miles through Macedonia and Greece very tempting."

Then they top off the gas tank and load the trailer with ten forty-liter canisters of diesel fuel. Karl secretly adds five extra canisters for the tractor. In the meantime, they put mattresses into the front of the big straight truck's cargo space to serve as living area, a place to cook and sleep. Johann hides several handguns, hunting rifles, ammunition, and signal flares underneath the mattresses. The women pick out a selection of dry and non-perishable foods and add some fresh produce for the first few days. While Karl is looking for tools, Johann and his sons search for medicine and tents. They plan to stack these goods in a manner affecting that of an emergency relief shipment.

Johann's wife is getting a bit nervous. Even though she is a manager of this very store, she would find herself with a lot of probably ineffective explaining to do if one of her superiors were to show up. But everything runs smoothly. When they leave the garage at 8:30, the streets of Graz have already filled with people. There are animated discussions going on all over about the reasons for the collapse of the network and how long it could possibly last. They all regard the truck-trailer combination warily and several times men try to bar their exit shouting, "What's happening? Where do you think you're going?" Not even Johann would have assumed that the general mood would heat up so quickly. He tells the women and children to hide down by the mattresses in the cargo area.

They drive slowly and carefully back to Johann's apartment, always aware of the fact that people are keeping a close eye on or even following them.

When they get back to the apartment, Johann decides to conceal their personal belongings in some old potato bags he discovered in a forgotten corner of his basement. By concealing their luggage, he hopes none of the bystanders will suspect their true motives.

The actual loading turns into a kind of running the gauntlet: a crowd surrounds the truck, some of them even following Johann and Karl into the basement, bombarding them with questions.

15

The only thing they have for an answer is, "Would you stop asking questions and help us instead? We don't have much time!" In the end, they manage to convince a few of the bystanders to help them load the truck, but the atmosphere soon becomes rough again. Johann and Karl realize that they'll have to leave some things behind in order to get out of there alive. The two jump into the cab and lock the doors. There's a huge crowd blocking the street. Some of them have even sat down to prevent their departure. Angry young men jump onto the running boards and try to force the doors open. A thrown stone creates a spider web of cracks in the windshield. Karl sits paralyzed behind the steering wheel but Johann quickly takes control of the situation. He tries honking the horn to warn the men off and the van slowly begins to roll.

But this seems to only stir up the anger of the mob. Suddenly, the crowd quiets, and parts to let an older man through them toward them. Heinz Stoeger, the governor of Styria grins at his friends then turns to address the crowd.

"My fellow Styrians, have you failed to notice that our entire computer and power network has collapsed? We don't know exactly why this has happened, but apparently the Wildon power plant has exploded. This truck is on its way to Wildon to provide the injured with food and medicine. Who in God's name came up with the ridiculous idea to obstruct this operation?"

"We only wanted to know what's going on!", a man shouts from the crowd.

"None of us know what's going on exactly. There will be an emergency meeting of the state assembly at 9:00 and we will provide information as soon as possible. Now please make way for the vehicle."

The governor omits telling them that only 15% of the assembly members will be present.

The people back up. Karl puts the truck back in gear and gives a respectful wave of thanks to the governor as he begins to drive slowly out of the street. "He lied to save our skins.'

The governor continues to speak. "At 1:00 p.m., the Army will begin providing food for all of us in the main square. But let's hope we'll have the electricity restored by then."

16

Johann and Karl look at each other. "So that's why the governor asked about our exact time of departure. He knew there would be trouble." But they both wonder how he managed to get the army functioning so quickly.

"It's going to be the hardest work of his life to keep this city and province from falling apart over the next days and weeks," Karl predicts. Johann nods in agreement.

It's only twenty-five km from Graz to Wildon and the farm can be reached without having to go through town. They manage to load the tractor onto the trailer without attracting a lot of attention. The others complain about how much time Karl takes preparing loading and unloading mechanisms for the tractor. He knows that it might be important to be able to get the tractor off fast in the event of trouble.

When the others start complaining, Karl reacts quietly. "You know your stuff and I know mine. The tractor has to be loaded in a way so it cannot be recognized at a glance. But we still have to be able to get it off and on quickly. I hope it won't come to it, but from what we've already experienced in Graz today, we really can't exclude the possibility." He then calmly resumes his work.

It's almost 10:00 a.m. by the time they get back on the highway just south of Wildon. They drive south at a steady eighty km/h. More and more often, they see people waving their fists at them threateningly. After all, it was the local population who turned the highway into a playground and inline skating track decades ago.

"According to the satellite pictures on my XP, the detour around Zagreb could be a little difficult," notes Johann when they are about ten km away from the interchange with the road to Rijeka. "The bigger the cities, the more they tend to come up with alternative uses for the highway."

When they reach the first sign for the highway to Rijeka, they notice a police motorcycle with its siren on and lights flashing behind them. "He must've dug that out of a museum," mumbles Christina who is sitting between the two men. All three of them feel uneasy about the situation.

In an attempt to shake off the gendarme, Karl takes an exit going in the wrong direction toward Rijeka, but no avail.

Apparently the policeman was after them in particular. He pulls up alongside them and they have no alternative but to stop. Karl slowly rolls down the window and shows the governor's certificate to the officer. He has a quick look at it and begins speaking to them in Croatian. Normally, Karl and the policeman's XPs would have been able to converse with each other, but in this situation they are not able to connect. For one moment, Karl fears that this is only the beginning of a massive language problem. However, he underestimates his XP's "intelligence." It has apparently managed to restart the translation programs that were damaged by the virus, and Karl's XP easily translates the policeman's sentences into perfect German and amplifies it over a loudspeaker. 'Wow! Finally a good old simultaneous translation,' Karl and Johann think, impressed.

The result of the conversation is both comic and tragic: the policeman will escort them for a stretch on the way to Rijeka. They have no choice but to go the wrong way until they reach Karlovac, where the policeman waves them a friendly good-bye. Now, they have to leave the highway to go east. They cross the Save River near Sisak only to be stopped again an hour later. Again, the certificate helps. Before they get back on the highway towards Belgrade, they decide to exit onto a regional road, then turn onto another small road which they follow into a wood out of sight of any houses or streets, in order to take a short break. It's only just after 2:00 p.m. but they've already got a good idea of some of the difficulties they are likely to encounter. Because of the unwanted detour, they are only 230 km into a 1300 km journey.

Nevertheless, they all enjoy the rest: the blooming flowers, the hammering of a woodpecker, and the sparrows that search the ground for the crumbs they left behind. Neither the sunbeams nor their own presence can keep the doe and her new fawn from grazing nearby. Apparently nature has not yet given in to human stupidity.

In this peaceful setting, Johann's wife decides to relate a joke she heard at work a few days ago. "Two planets meet out in space. One says to the other, 'I really haven't been feeling too well lately; I've been infected by billions of humans.' The other pats him on the ice cap and says, 'Don't worry old man, I've had the same thing myself. It passes very quickly.'"

Even though the atmosphere has lightened for a moment, they know that there is no time for further cavorting. Christina insists on contacting her father via the Mindcaller to tell him that they are on their way but that it will probably take them another two days.

But now it is time to continue the trip. They reluctantly board the truck and get back on the highway. In the meantime, Johann's sons have found the weapons underneath the mattresses. There is still enough boy in them to get them excited about their discovery. Little do they know how dangerous the situation will soon become.

After a relatively calm four hours and 300 km, they are only fifty km away from Belgrade. According to the information they have access to, they will have to switch to driving on smaller streets from now on. In Ruma they leave the highway towards Sabac. When they reach the town thirty km later, the police stop them, telling them to hand the truck over.

"We need it to guarantee that we can distribute emergency items to the population. You may stay here in Sabac and we'll give you the truck back as soon as the situation has normalized," the police offer.

Neither the certificate nor a long discussion helps. When the police become more threatening, Johann whispers to Karl, "We have to get through here. Go! Just go! They don't have a vehicle to chase us!"

Karl pretends to give in. He starts to open the door but then suddenly steps on the accelerator. The truck lurches forward and barely manages to reach fifty km/h on the narrow street. But this is still faster than the police can run. The police chase them for a while, then draw their ancient pistols to shoot after the vanishing truck. Apart from two holes in the tarpaulin over the tractor, the pistols cause no damage. Nevertheless, the refugees are shocked. If something like a functioning European Union still existed, then they would be wanted across the continent and immediately captured. The boys' excitement is dampened as well.

But Sabac holds another surprise for them: there is no police at the other end of town, but a barricade impassable to the truck. "It'll take them ten minutes at the most to catch up with us here. You take over the truck," shouts Karl, "It's my show now."

Karl opens the tarp, starts the tractor, and drives it off the trailer. He lowers the front blade and rams it repeatedly into the barricade. Several locals have gathered at the site but they don't interfere.

Suddenly, Johann's oldest son shouts, "There's a rifle in that window! They're going to shoot us!"

"Hand me a gun! Quick!" shouts Johann. Armed with two pistols, he jumps out of the truck and fires into the air. The locals scatter and the threatening weapon in the window disappears. The hole in the barricade seems large enough now. Karl gives Johann a sign to start the truck and drive through. Karl follows with the tractor. Once they are five km from the village, Johann stops the truck and Karl drives the tractor back onto the trailer, tying the tarp back in place.

"There should be an intersection coming up. It's about two km from here. We'll have to take the road south towards Valjevo. That road will be pretty bad. It'll lead us through the hills and with our luck there will be another unfriendly surprise waiting for us there," says Karl.

The light is waning by the time they find the exit. "I don't think this road has ever seen a truck with a trailer," comments Johann.

Karl does his best to maneuver on the narrow road, but when they reach a bridge with a two-ton weight limit, he has to stop. "There's no way we can drive over this. I'll have to make a track with the tractor on both sides so we can ford the creek, then I'll guide the truck through and destroy the bridge behind me. We'll drive a few more kilometers until we reach a place where we can hide the truck in some trees or brush. Maybe one of you can walk ahead to find a suitable place to spend the night."

Johann admires Karl: how naturally he has taken command! The boys watch with interest as Karl creates a new ford through the creek. Johann disappears and returns fifteen minutes later. "I have good news. There's an ideal place for us only two km up the road. Without difficulties, they manage to pull the truck across the creek. Karl destroys the bridge and manages to block his new path as well. No one will be able to get through here unless they have a giant tractor or a bulldozer.

The place that Johann has found is almost a perfect campsite. It is very tempting to consider starting a campfire, but obviously this is out of the question. Karl starts cooking "astronaut food" but–surprise–he has two bottles of Schilcher wine with him to complement the otherwise bland meal. Soon, the light of the moon shines strongly from the gloomy night sky. They can still sit outside and would like to forget about the terrible scenes that might trouble the rest of the world. Altogether, this creates a very strange atmosphere. After all, there is still peace in the world, so why do they have this feeling in the back of their heads that they are in the middle of a war? Is it simply because they are fleeing?

Christina relives the day in her head. Twenty-four hours ago she and her husband were still partying in Graz, and now here they are worrying about all the things that have happened since. Can it be that it was only twenty-four hours ago? Soon she comes back to reality. "Tomorrow we'll have to face about 120 km of dirt road and it's very likely that we'll also have to pass through some troublesome villages. But afterwards we should have an easy ride until we get to Skopje and from there we'll only have 300 km left to our destination." She knows that it is better to remain silent about the fact that those last 300 km may very well be the most difficult.

They all sleep restlessly in the back of the truck. It also doesn't help much that the mosquitoes are having a feast on them and that Johann is snoring like a buzz saw. At 5:00 a.m. they all awake listlessly. They all wonder if it might be possible to reach the General's castle today, but no one dares articulate their reservations.

After a quick breakfast, Karl draws the truck back up onto the dirt road with the tractor. "It doesn't make sense to load the tractor back onto the trailer. It shouldn't be more than thirty km to Valjevo, and that'll be the last big settlement before we reach the highway to Nis and Skopje. I suggest that I go on ahead and

21

show the certificate if we get stopped again. If this doesn't help, we'll just keep going like we did before. If there's another barricade, I can get it out of the way before you even get there. There's only one potential problem: if we have to face an armed blockade. So I suggest I take one of the boys with me, armed with a pistol. It's not about shooting anyone, it's just so we can scare people off by shooting in the air like we did yesterday. So which of the two of you would be willing to come along?"

They are both courageous enough to volunteer, so Karl asks their parents.

"I won't let either of them go!" Christina objects. "I'll go. They can both have a pistol but make sure to keep them out of sight."

When they near Valjevo, they can make out a big barricade in front of them, but it doesn't appear to be guarded. "There's no way we can get through this one with the tractor," says Johann, who is close to desperation.

But for some reason, Karl doesn't agree with this and laughs. "They and you are in for a surprise. This'll be child's play. Stay 100 meters behind me until you can get through."

All this happens so fast that Johann can't even react to what Karl has just said. Karl drives off with the tractor, stops in front of the barricade, jumps off, and opens the big utility box to take out the chainsaw. He revs it up and doesn't even seem to take any interest in the barricade. He is after the tree standing between the barricade and the front of the adjacent house. He takes down the tree and easily pulls it out of the way with the tractor. He signals Johann to come and drives through the breach in the obstruction. The truck follows him through. There are no people around and when they reach the end of the village, they find it unblocked. However, Karl notices deep ruts in the grass next to the street.

"Why did this truck drive over the field when it could've just taken this perfectly good street?" Karl asks.

Christina's and his XP both respond almost simultaneously, "Because the street is mined. Go through the field!"

Karl manages to get the tractor off the road and into the field just in time. Then he stops it to warn the truck. While they are driving through the field, Johann's XP keeps them informed about the location of the mines. After several hundred meters, the tracks lead back onto the road. The XPs signal all clear. Karl loads the tractor back onto the trailer and Johann keeps driving safely until they reach the highway to Nis.

The atmosphere is depressing. Johann's wife speaks for everybody. "Well I understand our truck would be useful to them, so the barricades make sense, but why would they want to blow vehicles up?"

Johann's older son observes, "Maybe the people here aren't really interested in commandeering the cars, maybe they're just scared that some intruders might come to steal their stuff. Maybe that's the reason they mined the road, d'ya think?"

Johann's wife hugs her son. "I'm happy that there is an explanation that doesn't assume the worst about everyone."

They are sure to have learned at least one lesson: Whenever they have to pass through a village, there will be the danger that either someone will want their vehicles or someone will be so afraid that they will try to kill the group, just in case.

Deep in thought, they drive down the highway, passing both Nis and Skopje. Before they get to the most difficult and final stretch of their journey, they take a short break. What awaits them now are several larger towns like Prilep, Pitola, Kosani and the Konitsa Pass over the Pindos Mountains. They have no problems passing both Prilep and Pitola, and once again, the certificate comes in handy. Soon after Pitola, they cross the border to Greece[10], and from now on there are only about 1.5 hours left to Kosani, an important intersection of the North-South and East-West roads.

As they expected, they find a major checkpoint at this intersection. Dozens of police guard the barricades and pass gates. Christina steps out to talk to her countrymen. She mentions her father's name because she assumes that it will be familiar in these parts. But neither her charm nor her persuasiveness help; the police confiscate the vehicle and threaten to arrest the potentially dangerous foreigners.

---

[10] This was the Greek border before Macedonia joined the EU.

After intense discussions, Karl realizes that again they will have to use naked force. "Everyone lie down in the back of the truck. Johann, you'll have to steer the truck. I'll jump on the tractor, shoot around like crazy in the air, and smash through the barricade. I won't be able to destroy the whole thing in one go so you'll have to just drive through it no matter how much you fuck up the truck. You'll make it somehow. Then just keep going. Go as long as you can. As long as we can make it at least ten km we should be in the clear. They don't seem to have any vehicles to follow us. If the truck breaks down for good, everyone jump on the tractor. And if that breaks down too, we'll only have about 100 km left to walk until we reach Konitsa. We should be able to do that in three days at the most. Christina's father promised to help us from there. I'm not willing to let them lock me up here. See the shackles they have out for us? Tell Christina to agree with whatever they ask for and to say that we only have to get some personal things out of the truck and trailer."

There seems to be no other solution.

The tractor takes the policemen by surprise. Shooting into the air like a cowboy, Karl drives the blade into the barricade. The guards instinctively fall to the ground. When Karl has almost gotten through the barrier, a bullet rips through his left arm. He barely manages to keep the tractor under control with only his right arm, but finally, he breaks through. As the truck follows, bullets hit the radiator and one of the rear tires. Nevertheless, they gain a head start over the police, who can only run after them. Once they seem to be far enough ahead, Karl stops the tractor in order to attach a rope to the truck, which appears to be losing speed. With this new load, the tractor can still make thirty km/h. Their pursuers remain far behind due to the tractor's downhill route. Just when they believe themselves safe, they suddenly notice a motorcycle following them. So the guards had a vehicle after all! Angrily Karl shouts to Christina, "Take this rifle. You know how to shoot. Aim at the front tire, but please try not to hit the driver."

With no other choice, Christina does as Karl has told her. She aims carefully and with her third shot finally hits the wheel.

For ten more kilometers, Karl pulls the truck with the tractor. But when they reach the first hill, it becomes clear that they will have to say good-bye to the truck. Karl is not willing to leave the cargo to their pursuers. Around the next curve he finds what he is looking for: a deserted house.

"From now on, we just have the tractor. Let's try to attach the back seat of the truck to the back of the tractor. Then we'll at least all be able to sit. Let's only take food for a day and the tents. We'll have to leave the rest of the things in this house. Maybe we'll be able to pick it up eventually. I'll pull the truck up to the next curve and let it go over the cliff. Whoever finds it can make their own conclusions. It's getting dark and I'm still worried about the police, so let's hurry up. Let's fix up the tractor before we hide the cargo. I can't really help much because I took a bullet in my left arm."

Only then do the rest of them notice Karl's wound. "The bone seems to be all right," Christina says as she bandages his arm. Then they do as Karl suggested. In addition, they cover their things in the house with straw before they push the truck into the ravine. They keep going a little further uphill until they find a spot where they can hide the tractor. They are so exhausted that it takes all they have to set up the tents before they disappear into their sleeping bags.

The following morning bright sunlight wakes them. The group feels surprisingly refreshed. Karl's wound is not as bad as they thought. Christina tells them that she has informed her father about their present situation so there will be no further surprises in Konitsa. After a rich breakfast, they get back on the road. When they reach the pass north of Bogdhanis, the highest mountain of the Pindos Range, they realize that there is a police truck several turns beneath them on the switch-backed road. They are sure that they have been identified when shots ring out in the morning air. After such a long way, their goal seems suddenly far out of their reach again. Only Karl remains calm. "They're not going to get us. I'll make the street behind us impassable." In fact he manages to start a small avalanche of stones with the tractor, blocking the road beneath them.

"Way to go, Karl. Sorry that I didn't believe that the tractor could be of any use on this trip. We wouldn't have got anywhere near here without it," says Johann.

They soon approach Konitsa. Christina keeps praying. "I hope my father was able to arrange something for us here. He knows we're on a tractor." When they take the last curve into Konitsa, their hopes seem shattered for good. Fifty meters ahead of them stand thirty heavily armed soldiers apparently prepared to open fire.

"Oh for God's sake! That's it!" Johann's wife wails. But then unexpectedly, one of the soldiers begins running towards them.

"It's my father!" a jubilant Christina exclaims. "Those must be his soldiers! We did it! We're safe!"

2 Stranded and Rescued

Vava'u, Tonga, South Pacific
Sunday June 9, 2080, 4:30 p.m. (4:30 a.m. Central European Time)

Takis and Mary, both traveling on their own, are the only tourists on the little whale-watching boat, which left the Tongan Beach resort this afternoon. Most visitors have left the resort after weeklong vacations to return home via Tonga's capital, Nuku'alofa, or via Fiji. The skipper of the boat, Nufa, is a tall, dark Tongan. He smiles at his guests. He is happy because once again he has been able to lead the tourists close to several pods of whales. They were so close that fear was sometimes noticeable alongside the general excitement of the tourists. From here on, he can switch to the automatic navigation system, which guarantees that the boat will avoid coral reefs. Nufa has known this passage through the reef since he was a small child. That's why he's still fascinated by this super accurate Chinese GPS which was based on the European Galileo system. In connection with the steering system of the boat, the GPS takes the tides, the height of the waves, and the ever-changing coastlines and water depths into account.

Nufa's job is done for the day, so he opens a can of beer to celebrate. It's now 4:33 p.m. They'll get back to the resort just in time to deliver their catch of small tuna fish to the kitchen. It will be turned into sashimi and served to the guests as an appetizer.

The skipper and his guests gasp with surprise when their XPs simultaneously signal "Help!" How is this possible? Nothing like this has ever happened before!

Nufa reacts as fast as lightning. He realizes that the navigation system of the boat has collapsed as well. Fortunately he still knows how to navigate the reef manually, but this is the first time he's ever cursed the navigation system: due to the high tide, it has left the widest and deepest passageway through the reef and taken a short cut that demands very precise steering.

Nufa steers the boat to the right in order to reach the ideal channel. The whole maneuver calls for a very high degree of concentration. After he has already been forced to retrace his path one time, he finally finds the point in the sea where he has absolute confidence in his navigational skills for the remainder of the trip.

Suddenly Nufa is distracted by a huge explosion on the hill behind the village by the airport. A huge column of flame and smoke rises into the sky. Even though they are still six kilometers away, the sight is overwhelming. The boat scrapes a head of coral. Nufa tries to steer away from it, but too late. The next unfortunately large wave lifts the boat and smashes it back down on the coral head. The boat begins to leak.

Nufa notices the fearful faces of his passengers. "We are not in danger. The tide is going out. Unless there is a very big wave, we will remain aground here. At low tide, the coral head is only a few centimeters under water. They are expecting us to be in by 5:00 p.m., so if we're not back in time, they'll send a boat out to look for us. We're only twenty meters away from the deep reef canal, so they'll definitely see us and bring us aboard. So all it'll take is a bit of patience. If a big wave gets us off this coral, we'll make it back ourselves. Don't worry about the leak. I'm sorry for this whole thing. First the navigation system broke down and then I got distracted by that explosion."

"It's not your fault," says Takis, "Apparently something very unusual has happened. What do you think that explosion was?"

Nufa hesitates. He is fairly sure that he knows what has happened but should he really tell the tourists?

Mary notices Nufa's thoughtfulness. "Nufa, do you know something that you're not telling us? I think we have a right to know."

Nufa nods. "You know, it's only a guess, but the airplane coming in from Tongatapu lands at 4:35 every day and it always brings guests for our resort. If the navigation system of the airplane crashed like my GPS, then probably the plane crashed. That might have been the explosion. Just look. You can still see the fire burning over there."

Nufa keeps to himself his fear that the fuel depots have gone up in flames as well.

There are no more large breakers and the tide continues to ebb. The three on the boat discuss the implications of the latest developments. Suddenly, their XPs reactivate. They explain why they failed. "A virus hit us all at 4:34 p.m. sharp. It took the entire computer network down and rendered several of our individual programs useless. Fortunately, we have been programmed to regenerate and were able to restart most of our programs. Despite some important functions having been nullified, we are now partially functional again."

"Which functions do you mean?" Takis wants to know.

"First of all, the whole computer network is down. This means that we can communicate neither with other XPs, nor any other electronic devices because all the transmission protocols and drivers have been destroyed."

"Did this only happen here in Vava'u?", asks Mary.

Her XP answers for all to hear, "This problem definitely extends beyond Vava'u. We used to be in contact with stations ranging from Nuku'alofa, Fiji, and the Cook Islands, as well as with satellites. But these are all now mute."

"So this could be a large-scale collapse of all computer networks?" Mary speculates.

"Let's hope not. That would mean that thousands of planes and boats that have automatic guidance systems are in great danger."

Takis doesn't even know how right he is. In the last ten minutes, more than 2800 aircraft have crashed. Several thousand more are still being flown manually without any support from air traffic controllers, tracking devices, navigational lights, or radar. The same is true for tens of thousands of boats, from the Queen Mary IV, *with her 6300 passengers, down to small sailboats across the seven seas and in waterways across the globe. Only those vessels with experienced skippers, or pilots who know the area well and can still navigate without technological support have any chance of survival. For example, the captain of the* Queen Mary IV *immediately lowers her speed and realizes very quickly that he will now have to rely on ancient astronomical methods in order to keep his present course.*

But still, the danger for the passengers and the crew is very real. The entire internal computer and communications systems have collapsed too. While the generators on board are still able to provide enough electricity for lighting and ventilation, all control systems are unusable. This has some unusual effects: the doors to the passenger cabins open, the lights go on and off, and the elevators are no longer reliable. All this happens at 11:34 p.m. Caribbean time, when most passengers were just about to go to bed to be ready for tomorrow's port of call. On top of this, the captain cannot inform the passengers about these developments because the public address system is no longer operational. Soon panic breaks out. The world will never know any details about this. Those few that will survive will only be able to provide a few shreds of a story that was triggered by malfunctioning systems and irrational humans.

Dieter Eyck, the great-grandson of Vava'u Beach Resort's founder, is sitting at his office computer. His brother Max is the head chef at this little pretty vacation spot. He and his helpers are just preparing dinner for Takis and Mary, the awaited new guests, the crews of several boats in the harbor, and the other resort personnel. Many of those yachts only dock here because of the famous cuisine at the resort. This is the only restaurant in Tonga that has been honored with a Golden Spatula. As far as the South Pacific is concerned, the quality of the food is only matched by the 'Bloody Mary' restaurant on Bora Bora. The King of Tonga himself regularly flies from the maim island to Vava'u just for dinner.

At 4:34 p.m. Dieter's peace is suddenly disturbed by a wave of problems: his XP crashes and his computer goes crazy. Before he can even react to this, he hears a massive explosion. His beautiful Tongan wife, Sakuafo, storms in from the restaurant. "Dieter, all the XPs are down and there was a huge explosion at the airport just now! It must've been the airplane from Tongatapu."

Dieter rushes out of his office. He looks out over the lagoon with its glass-clear cove that stretches far into the island. Everything seems peaceful at first. A school of barracuda swims seaward through the individual coral heads, which protrude colorfully in the late afternoon sun. But when Dieter turns to look inland, he faces a huge wall of flame and smoke rising from behind the village.

"I hope it wasn't the plane, but whatever it was, it hit the fuel depots. I have to find out what happened."

He decides to send out one of his employees in a motorboat to the village. "You find out if the computers and communication systems are down all over the village. If they are, then spread the news that Kana-tu (the village elder) and I will inform the public at 9:00 a.m. tomorrow about what's going on. Please ask Kana-tu to come with you when you return. It would be best if you could take a bicycle along to get to the airport to find out what happened there."

Dieter asks the head of the diving school (which for almost 100 years has been managed continuously by American women) to go to the reef channel. "Nufa's out there whale watching with two guests. His XP and navigation system must've broken down too. He'll try to get back here through the main channel. It's very likely that he's in trouble. Take someone along with you and don't forget to bring the inflatable dinghy in case you have to get into the shallows. Please get Nufa and those guests back."

She nods when Dieter gives her an encouraging handshake. Soon afterwards, Dieter's XP reactivates, and appears to be partially functional. At first he is relieved, but when he is informed that apparently the computer network has been extensively interrupted, he gets more worried.

The head of the diving school has no problems finding and rescuing Nufa, Takis and Mary. She decides to tow the damaged boat in later, when the tide is again high.

When they return to the resort, Dieter is waiting there to meet his guests. He congratulates them and opens a bottle of champagne to welcome them back.

"Here's a toast to your first shipwreck. May you never have another." They all raise their glasses and drink it down like water. Dieter continues, "Of course, all the drinks are on the house tonight. We're just about to find out what happened at the

31

airport and how long we'll have to live without the network. I'll keep you informed. But I'm sure now you'd like to relax."

But Mary draws him aside. "Dieter, I don't think I can really relax now. You should know that I'm a computer scientist. I think you should show me your computer now. Maybe I can figure something out from it. I'm afraid I have to dampen your optimism, too. The way the network and the XPs broke down, I don't think that this'll be over soon. I think we're all very lucky to be here on this resort. We have our own water and generator. You still have an old truck, don't you? I suggest you drive it to the village to get fuel for the generator, food and medicine. Honestly, I think this'll be a matter of weeks."

Dieter shrugs at this.

Mary continues, "This means we'll need supplies that'll last weeks. Everything will be sold out soon."

Tonga has refused to give up coined money, so with the given situation, buying and selling will be easier here than in most other countries where you can only find cash in museums. The resort is also somehow in a privileged situation. Not only do they have in Mary a computer scientist, but also, in Takis, a doctor. The two of them have become friends over the last week but even though they only came to Tonga to relax, they will now both have to exercise their professions.

Dieter looks at Mary thoughtfully. "I'll soon know what's going on in the village. Hopefully Kana-tu will come over here to discuss the situation. He's the village elder. I suggest you and Takis be present at the meeting too."

Mary nods.

There is only bad news from the village. The network has collapsed completely. As everyone feared, the crashing airplane caused the explosion. There are no survivors. Also, the plane hit one of the fuel tanks, which burst into flames and ignited all the other ones. Most of the airport buildings are burnt to the ground. The only things that did not explode were the depot-tanks for diesel fuel, which are located further away from the crash site. This last bit of information gives at least some hope to Dieter. It seems that they will be able to keep the generator running for a long time.

One hour later, the emergency meeting takes place. Dieter, his brother, his wife, Kana-tu, Mary, and Takis all agree that it will be necessary to place guards at shops and storehouses. All the shops will remain closed for the entire next day. They will first have to make an inventory of the goods and then create a reasonable rationing plan. Takis agrees to see patients once a week in an empty suite in the village hotel. Of course, he will also be on call in case of an emergency. Maru'ofa, a local New Zealand trained nurse will act as his assistant.

"Kana-tu, are these precautions sufficient? We'll soon begin to feel the first shortages. Will we be able to keep the people in control? Will they all go along us?"

"Dieter, my friend, you know that you are well appreciated here among the locals. Keep reading the Bible every Sunday morning like your father and your father's father always did. We need faith now. As long as we stand shoulder to shoulder with you, your wife (who is one of us) and the doctor, who can help our people, then the people of Neiafu will stand with us too. I still believe that we should do as Miss Mary has suggested. We should bring the most important goods to the resort with the truck. We need them as a reserve. We have to have some backup here. I am not worried about the next couple of weeks, but if this going to go on for longer, then..."

"Then what?" insists Dieter.

"Then it will be the Tongan law that will save us. Every male Tongan older than sixteen has the right to use 3.3 hectares of arable land, but in return each "landowner" must plant 200 coconut palms. This law has been the reason why so many Tongans have had to emigrate. There was just not enough land left. But those that stayed are now self-sufficient and if necessary could survive forever living off this land. Of course, under conditions that I hoped would long be over."

June 10, 2080 and the next days

The inventory turns out to be a sobering experience. Because the village has adapted to the special needs of a growing number of private boats sailing to Neiafu, fuel is not a problem: there is enough to keep the generators running for several weeks, and to cook with for three months. But if the Tongans don't change their lifestyle, shortages in other areas will start to occur in as little as three days.

In the evening, everyone agrees on a two month rationing plan. Only the computer specialist Mary favors a longer period. For the majority, two months seem long enough. Also, this will only bring with it light cutbacks in supplies. They hold a gathering at the main square of the village to explain the measures. Kana-tu gives a speech and is smart enough to play his best card, the presence of an experienced doctor, only at the end. The population accepts the measures without complaint.

After the gathering, Takis withdraws in order to concentrate his thoughts on his brother, General Paul Kalkias. He knows that his brother will be able to read his thoughts over the Mindcaller. Takis informs him that all the computers and networks in the South Pacific have broken down. He also tells him that they will get a grip on the situation for the next two months and that he will be working together with a young Tongan nurse. What Takis does not notice is that Maru'ofa has followed him and is now standing next to him admiring his nice round beer belly.

The Mindcaller transfers this message and the image of Takis and Maru'ofa simultaneously. The General receives the message shortly after the group with his daughter has made the street into Konitsa impassable for their pursuers.

'Ah hah! Also in the Pacific,' the worried General thinks. Despite the seriousness of the situation, the General doesn't fail to notice the beautiful young woman at his brother's side. For one moment he would like to be with his brother in Tonga. But deep inside he wishes for his brother to be here with him, or at least among his friends in Canada.

Mary digs into the XPs' problems. She finds a way for them to communicate with each other and other electronic devices as long as they are nearby. Now at least local communication and shopping will be simpler because they won't have to use the Pa'anga, the island currency, any longer.

Takis quickly becomes very popular among the Tongans. He falls head over heels in love with Maru'ofa, who is much younger than him. During their first intimacies, Takis feels a bit embarrassed about his "spare tire." But soon he realizes, to his astonishment, that this actually brings him close to the Tongan ideal of beauty.

In order to relax after their days with patients, Takis and Maru'ofa get their PADI SCUBA diving qualifications at the diving school. This allows Maru'ofa to introduce Takis to the warm and colorful world of the lagoons. Their first dive takes them into the famous "Cave of Lights" on Vava'u. The caves can only be reached from under the water, but nevertheless, light pours in from above, which creates an unreal beauty only comparable to the Blue Grotto in Capri. Inside the caves, they are able to stand up on a small sandy beach. When they get there, Maru'ofa removes first her wetsuit, then the bikini beneath. At this point Takis is not sure if he ever wants the net to work again. Soon he will regret ever having thought that.

At the General's Manor, ten km northeast of Monodendrion, NE Greece
June 11, 2080, 12:00 noon.

The last part of the Graz group's journey from Konitsa to the General's manor is practically a victory march: people are waving everywhere and Christina switches from riding in the back of the tractor to the back of a horse. They soon reach the old stone bridge across the Aaos River with its famous canyon. Not much later they cross another bridge across Vikos Creek and take a narrow street east.

After they pass Monodendrion with its many big trees (contradicting the name of the village), they soon reach a very high fence topped with loops of barbed wire. This is where the General's property starts. They reach a wide and well-guarded gate. Inside the gate, there is a veritable village of tents. The soldiers that had accompanied them live here. From here on the path gets steeper. They reach a road that has been blasted through solid rock, which is again blocked by a gate. The other side of the man made canyon feels like an old castle courtyard. It has a grass surface with several olive trees. Karl notes that they must be very old. Despite the cold winters that these trees must have lived through, they're still covered with blossoms. But there are also nut and mulberry trees and mountain goats standing among the bushes. A large plain tree marks the beginning of the footpath leading to a great villa with many additions. Oleanders flank the path on both sides.

"It's so nice to be back here with you daddy!" Christina exclaims.

After a long series of ceremonious hugs and welcomes, the General takes command again. "Christina and Karl, you'll occupy a room in the main building. Your friends will move into the bungalow. Clean yourselves thoroughly and rest a bit. We will have lunch in exactly forty-five minutes on the terrace behind the house. We *will* have a lot to talk about.

They have stifado[11] for lunch. The General's wife, who they all call Popi, and a young woman serve the food.

Christina explains why they accepted this invitation instead of taking refuge at their farm in Wildon, despite the great distance. Johann presents the General with a bottle of pumpkin seed oil and a flacon of *Eiswein*. Despite the kind intentions of this gesture, Karl can't help but to feel angry about it. There they were yesterday, all in a hurry to hide goods from the truck in the deserted house before dumping the truck, and this guy was wasting time and energy just to be polite?

"I must say again that I'm very happy that you're all here now. And I have to say that I expect you will be a great help. It's very important to have a doctor here." Full of pride he looks at his daughter Christina. "But I'm afraid you'll have to deal with complex problems with very simple means. I am sure it was the right decision to come here, despite the difficulties you encountered in your journey. From what we know now, we

---

[11] Typical Greek food consisting of tenderly cooked meat and onions.

36

won't have a computer network or sufficient electricity supply for a very long time. Unfortunately, this reduces all kinds of transportation possibilities. As you know, the Mindcaller enables me to receive information from many different parts of the world. Fewer than three days have passed since the breakdown. There are two things we know for sure: First, the breakdown affects the entire globe. My brother, who is presently on vacation in the South Pacific, has let me know that the situation is just the same there. I guess he'll have a very long vacation. Second, every community around the world needs someone to take control over the situation. If nobody takes responsibility, chaos will reign. I don't want to spoil your well-deserved meal with more unpleasant details, but as a matter of fact, I've already received news about large-scale looting. But let me now tell you about one positive thing. Christina's brother Alex is safe in Alberta, and so are the families of both her sisters, who also reside in Canada and are presently trying to get together. I'm in constant contact with Alex, who also possesses a Mindcaller. The telepathic information I receive should help our friends and us to feel relatively safe. Emergency assemblies have only begun in small sections of Greece..."

Christina interrupts him, "How do you know all this, father? Do you also still have direct contact with anyone?"

"Yes I do. It's pretty ironic, actually. Here we are at the end of the twenty-first Century, but are lucky that we still have 20th Century technology around. And in addition to that, now, all of a sudden, the best means of transportation that we have at hand are horses, bicycles and tractors. Now we can be grateful that technology has not found an adequate way to replace these tractors in certain important agricultural milieus. I was very surprised to hear that you managed to get your hands on a truck. At first I was certain that you wouldn't make it here. But thank God you had that tractor! But I digress. On Sunday I had already realized that we are facing a very far-reaching problem, so I decided to send three of my men to the Greek military headquarters north of Athens. Including the two hours of negotiations, it took them fifteen hours to get there and back on the tractor. They brought back a ham radio and crank generator.

That made me laugh! They really thought I would be stupid enough to have come up here without my own emergency outfit! The army distributed a number of those two-way radios to some people; retirees like myself were reactivated. This is the reason my men are allowed to wear army uniforms.

"This is now an official military post and like all other posts, we have been equipped with horses, bicycles and tractors. It's our job to guarantee the safety of everyone in the area. My area reaches as far as the Ioannina plain. Ioannina itself, Igumenitsa, and the Korfu harbor are under the control of General Panpandraki. Do you still remember him, Christina?"

Christina is not sure.

"So anyway, officially, I should not be concerned with the situation in Ioannina, Igumenitsa, Trikala, or Kosani. I'm only responsible for the area of Konitsa and its surrounding villages, which 'only' consists of about 10,000 people. Nevertheless, it will be difficult to absolutely guarantee their safety. I would not want to trade places with Panpandraki, who governs an area with ten times the population of mine. I really hope he can keep control of his district, otherwise we will have to deal with thousands of refugees here in the mountains."

"Aren't you perhaps a bit too pessimistic, father? Shouldn't it be possible to feed everyone here and to get them through the winter alive, if we all work together, I mean?"

The General sighs. "You used the right word there Christina, *if*. Unfortunately, most people only think about themselves."

The Loukoumades they have for dessert calm them and make them, for a short time, feel more optimistic about the situation. The food and the Retsina, as well as the increasing heat, has made them all tired. Nobody wants to bring up the topic of the catastrophe again. They agree that they should all retire for a short afternoon nap.

The short nap turns into a several hour sleep. After they awake, they gather around the table again to drink strong Greek coffee. Popi introduces them to some newly arrived comrades and explains that the General has gone to Konitsa, but will be back later to show them around.

The General returns at about 5:00 p.m. Without giving them many details, he assures the group that everything is O.K. down there. Then he shows them his "castle" and the storage buildings and explains all the defensive precautions they have taken so far. He also points out the path down to the canyon and introduces them to more of his comrades and soldiers from the tent village. It turns out that the tent village was planned for 1500 people, but at the moment it is only home to fifty men. "This will provide adequate room for refugees, if need be. We would've liked to create a bigger village, but we simply didn't have the necessary infrastructure and equipment."

Karl and Johann look at each other: 'Could all this really turn out so bad that a village like this wouldn't even suffice?'

June 12, 2080

Late next morning Karl and the General visit Konitsa to get an overview of the small local factory. Karl is a mechanical engineer and a devout do-it-yourselfer. For the General, it is most important to find ways to improve the transportation and communication devices. Karl believes that the materials at hand will allow them to piece together about eighty simple radio receivers. Unfortunately, they lack many of the necessary components for the actual radio station.

"There may be a solution to this. I will explain later", says the General. "Eighty receivers would be enough to equip all the taverns. That would be the best way to keep the public informed."

Karl starts to sketch simple plans for the construction of the receivers and compiles a list of items needed to complete a radio transmitting station. He knows that as communications and computer experts Johann and his sons will be of great help in constructing both receivers and transmitter.

During the visit, the General also shows Karl one of the few remaining Mollers from the fifth decade of the twenty-first century. Its owner proudly assures them that it is still 100% functional. Karl's eyes glimmer. "This model can still be controlled manually. We just have to disengage the navigational system."

The General can't believe his ears. "Are you serious? That would be... Could you turn the system off?"

"I think so."

"That would be great! All our transportation and motoring problems would be solved. We could also easily pick up the things you left at that abandoned house."

""Let me add the things I need to get this flying to the list for the transmitter. Then we'll know for sure." Karl jots down a number of items on an old gyros wrapper and hands it to the General.

"Except for a couple of the more exotic components, we have everything here," says the General, "and I think I know where we could get those other pieces. But let's go back to the castle now. As long as we still have food, we might as well eat. I'll explain the rest to you on the way back."

Once they are on the tractor again, the General begins to elaborate. "Several years ago, I found a hidden cave in the mountains on the other side of the Vikos Canyon. It's pretty high up there–I'd say about 2200 meters. It's an ideal hideout. The entrance is extremely hard to find. The cave is pretty spacious and it has several holes at the top that allow in enough light for it not to be pitch black. Those holes also let in the rain, so there's always drinking water. You can even start a fire in there because the smoke rises up through the holes. If you have dry wood, the fire cannot be detected from the outside. I consider this cave the "last bastion." In case of emergency, the entrance can be sealed through an explosion. I've met all precautions for such a case. The cave is equipped with everything you could hope for. There is food, weapons, tools, clothes, blankets, even furniture and books. Ten people could survive there for up to 100 days. The components that you're missing for the transmitter and the Moller should be there, too. I'd like you and Christina to hike there very soon—today if possible. About 400 meters below the cave, you'll find a bivouac. You should be able to make it there before nightfall if you leave right after lunch. It's near the Drakolimini, the Lakes of the Dragons. You could easily be back here tomorrow. One more thing: I hid a little sack with gold coins in a certain crack in the Vikos Canyon. I think we could really use them now. But that would mean that you would have to spend another night."

Karl doesn't think this over for too long. "If the situation weren't so serious, the whole thing would actually be a pleasure for us. Christina and I hike in the mountains quite often. I'm sure she'll be up for it. Don't get me wrong, but why do want us both to go?"

The General's face turns very earnest. "In case of emergency, I want to make sure the two of you can find the cave, even if you're separated."

Christina and Karl start their hike at 3:00 p.m. They take food for two days, a gas stove, appropriate clothing, sleeping bags, and a tarp. They also take climbing equipment so they can reach the "treasure crack" as Christina jokingly calls it. They plan to leave this equipment behind in the canyon to keep their load light for the more difficult part of the climb. The sketches and instructions the General gives them are so detailed that they both have no doubt that they'll be able to find both the cave and the gold coins.

At first, they have to hike on a steep path into the Vikos Canyon. Up here, the creek bed is already dried out. The creek is dry from the end of May through the entire summer. It's very hot on the floor of the canyon. They follow a well-beaten trail[12] downhill, until they reach the first *voithomati*[13], where a huge cold well emerges vertically from the ground, forming a pond: at this time of the year, the Vikos Creek starts here. Later on, this spring will also dry out and the creek will start much further down the canyon. The first *voithomati* is apparently a popular place to stop. The water looks tempting as they are both already sweating profusely. No one seems to be nearby, so they undress and jump into the water.

"Jeeezus! Cold!", Karl shouts. He quickly finds his way out of the pool. He's used to cold water in the mountain lakes of Austria, but these are in a whole different league.

---

[12] This has been a national park for almost ninety years.
[13] Voithomati means "Ox's eye."

"Maybe I should've told you. They say the water is about seven degrees Centigrade all year long," Christina says, laughing.

Karl watches Christina's perfect body, her long, dark, wet hair, and her nipples that have hardened from the cold water. Karl decides to take out his holocamera for a few pictures. Christina notices and tries to hide her nudity. 'This will only make the pictures better,' thinks Karl.

After the swim, they warm up a little before continuing to the path leading down the right side of the creek. They know that they have to be careful not to miss the trail up to the mountain. Surprisingly, this trail is marked better than the General told them. They leave their climbing equipment here. The trail becomes steeper and steeper. They slowly make their way uphill. Fortunately, most of the path lies in the shadow of the trees. When it evens out, they get a glimpse of the little mountain village where most tourists would start their hike. They will soon reach the path coming from this village, which leads to the Dracolimni, where they will bivouac.

It is almost 7:00 p.m. Since they left the floor of the canyon, they have already gained 1200 meters in altitude. According to the instructions, they have another two hours of uphill hiking. At around 9:00 p.m. and with little daylight to spare, they reach the bivouac that turns out to be a crude lean-to. As expected, no one else is around. In the last minutes of daylight, they enjoy the view before they sit down to heat up some soup. The little village below is almost completely dark. Normally, hundreds of light would be visible, but now they can only see light and smoke from a couple of cooking fires. Christina points out impressive walls of rock to the left. This must be Mt. Gamila. There is even still some snow near the peak. Tomorrow they will have to hike around the northernmost foothills of Gamila and even get very close to the peak. Further to the north, they make out the pass into the Aaos valley. Not far from there, the path that will lead them to the Dragon Lakes begins.

"Should we have our morning bath there tomorrow?" suggests Christina. They are both very hungry and tired after six hours of intense hiking. The warmth of the soup feels good at this high altitude. They also have olives, feta cheese, and white bread that Popi baked herself.

They find enough water in a cistern to wash the sweat off each other before they slide into their sleeping bags. Their goodnight kiss turns into something more...

June 13, 2080

Before they have breakfast, they run up to the Drakolimni. The lakes turn out to be both a surprise and a disappointment. These flat ponds hardly deserve to be called lakes. But on the other hand, they see an uncountable number of "dragons" there. These medium-sized reptiles have high scale spines on their backs. They really look like fairy tale dragons shrunk to one hundredth of their original size. They are also surprised to find a soft lime beach there and very warm water for the altitude. They excitedly jump into the water and cavort like children. After they have bathed enough, Karl lifts Christina out of the water and lays her down on her back on the soft beach. They make stormy love, rolling in the sand in their passion. Later, they lie together in the afterglow of post coital bliss, but discover that they are covered head to toe in white powder. So it's back into the lake for them!

After a short breakfast they continue on the trail to the peak. But soon the trail peters out and the ascent becomes more and more difficult. When they reach the windy gap below the peak, they find a marking which the General himself put there. It's a big red arrow reading, "Gamila Peak." They know that from here they have to turn exactly ninety degrees to the right. After about 200 meters of a challenging climb, they reach a field of broken cliff rock, characteristic for this area. They look for a specific rock resembling an equilateral triangle with sides of about one meter. They soon find it and carefully lift one side vertically, creating a slit, through which a hole becomes visible; it's the entrance to the cave. Carefully, they climb in and lower the triangle into its original position. They slowly crawl inside. It's not getting darker, but to their surprise, lighter! Where the cave is high enough, they stand up and find a fairy tale world around them. Light streams in from above and they can see a baby drakolimni. They can make out furniture covered in plastic tarps, just like in a long-deserted house. Many boxes stand around, carefully labeled indicating their contents.

Both Christina and Karl are speechless for a moment before Christina notes, "How could he even find this place? And how the hell did he manage to get all this stuff up in here? Even a cargo Moller couldn't land on the steep slope outside!"

Telepathically, Christina informs her father that they have reached the cave and that he owes them a couple of explanations.

When the General gets the message, it's the best news of the day. He can't keep a smile off his face. Of course a Moller couldn't land up there. It had to hover above the rocks. Of course, they also didn't move all the furniture into the cave completely assembled. The pieces had to be assembled inside. All this work was only possible with the help of several visiting Finnish soldiers. They were here for maneuvers and there was absolutely no risk that they would ever find their way back to the spot. Since then the cave has remained the General's secret, which he is now sharing with his daughter and Karl.

After Christina and Karl have marveled at the interior of the cave, they start unpacking two of the crates: one containing weapons, which they check and oil, the second containing the parts needed to repair the Moller and construct the radio station. When they are finished, they take the tarp off one table and two chairs and fix themselves the best lunch possible under such conditions. They create a cozy atmosphere and even take a couple of holo-snapshots as a surprise for the General.

Unfortunately they cannot stay long. If possible, they want to make it to the treasure crack and hopefully even back to the castle today. The descent is fast. When they reach the Vikos creek, they pick up their climbing equipment again, cross the creek, and follow it downstream. The canyon gets narrower and narrower and there's no longer enough room for them to walk beside the fast water, so they have to move higher and higher up into the rock-face lining the canyon. The General had warned them about the difficulties of the climb, and indeed, without the rope and pitons it would be much more difficult. They reach the plateau mentioned in the sketch. From here they have to climb about 200 meters almost horizontally along the vertical wall. They know that they will come across a group of dwarf pines that grow directly out of the rock. From there the "treasure crack" should be easily visible.

This turns out to be the most difficult section, partly due to the worsening of the light: strange clouds have formed and the wind has picked up. Just when they are back at the plateau with the coins in their backpack, they become aware of the change in weather. They were just too busy concentrating on their climbing. Suddenly they are facing a storm rolling in down the mountain and into the canyon. Thick curtains of rain become visible in the distance and the wind gusts hard. Protected by an overhanging rock, Karl fastens the tarp to the weather ward side of the stone. They barely have time to get underneath it before the storm rolls in. They each hold a corner of the tarp down with both hands. The tarp rattles in the heavy wind. It rains buckets and they find it hard to protect themselves and their backpacks from getting completely soaked. And suddenly it is all over. Despite the tarp, they are wet to the skin. The rain has cooled the air considerably. They are lucky to find some nearly dry clothes in their rucksacks and change into them. It's still light enough to try to make it to Monodendrion.

All of a sudden, Karl screams fearfully, "The storm is coming back!" Miraculously, the wind has shifted 180 degrees and is coming right back towards them.

Taking control of the situation, Christina shouts, "I've never seen anything like this. We'll have to find another shelter, and quick! Let's get on the other side of the rock." Again, they have some luck. They find a small cave that first leads a bit downwards, and then back up to where the floor is completely dry. "We'll be completely safe here. It wouldn't be a problem to spend the night here, either," exclaims Christina before she sends the following telememo to her father's Mindcaller: *'Mission accomplished. Must spend the night in a cave on the plateau. Be back tomorrow morning.'*

By then the rain is back. It's not quite as dramatic as before, but it lasts longer this time. It keeps raining and raining as it gets darker and darker.   The excitement over the cave diminishes when the roof begins to leak. The once bone-dry floor turns into a slippery mass of clay.   Water collects in the lowest point, between the entrance and the two hikers. Their sleeping bags are soon filthy and soaking wet, despite the tarp underneath them. The rising water by the entrance threatens to cut off their exit.

Karl shrugs his shoulders. "Sorry Christina, but we have to get out of here."

Christina nods.

They have to wade through waist deep water. It's still raining. Eventually, they find a half dry place under another overhang. Karl manages to cook some tea on their small camping stove, but despite their repeated attempts, they do not succeed in starting an open fire. Will they have to stay here and freeze all nightlong? Christian's XP announces, "I'm sure we can provide enough light with our infra red lamps for you to make the short walk back to Monodendrion." Christina and Karl wonder why they didn't think of this themselves.

With the help of the XPs, the climb turns out to be less dangerous than they thought. Despite the late hour, Christina decides to telememo her father: *'We got ourselves completely soaked. Can someone come and pick us up with the tractor at the Monodendrion exit of the canyon at half past midnight?'*

They both hope that this message will reach the General even if he is already asleep.

But the General hasn't even closed his eyes yet. He keeps receiving telememos, which sound more and more like SOSs. Most of them come from the USA, especially Los Angeles. By now the looting has escalated from rioting into a full-scale civil war. With the racial tension stirring up the situation even more, there seem to be never ending battles with heavy weapons involved: there is no more organized collection and distribution of food. It's all down to hoarding and defense. The General desperately hopes that this behavior is mostly due to the racial conflicts.

Christina's father picks them up personally in Monodendrion. "You two look like shit," he welcomes them.

Christina would love to say, "And so do you," because she has never seen him so exhausted.

"How's the world doing?" asks Karl.

"So-so la-la. Here in Greece, we still seem to have everything under control. But in the megopoli, everyone seems to be fighting everyone. It's really bad in Los Angeles, Tokyo, and Hong Kong."

There is a moment of silence before Christina breaks it with an optimistic word, "We found everything we wanted. There you go." She hands the bag with the gold coins to him.

"And I got everything for the radio station and the Moller," adds Karl. For now, all I can do is go to bed. But tomorrow morning you can tell me what you want done first: a flying Moller, or a radio station."

"Which will be quicker?" the General asks in excitement.

"The Moller. If I can get it going at all, it'll only take me about ten minutes."

"Then fix it the Moller first. The radios aren't fully functional yet anyway. By the way, without your three friends from Graz, we wouldn't be nearly as far as we are now. Those guys are good. Must be a pretty good university you have there."

But now they are all too tired to talk any more.

June 14, 2080

The General can't wait for Karl to get up and have his breakfast. Popi has to restrain him twice from waking Karl up.

Finally, the General, Karl and Christina drive down to Konitsa. Karl immediately stars to modify the old Moller. After a few minutes he observes, "It should be working now. Should I try it out or are you a better test pilot?" he asks the General.

The General doesn't even answer him but rather swings into the pilot seat. Just when Karl and Christina are ready to join him, they hear the screams of an approaching woman. She holds a little girl in her arms, whose face looks terrible.

"My daughter, my daughter! She has poked her eye out with a butcher knife! Just look at her! You're a doctor, please help!"

Christina curses herself for not having her medical bag with her. From now on, she'll have to remember to always keep it with her. Without a word, she takes the child and orders her husband to rip a piece of fabric from her blouse. She then uses it to carefully push the eye back into the socket. Neither the artery nor the optic nerve seem severed. Everything should work out fine. "I'll have to take her back to the castle right away. If we're lucky, it won't be as bad as it seems. We'll bring the child back to you as soon as possible."

"What kind of doctor are you?" thunders the General. "You want to separate the child from her mother. She'll come with us, of course." He quickly hands five of the gold coins to the owner of the Moller. "That's 200 Euros rent for the Moller. Go and inform the child's father. Tell him that we'll bring them back quickly and safely."

Now it is four adults and one child in the Moller. The motor starts. There was no time for a test flight so this will have to be it. Luckily, the Moller lifts itself, light as a butterfly. The General turns out to be a talented pilot and it only takes five minutes to fly the twenty-five km to the castle.

While Christina quickly gets the child into the house to further care for her wound, Popi takes care of the crying mother. She talks her into drinking a double shot of Ouzo and talks to her continuously, not allowing the mother to dwell on the state of her child.

Soon Christina is back, with the child in her arms and a happy smile on her face. "Everything will be all right. I put a good bandage over the eye. I know this looks pretty grim now, but nothing essential has been damaged. Your child will have completely normal eyesight again and only a tiny scar will remain. I've just given her a sedative. That should keep working until this evening. I'll come and check on her later and replace the bandage with a smaller one. There is absolutely no reason to worry any more."

The mother can't stop thanking Christina but Christina waves her off. "We all have to help each other–it's the only way we can get through this. Who knows? One day I may need your help."

The General has the woman and child taken home by one of his men. Then he turns to Karl. "Good job on the Moller."

"We were lucky. We really need the medicine from the abandoned house, remember?"

"We'll take care of this if not today, then tomorrow. I just got the news that the first receivers will be operational this afternoon."

"Well, good. We should begin distributing them right away to all tavernas and tell people to listen every day at 7:00 p.m. I'll have the transmitter ready by then."

For the General, this Friday thirteenth is the first good day since the breakdown: Christina just saved the eyesight of a child, and they have gold now for purchasing important goods. They have a flying Moller, and will soon have an operational radio station. In addition, he has just been informed that the families of his daughters, Felitsa and Melissa, have boarded to Alberta. His eyes are gleaming and yesterday's fatigue seems to have vanished.

But again he seems distracted. Apparently he is receiving another telememo.

After a few seconds, his positive tone has disappeared. "There have been lootings in Athens. Many people have died. They had to give up the whole airport district. Sixteen airplanes have crashed there since the breakdown. The few official helpers and security personnel have withdrawn. Those that are still alive are at the mercy of fate. For God's sake! This country could've been saved if everyone had pulled together. But instead, they're fighting over breadcrumbs. And we'll have to fight too eventually. As soon as the refugees overrun us, we'll have to waste a big part of our energy to avoid being robbed or stampeded. Let's hope that the situation in Ioannina remains stable. It's only sixty km away, and its 80,000 inhabitants could become a huge threat for us if they hear that we're not yet having any serious problems here."

For the first time, Popi has something to say about the situation. "Paul, don't be naive. They will definitely hear about us. You know how many people from here have family in Ioanninna and vice versa. You'll only have two alternatives:

49

either make sure that Ioanninna stays under control, or stop the people from coming here."

"As usual, you're right, of course," the General admits quietly.

3 Eastern Canada

Churchill Falls, Labrador, Canada
Saturday, June 8, 2080, 10:34 p.m. (Sunday, 4:34 a.m. CET)

Churchill Falls lies in the North Canadian wilderness about 300 km from Goose Bay and 200 km from Labrador City. From 1992 to 2040, those two cities were still connected by the Translabrador Highway. The era of the Mollers slowly turned this thoroughfare into a disused dirt road, which today is no longer drivable, even by off-road vehicles.

Frank and his wife Melissa sit in their holoroom watching a comedy film on one of the holochips they have rented from the library in the Donald Gordon Center. At 10:34, the lights flicker for a moment.

"Hey honey, would you mind if we stopped the film for a minute?"

"Too much beer, huh?" Melissa chides him.

"That too. But I'd like to check my computer real quick. Did you notice the lights, maybe there's some kind of problem with the power. I might have to restart the computer."

Not only has Frank's computer crashed, but also it can't be restarted. Frank wants to ask his XP for advice, but that doesn't work either. While he is still attempting to fix it, Melissa comes in. "What're you doing?" she asks impatiently. "Let's watch the rest of the movie before the kids come back. Some of the scenes might be a little racy for them."

Frank nods absentmindedly. "Yeah, yeah. Could you try your XP for me? Mine is dead. I've never seen that happen before."

She leaves the room and returns a half a minute later. "That's weird. My XP is dead too and so is the spare one. We'll have to take care of that first thing tomorrow."

Frank quietly agrees and they go back to enjoy the rest of the film.

But Frank's mind is elsewhere. As the head programmer of the Churchill Falls Corporation, he is naturally deeply concerned about this strange situation. Churchill Falls Corporation is one of the biggest underground hydroelectric plants in the world. The plant is the reason the family moved to this backwater in the first place. The capacity of the plant has been continuously increased over the years. More and more dams have been built, creating a huge lake that makes up an area of 6,500 square kilometers altogether. It has the capacity to produce eight gigawatt hours[14] and provides large parts of the Northeast of the continent with electricity.

Melissa is the oldest daughter of the Greek general, Paul Kalkias. Frank has always admired his father-in-law and is very happy with how much her family has accepted him. Due to the fact that her father and her brother Alex in Alberta both own a Mindcaller, Melissa is able to send telepathic messages, so-called "telememos," to both of them.

When Melissa became worried just now about those inappropriate scenes in the film, it gave away the fact that she is a typically protective, conservative Greek mother. Melissa still cannot accept the fact that both her seventeen-year-old son and her sixteen-year-old daughter have grown up and will soon graduate from high school and go on to university.

Her son has already been accepted at the medical school at Calgary University. His decision to attend was also heavily influenced by the fact that his favorite Uncle Alex, Melissa's brother, owns a farm near there.

Frank continues to dwell on the strange and simultaneous breakdown of his computer and the XPs. Apparently, the big computers at the power plant are still running; otherwise, they would be sitting in complete darkness by now. This eases his mind somewhat. However, their kids rush into their Cantle Avenue house earlier than expected. The Donald Gordon Center, where they were hanging out with friends in the bar of the only restaurant in the village, is only a stone's throw away. Teenagers are welcome to make use of the small dance floor there as long as they stick to alcohol-free beverages. The kids excitedly tell the

_____

[14] This is the equivalent of about twenty large river based hydroelectric plants. After its construction in 1971, the plant's capacity extended rapidly to 5,4 Gigawatts by 1990 and continued to grow a bit after that.

parents about the simultaneous breakdown of their XPs and about rumors that the village is now completely cut off from the rest of the world.

Frank reacts quickly. "I think I should go check on the plant. I'll take the ATRV[15]."

As compact as this settlement may be, such vehicles are still a necessity in bad weather, especially in the winter, when it sometimes gets down to minus forty degrees Celsius or below. Before Frank gets in, he checks on the large family Moller. His fears are confirmed: the entire navigational system is down. The security system of the vehicle would not allow it to be started.

When he arrives at the plant a short time later, he is informed that all the secure data lines leading to the outside are down too. The plant manager and the chief of security have already been discussing the situation: they are sure that the town is both physically and communicatively isolated from the outside world. Even though this breakdown seems to be more serious than any other before, the village is not in any immediate danger. Both electricity and water supplies are secure and the cool rooms and storage buildings are packed with goods. Remote areas like this one have always been more careful about certain precautions. There is word that there will be a gathering in the theater tomorrow morning.

Frank makes sure that his help is not required at the plant. He thinks that he will be able to get more information using his old ham radio at home. His brother Greg, an officer in the Canadian Navy, is also a hammer. A lot of people have laughed at their little hobby, and they tend not to mention it much anymore. However, this archaic foolery could now prove very useful.

---

[15] All Terrain Recreational Vehicle—these small vehicles are built mostly for short distances and off-road travel, and are especially used in the Moller-free zones of the national parks. They can only travel at a maximum of forty km/h. They can be coupled and don't require a driver's license to operate. They are small enough to fit into cargo Mollers. See the "Xperts:The Beginning", Chapter: The Mauto.

When Frank arrives home, the kids have already disappeared into their bedrooms, but Melissa is still up, eagerly awaiting her husband's arrival. "Do they know what's going on?"

"Not yet. I'll try to reach my brother over the ham. He should be on his frigate in St. John's[16] Harbor." Absentmindedly, he puts on his XP and notices happily that it seems to be functioning again, at least locally. But this will not help in analyzing the situation.

"Will you still be able to reach Greg? It's already after midnight, and half an hour later where Greg is."

"If they also had a crash like this, they must've realized it by now too. I'm sure they would have woken him up. It would actually be a good sign if I couldn't get hold of him. That would mean that the capital wasn't affected."

For a change, Melissa accompanies her husband to observe his work on the radio. Frank reaches Greg right away. "So there too," is Greg's unusual greeting.

"Right. All the XPs and the entire communication network are dead here. Well, locally they're working, but with no communication facilities," explains Frank. "What's the situation like there?"

"It's a catastrophe in the city. They don't even have electricity. They say that parts of the city are without water, especially where they need pumps for it. Here on board, most navigational instruments and certain sensors have collapsed. The computers are going nuts. But you know what's the good thing? Remember how I was complaining about how Canada has never really spent enough money on renewing military equipment? Well, everything we have is hopelessly ancient, and that's exactly the reason that a lot of it still works. We do have electricity, the sonar and radar still work; we still have paper charts and those good old nautical instruments. So I guess you could say we're only half-crippled. We don't have any connection with the

---

[16] St. John's is the capital of Newfoundland. This province consists of Newfoundland Island (108,860 km^2) and the eastern part of the Labrador Peninsula. The two parts are divided by the St. Lawrence Gulf. St. John's is situated about 1,100 km South- East of Churchill Falls.

admiralty, which means that I'm the boss over here now. Our specialists here on board aren't very optimistic. They're pretty sure that this'll last for days, if not weeks. If..."

"If what? Why did you stop there?"

"Well, I just realized that I really shouldn't be stirring up panic. But just between us, if this lasts three weeks or longer, we'll be facing a state of emergency, at least in the metropolitan areas. If that happens, I'm not even sure we could ever really get back to normal again. Man, if this is going on worldwide, then it could change all of humanity."

Frank and Melissa exchange distressed looks. They never really thought it could ever get that bad. But Frank wants to hear more from Greg.

"You know Frank, Felitsa and I are planning to make our way to Alex's place out in Alberta. We should be pretty safe and self-sufficient on his ranch. We've already figured out how to get there. I highly recommend you come along. We could pick you up, sort of. All of us really belong together there in these difficult times. It could be just like those days when we met those pretty Greek sisters," says Greg with a little chuckle. "But you have to decide this for yourselves. Anyway, I'll leave for Goose Bay at dawn tomorrow."

"You still remember that docking area, Terrington Basin? From there, I'll try to take those people who decide to leave to the main island quickly. I really hope to see you there. It'll take me two days to get the frigate to Goose Bay. It should take you just as long if you decide to leave tomorrow with your motorboat and go down the Churchill River. I'll only stay in the harbor for the day, then we'll have to go back. I'll definitely have to be back here within five days because I'm afraid by then there could be chaos breaking out. Let's stay in contact over the radios. Please let me know before 10:00 a.m. tomorrow whether you're coming or not. I have to stop now. There's a lot I have to take care of here. I really think that Alex's ranch would be the best option for all of us. Greetings to Melissa from her sister. Out."

Frank and Melissa just look at each other for a while. Melissa is the first one to speak. "I know this doesn't seem the right moment for any games, but I really think we should have a secret ballot so as not to influence our decisions. So it's either "Alberta" or "stay." We'll each write our decision on a piece of paper, then we'll know if we agree or if we have to discuss this further."

When they show their votes to each other, they both have Alberta written on them. They embrace each other. Their decision-making technique has proven to be successful one more time. Whatever may happen in the future, neither of them will be able to blame the other for having made the wrong decision.

They start the necessary preparations. Tomorrow they will let their friends know about their decision at the community meeting. They also decide to ask their friends if any of them want to come along. But now it's time to get some sleep. They have a tough day ahead of them.

Against his will, Frank remains awake much longer. He thinks back to a year ago when they decided that he should sign a three-year contract with the power plant. This decision had been strongly influenced by the problems they were having with their son, who was on the verge of going down the wrong roads out in Montreal. Frank is aware of the fact that this was also partly his fault. The affair he had been having with pretty, young Greta from Alberta had been keeping him from taking enough care of his children for years. Greta and he had a great time together, but always accompanied by a guilty conscience. He was really in love with her, though, and probably still is. Nevertheless, he could never talk himself into getting a divorce. Maybe he was just too cowardly, maybe just cynical, or maybe he just thought that a new marriage would lead to the end of their love. After several warnings, Greta started to withdraw more and more and eventually found herself a boyfriend closer to her age. They had a baby and got married, but even before that, she started to refuse having any kind of contact with Frank.

Her parting words still ring in his ears. "You're no longer part of my life." She even insisted that there should be no more e-mails between them. How could she just erase those beautiful years from her life? He never could. Time and again he is hit by dreams and loving memories of Greta, even though they haven't spoken in three years.

Because of the situation, the job offer at the plant was tempting in several ways. It offered the opportunity of a new life for him and his family in a beautiful, essentially free house in a remote but pleasant settlement of around 300 adults and 300 children. There was an unusually well-developed infrastructure with good schools, a holocinema, a theater, an indoor pool, a skating rink, a large library with a enormous selection of holochips, a ski lift, fifty clubs, and all for free. There was also a nice, heavily subsidized restaurant, a supermarket with a great selection of international cuisine, and a small hotel for friends and relatives. All of it was surrounded by beautiful wilderness in which to hike, fish, hunt, and snowmobile in the winter. It was really good for the kids. After they were there for several months, they realized that, due to the wide range of activities available at Churchill, the urge to get away from the community was less than they had expected.

However, they also had to face certain unexpected complications: they soon learned not to make friends too quickly because those "friends" could be very difficult to avoid in such a small community. Picking a friend was almost as difficult as picking a spouse.

Many of the residents had spent all their lives there. In the beginning, Frank and Melissa could not understand how they could endure this, but after a year living in Churchill, and despite the long and extreme winter, this didn't seem so absurd anymore. Life in an extended family had its good side.

Unfortunately, it was not possible to own a piece of land or a house here. Everything belonged to the plant. At first, it seemed strange and unfair that you had to leave all this behind after you retired, but they soon realized that most retirees were able to buy themselves a little house in the nearby southern areas close to where other retirees they liked would live. Of course, there were also other problems: the winter was too long and as soon as it warmed up again, huge swarms of mosquitoes and black flies rose from the earth. Only a short period after the first frost was both free of insects and warm enough to enjoy the outdoors.

The kids enjoyed the life there though. The only thing they found a bit problematic was romance. Where were they to go? Everyone knew everyone everywhere. And what was even worse was the very limited selection of potential partners. They had all known each other for years. "It's like dating your sister," Frank remembers his son complaining once before he finally glides into a troubled sleep.

Sunday, June 9, 2080

At 9:00 a.m. sharp, the siren in Churchill Falls howls three times. This means that an emergency meeting will take place at the theater in one hour. Even before that, Melissa and Frank informed their kids about their plans to go to meet Uncle Greg and Aunt Felitsa at Goose Bay, and from there try to get to Uncle Alex's farm in Alberta together. "This could be quite an adventure for all of us, and we can't be sure that we'll ever be able to return here. Nevertheless, you can only bring one backpack each in addition to the things on our list. Don't forget, we only have a small boat and we'll have to portage everything around Muskrat falls between here and Goose Bay, and that'll be no piece of cake. The kids understand the gravity of the situation, and do not protest. The thought of the ranch keeps them focused. While they begin to pack, Frank informs his brother over the radio that they will be coming to meet him. Then he and Melissa hurry to the meeting.

When they arrive at the theater, Newmoser, the plant manager, and Fred, the security chief, are already up on the podium. The theater is packed. Every family is represented by at least one adult.

Newmoser first summarizes the situation. Then he lays out the inventory list and explains that food, electricity, and water supplies are guaranteed for at least twenty days, but afterwards they may have to face shortages. "Are there any questions?"

Frank stands up. "There're a couple of things I'd like to say here. Some of you may know that I'm a ham radio operator. I contacted the commanding officer of a navy frigate in St. John's last night, right after the net imploded. Apparently, they're facing a similar situation there, but on top of that, they don't even have electricity. It's very likely that this is also true for all of Canada, if not the whole world. There seems to be absolutely no contact anymore with any satellites. The frigate no longer has a connection to Navy headquarters or to the government. However, I was informed a couple of minutes ago that the provincial government is holding an emergency meeting in St. John's right now. The navy specialists assume that it could take several weeks for the situation to normalize. The frigate I mentioned is on its way to Goose Bay to pick up any people who wish to leave Labrador and take them to the main island. My family and I are leaving for Goose Bay by motorboat soon. We feel that we might be safer at one of my relatives' farm in another place. Don't get me wrong, I think that Churchill Falls might also be one of the safest places at the moment; we all know why. Nevertheless, we just heard from the boss that certain important goods will also get scarce here. If some of you want to leave, I feel we'd be safer traveling as a group. We'll be leaving soon, so if any of you want to join us, you'll have to make it fast. Just for your information, we'll be leaving at 11:30 where the water from the plant flows into Churchill River. I wish everyone the best."

After a few handshakes and quick good-byes, the attention goes back to the podium. No one seems to be seriously considering leaving Churchill Falls at this point. The people still feel strong as a group and have no reason not to trust those in charge. Newmoser begins to speak again, "Would anyone else like to talk before I hand it over to Fred?"

No one does, so Fred begins to speak, "It's true. This could last a long time. Maybe even into winter."

Murmurs and whispers run through the crowd.

"I think we'll just have to prepare for the worst. That's why we have rationed all the goods we have according to the size of every family for a period of ten weeks. Every Monday you can pick up your ration of goods. Some goods will run out faster than others. We don't have much sugar or alcohol, for example," he says with a smile to a few boos from the audience. "We'll concentrate the workforce, including the older children, on foraging for and gathering food. We're working on a detailed program, which we plan to announce here tomorrow at the same time. Thanks for your attention and let's keep cooperating. If we stand together, we'll get the best out of the situation. Back to you, Jack."

Newmoser continues, "As long as we're only using the electricity for ourselves, we only need to keep one turbine working. That'll save us a lot of work. I know all of you are highly qualified programmers and engineers but there won't be a lot for you to do now, so of course you'll be paid as usual, but please agree to do those jobs that are most crucial to the running and maintenance of our village as a whole. Of course we'll try to arrange this according to your wishes as much as possible."

"But one thing should be clear to all of us: we are strong enough to survive here, but there won't be any room for parasites! No work, no food, just like in the Bible. There's another delicate topic that I feel I have to address now and that we should vote on. As you know, Goose Bay is the nearest large town. It is important to find out what the situation is there. If everything is normal there, then we shouldn't have any problems either. All we'd have to do is find a way to transport things over here. At worst, we'd have to repair the road. But if they have had a complete breakdown too, including electricity, then we'll be facing a serious problem by the time it starts getting cold."

"They'll try to come here, where there is electricity and hence warmth, by snowmobile. Our little settlement will definitely not be able to cope with thousands of refugees. Apparently, right now there's only one way to get to Goose Bay and back, and that's by snowplow. A motorboat wouldn't be able to fight the strong current coming back upstream. So, you could only come back here in about five weeks, once the water's lower. The ATRVs were just not built for such a rough 300 km journey, one-way. I suggest that two people who can operate the snowplows try to get near enough to Goose Bay to find out what's going on there. If necessary, they'll destroy all the bridges and obstruct all the trails on the way back. Is anyone against this plan?"

This plan comes as a shock to the audience. No one dares to raise a hand despite the fact that several people present have close relatives in Goose Bay, and this could be a virtual death sentence on their families.

Newmoser's scheme works as planned and he is happy that his speech was so effective. For quite some time, he keeps talking about thankfulness, standing together, friendship and the like. He enjoys not being just the plant manager, but also the undisputed "chief" of the village: a village, which has become his own little monarchy. He is already dreaming about the time when they can start printing money, bills with the plant on one side and his visage on the other!

Finally, Newmoser closes his bombastic speech. "Now we should perhaps try to enjoy this beautiful Sunday and pretend that nothing has happened before we start our new lives tomorrow."

The audience applauds. They feel they will be well cared for under Newmoser. Fred is the only one who is uneasy: 'Of course everyone in Churchill Falls should have the right to leave,' he thinks, 'including that Frank and his family, but shouldn't they check to see that they are returning the company's house in good condition? And shouldn't that ham radio-station stay here in the village, whether it is private or not?' He decides to keep it here as a deposit until their house is once again in perfect condition. He'll have to catch up with Frank before 11:30, and there are only twenty minutes left...

With his speech, Newmoser has triggered a development following the same pattern as others around the world: defending your turf. Even where individual groups are working successfully together, a lot of their energy is wasted on segregationist activities. The world is in the fast lane on the road back to the feudal system.

After Frank and Melissa leave the meeting, they rush to pack up the rest of their things and drive them to the boat with their ATRV. "Why the rush? Didn't you just say that we're going to wait until 11:30 by the plant's outlet? We've got plenty of time."

"You're right, I did say that but I really don't trust that Fred. Maybe we should've just left without telling them, but I really thought we should tell them about the seriousness of the situation. That's why I had to tell them about the radio. I wouldn't be surprised if Fred tried to take it away from us."

"You really think that he'll try to take it from us by force?"

"He might come up with some kind of rationale for that," answers Frank.

So, the four of them leave a little bit before 11:30, but Melissa leaves a message on a piece of cardboard: *Had to leave early. Will wait by Moss Bay until noon.*

Only minutes after they have cast off Fred arrives but finds them already 100 meters downstream. He reads the sign and curses, realizing that he would not be able to get back from Moss Bay due to the strong current. But Frank must not escape!

Fred is now more interested in punishing Frank than retrieving the radio. He takes his hunting rifle out of his ATRV and aims at the boat. He shoots several bullets but misses because of the increasing distance.

Melissa is terrified. "What a bastard! I don't believe it!"

Frank tries to calm them down. "It'll be alright. They can't hurt us any more. I just can't believe I trusted them this long. Maybe it's true what they said about the security personnel, that some of them are ex-cops who were kicked off the force. Maybe we should be happy that we're out of Churchill Falls."

Despite their worries, they stay at Moss Bay until noon. Frank is not sure if Fred would be crazy enough to follow them here in a motorboat so he keeps a rifle close at hand. Fortunately, he doesn't need it.

They try to put as much distance as possible between themselves and Churchill Falls. They don't have enough fuel to keep the motor running constantly and decide to turn it off where the current is strong. Under normal circumstances, this would be a dream of a trip: the bushes on the banks of the river are already in bloom, wildflowers cover few patches of grass, they even see young moose but keep a good distance from their guarding mother. They manage to catch a large trout. The sky remains cloudless and blue, and the birds are flying high, giving them hope for continuing good weather. As they are nearing the waterfall, the current becomes stronger and at times they come close to capsizing.

They reach Muskrat Falls late in the evening. They know that this is the most critical point of their trip. They decide to land the boat a good bit upstream of the falls themselves. Frank decides to land on the right side of the river. He knows that there is a path on the other side connecting the waterfall with Goose Bay that is only about thirty km away, but he believes it better to avoid contact with other people.

They leave the boat beached at the top of the falls and set out, only bringing their backpacks and those things necessary for spending the night. They'll get the boat and the rest of the gear the next day. To get to the bottom of the falls, they first have to cross a swampy forest, and then traverse a rocky slope. Sometimes the bushes are helpful as handholds; sometimes they just get in the way. After passing through another small wood they finally reach a suitable rocky bank near the river, They decide to make camp and prepare dinner.

"Can I start a fire to cook the trout?" asks Frank's son.

Frank hesitates. It wouldn't be wise to attract any attention and the smell of the trout could also attract bears. Nevertheless, Frank gives into his son. "O.K., but make sure to start the fire behind a rock so that no one can see it from the other side of the river. And stack our food near the fire for now. We'll have to hang it on a tree later to keep the animals away from it."

They set up the tents behind another rock and pick a spot for the toilet.

"Be sure you always have a shotgun at hand. The bears are really hungry this time of year. You have six shots."

Even though they are all used to the wilderness, they are a bit nervous now. The combination of the bears, hungry after a winter's hibernation, the smell of the fire, and the trout in the creek make an unwanted visit likely.

It's still light out so Frank and his daughter decide to go up again and get the motor and the radio from the boat. For now, the boat itself will remain above the falls. It will take all four of them to carry it down.

After dinner, Frank decides to contact Greg and tell him that they'll be at the frigate shortly after noon tomorrow. Greg is happy to hear the good news.

They make sure to thoroughly wash the pans and dishes so as not to leave anything that could be detected by sensitive noses.

Finally, they wrap all the food and cooking utensils into a bundle, tie a rope around it, and hang the bundle from a high branch. This "bear bag" will keep most wild animals from getting to their food. They say good night and disappear into their tents, the parents into one, and the kids into another.

It is still dark out when Frank and Melissa are abruptly awoken by screams from the other tent. Quickly, Frank gets out of his sleeping bag, grabs his gun, and crawls out of the tent. Only a meter away stands a large brown bear, tearing at the other tent with its huge paws. Behind the bear he can make out two cubs. There is no time to think; the lives of his children are at risk. He fires one shot over the head of the mother bear. She turns to face her new opponent instead of running away. Now he has to shoot again and hits her in her front leg. She takes a swipe at Frank with her good paw. Fortunately, she cannot support her weight with the wounded front leg, which buckles under her. With a terrible roar, she turns and runs back into the woods with her cubs.

"Is anyone hurt?" shouts Melissa, who is trying to assess the situation with the help of a flashlight.

"Only a little," groans her son.

The "little" turns out to be a large flesh wound on his upper arm. While Melissa is taking care of the wound, she doesn't fail to notice a fishy smell on her son. "Could it be that you neglected to wash thoroughly?"

Melissa and the kids spend the rest of the night in one tent while Frank keeps watch, his back against a tree and the shotgun across his knees. Fighting off the desire to sleep, he stays awake like this until sunrise. Then he starts the fire again and prepares breakfast before he wakes the rest of the family.

Monday, June 10, 2080

The incident with the bear was bad enough, but now only three of them are left to carry down the boat. This turns into a very difficult job. At the steepest point, Frank slips and they lose the boat, which rattles down the slope. Frank pales. Because of his carelessness, the boat might now be too damaged to get them any further. However, it seems to be only a little scratched up.

They reload the boat and get back on the river to find the boat leaking steadily. Frank decides to speed up as much as possible while the others bail the water out. They can only hope that they'll have enough fuel. They soon realize that not only will the fuel run out before they get to Goose Bay, but it is likely they will also be swamped. They have to land it several times to empty it out. When they reach the westernmost point of the Hamilton Inlet, the current stops completely. With the remaining fuel, they only make it just beyond the small settlement of Mud Lake before they have to land the boat for good on the north shore. Twenty kilometers remain between here and the dock. They'll have to walk it. The path wouldn't be a problem, but they would have to leave several important items, including the radio, behind.

Frank sets up the radio to reach Greg and explain the situation. "We could easily reach you by foot. It would take us four, maybe five hours. The only reason to pick us up would be to save the radio."

Greg doesn't have to think twice. "We have to save the radio. I'll send a boat over. It shouldn't take more than thirty minutes."

Soon the family members are embracing each other. "It's so good that we're back together again," Greg welcomes them. "Frank, I need your help right away. People are already going crazy down here. We'll have to drive through the streets with an ATRV and explain the situation to the people over a loudspeaker. The government has erected a tent village on an Air Force base between Lewisport and Gander. It should house about 5000 people. They have electricity there, hot and cold running water, and the food should hold for at least three weeks. No one knows what we'll do after that. We'll be able to fit a maximum of 400 passengers onto the frigate, and that's only if we use the deck too. I want you to stay on board the frigate and keep me updated as to how many people have already boarded or are waiting to board. Once we are at 300, I'll return to the ship. We have to make sure that we don't exceed 400. No matter what, I'll be back in no more than three hours. Then we'll know more."

"How much is everyone allowed to bring on board? How will they get to the dock?"

"I'll guess they'll use their ATRVs. Apparently, someone is even planning to run a sort of taxi service."

"And how're they going to pay for that?"

"I guess they'll use whatever they have: gold, food, beer, water, I don't know. The taxi driver seems to be building up a stash. You asked me how much they're allowed to bring: I'd say one suitcase and a piece of hand luggage each. But in the event we have less than 400 passengers, we could also allow them to bring more. We'll leave the dock at 7:00 p.m. We need some daylight when we get out to the open sea. The passage between the inlet and the sea is very tricky. Once we're out in the open sea, we can haul ass to St. John's, that is, if we have some moonlight. There're just too many icebergs still around in the early summer. We'll talk about all the details later. Now, let's get started."

With a bullhorn in one hand, Greg drives through the streets of Happy Valley and Goose Bay. "Every family has to decide if they want to stay here or go to the reception camp on the main island. If you have relatives or friends on the main island, it might be better to go. Please consider that there may not be any scheduled ferries for a long time."

Many people hear the announcement, but not many seem to react to it. Greg decides to also drive up to North West River, the only neighboring village, to advertise the evacuation. He understands the reservations of the people. After all, he can be sure to have a safe refuge in his brother in law's house in Alberta. But why would anyone exchange his own house, friends and neighborhood for a three-week stay at a reception camp? But on the other hand, how can one expect to survive the winter here at Goose Bay if the worst happens?

When Greg returns to the boat, only thirty people have boarded so far. Those are either tourists or stranded business travelers. This pattern hardly changes all the way up to 7:00 p.m. Only two Goose Bay families have boarded. All the other passengers, 100 all together, are from somewhere else.

"Why the hell do you think the locals didn't accept this opportunity? Goose Bay is getting more and more dangerous. Some of the shops won't even open up any more. There's no more buying, just exchanging goods. I don't even want to know what that place will look like in a week."

Felitsa, Greg's wife and Melissa's sister, thinks she has an answer. "So far, no one is hungry or cold, and the weather's great. Plus, they all know that the main island is not exactly Florida in winter either. And most of them are still hoping that things will soon be back to normal. We know that this isn't very likely, but let's hope we're wrong."

4 The Colony at Churchill Falls

Churchill Falls
Sunday, June 9, 2080, afternoon

After Newmoser's speech, most people do as he suggested: they spend a relatively normal Sunday with their families. But from now on certain things are handled more carefully. Not a single bottle of wine is opened on that day. Special privately owned "treasures" are reserved for special occasions. When a fisherman snags his hook in a tree, he doesn't just cut the line, but does his best to retrieve it somehow. Who knows when they will be able to get new fishhooks again? Children who come back from playing with scratches and scrapes do not get the usual bandages any more. They have to be saved for serious accidents.

Many inhabitants still do not believe that the situation is really so dire but others start inventorying their supplies, which are huge compared to those in other places around the world. Almost every house has at least two freezers and some have as many as five. This is due to the fact that electricity has always been practically free in Churchill Falls. It has become a habit for most of the locals to keep large amounts of frozen meat, vegetables and prepared food in their homes. Some of the freezers that were not completely filled up when the breakdown happened are soon filled with fresh-caught trout, filleted to save space.

Newmoser, Fred, Fred's lieutenants, Jim, Richard, the manager of the supermarket, her husband, the owner of the liquor store, the owner of the gas station, and the doctor get together for a meeting.

Newmoser starts it out with a short introduction. "The computer specialists and the technicians are all convinced that, for a long time, we're not going to have any kind of contact with the outside world except perhaps for unwanted contact with refugees from, say, Goose Bay or Labrador City. We think that Labrador City will be less of a problem because most people would probably go south from there to reach the settlements on the St. Lawrence Seaway or on the ocean itself, because those simply have a less severe climate than us. We should all be mentally prepared for the possibility of having to survive here for more than one winter. I consider all of you present here to be the "Emergency Committee," which I prefer to call the "Executive Committee." I think of myself as the Chairman of the Executive Committee and I would like Fred and the good doctor to serve as my Vice Chairmen. I see the rest of you as equal members of the board. Our relatives and us will be something like an "inner circle" which should be completely cohesive and should be obliged to accept the decisions of the majority. If there is no majority, the chairman will have the deciding vote. Are all of you happy with this?

As Newmoser had hoped, his proposal is accepted. He is pretty sure that Fred will always be on his side because of the survival chamber. On the other hand, Jim is completely dependent on Fred because of his drug problem (only the chief of security has access to confiscated illegal drugs). Newmoser can also be pretty sure of Richard's vote because of certain business favors. This always guarantees him at least four votes, which is the majority he needs.

He continues confidently, "It's the job of this Executive Committee to care for and distribute supplies fairly, and to consider measures that will allow us to enlarge our stocks. At the same time, I believe that it would only be fair if our relatives and us had certain privileges. We need to make sure that we don't become what others are surely becoming: egoists and hoarders. That's the reason why the transcripts of our meetings should be kept strictly confidential. This is what I propose. You who agree, please raise your hands."

Eight hands rise.

Newmoser is earnest about the equal distribution of resources and work, however, he considers himself and his committee to be somewhat more equal than the rest. Last night, he and Fred already gathered all the existing keys to the survival chamber. This chamber is located 200 meters below the surface in the bedrock of solid granite and contains everything necessary for a number of people to survive for a long time. "If necessary, the two of us can survive here for almost eighteen months and no one will ever be able to get to us. But this secret must remain between us," explains Newmoser. Both Fred, who is a bachelor, and Newmoser, whose wife is stuck with her daughter in Tucson, Arizona, would have no one to care for in this situation. The survival chamber is an enormous security factor for the two of them, but on the other hand, the supplies that are stocked there could never feed all the 600 people of the village for more than two days. "Two days won't make a difference," Newmoser justifies himself.

But even Newmoser is not immune to the hoarder mentality he talks about. And Fred has managed to keep an extra key to the chamber secret form Newmoser. The attitude of the doctor is not much different: He and his wife, who assists him as a nurse, have made sure to "put some medicine aside" for themselves, "just in case."

The other committee members also try to take advantage of the situation as soon as they realize that the condition could become critical: the restaurant owner reserves food for himself, the teacher reserves paper, etc.

After some further discussion, the committee carefully studies the inventory list. They soon realize that the original plan to hand out a 10% ration is not realistic. Many of the goods can simply not be divided into 600 parts. For example, how are they going to divide 800 light bulbs, or the three extra freezers? It also wouldn't make sense to hand out diesel fuel, which can only be used for the snowplows and their single tractor. It similarly seems to make no sense to distribute the latest supply of 500 sacks of rice because most of the families do not have enough space at home, and there would be a danger that such valuable food could go bad. Conversely, they are shocked at the small supply of flour and eggs: under normal circumstances, flour would have arrived in two days, and eggs would have arrived in small batches.

"Aren't you happy that we made this exception and allowed the Voller family to keep their own chickens? Now we'll at least be able to have the occasional egg," notes Fred.

71

"We? What do you mean, 'we'?" Jim reacts, "Why would the Vollers give us any of them?"

This leads to a longer debate on whether it wouldn't be a better idea to gather many of the private goods and add them to the collective inventory.

"I don't think we should become communists all of a sudden," argues Newmoser.

They end up agreeing against collectivism not out of reason but because the committee members know that they and their families own more than the average. Newmoser had earlier made clear that most of the regular work at the plant would be stopped, which means that they will close down the cafeteria there. The goods that are stocked there will only be distributed to the "inner circle." It is convenient that Richard is married to the manager of the cafeteria, who is the only one who knows exactly what is stocked there.

It is obvious that it will probably be best to distribute all the goods on a monetary basis, and not depending on how much somebody owns, but on how much the individual goods are worth.

They decide not to include the diesel fuel or most of the weapons and ammunition. Those supplies will serve the community. The diesel will only be used for the snowplows; the majority of the weapons and ammunition will be reserved for the defense of the village. They also decide unanimously that refugees will not be accepted in the summer and will only be allowed to spend one night in the winter.

The old, official value of all the goods is totaled and then divided by 589, the population size. From this they calculate the disposable sum per person. This is the amount that each family can use to buy whatever they want until the supplies run out. New goods they accumulate communally will raise the disposable sum proportionally. It will be impossible to use the XPs for accounting purposes, but Newmoser is sure that his experts will be able to create a local computer network within the next few days. Until then, no goods will be given out.

By 4:00 p.m. they all seem to be happy with what they have agreed. Only Newmoser regrets that they have not decided to print banknotes. But the hard work still lies ahead of them: how will they deal with the lean times? How will salt, sugar, eggs, milk, flour, spices, and vegetables be replaced?

At this point, all they are thinking about is food.

Undeveloped ideas swarm around the room. In the end, the committee agrees to implement work groups for the different issues. They will put those work groups together during the general meeting tomorrow morning.

"We should really clarify now how much every individual will have to work for the community and how much free time they'll get. I think that working at the plant, or in a work group, or wherever should count the same as long as it serves the entire community," suggests the doctor.

Mostly due to their own immediate hunger, they find it easy to come up with a formula quickly. Richard's wife is preparing a hearty dinner at the cafeteria for the committee members and their families. Altogether, this circle consists of only ten people because after an animated discussion, they decided to exclude the younger children for security reasons. Of course, the parents of those children will be allowed to take some food home to them.

The dinner is good, but at the same time, modest. It consists of meat (they all believe that meat will never get scarce given the abundance of wildlife), rice, and a salad made from dandelion leaves. They also open some bottles of beer and wine, well aware of the fact that the supplies of both the cafeteria and the liquor store are low and will soon be exhausted. How will they ever be able to replace that?

June 10-14, 2080

The next day's general meeting is mostly concerned with supply issues and goes fine for Newmoser. There is even occasional applause, especially when Newmoser explains that all the goods will be distributed equally, independent of how much money a family has. It will be possible, of course, for the families to exchange goods between each other on the basis of IOUs.

Before they get to the issue of workgroups, Newmoser explains the work hours agreement: "Only those who work for the community, and their families, of course, will be a part of the supply system. Working for the community means committing to a thirty-five hour workweek either at the plant or on committee-approved projects. In a moment we will put work groups together. Every one of you is quite welcome to suggest ideas for serving the community, but they have to be approved by the committee. The thirty-five hour system is in effect for everyone eighteen years or older. Children under ten have no work responsibilities whatsoever. Children between ten and eighteen can be drafted for work if necessary for a maximum of twenty-five hours of work per week. But now let's get going with the work groups..."

Newmoser does not allow interruptions or discussions. This tactic will save him several times in the coming general meetings. Once all the work groups have been put together, they agree to report back on June 13th, three days from today.

The continuing pleasant June weather seems to have a positive effect on the general atmosphere. What's also positive is that the computer network between the supermarket, the gas station, the restaurant, and the liquor store will be up soon, too. This means that everyone will be able to shop again tomorrow. People are looking forward to shopping without actually having to pay for anything, even though it will cut into their disposable sums, a term which people will quickly shorten to "DS". This DS will also become the main topic of conversation. All in all, the inhabitants of Churchill Falls feel well governed and Newmoser enjoys this new level of popularity.

They all get to work. Some of the locals have not yet been assigned to a workgroup and are collected together into the so-called "foragers." This group is initially so successful that the DS even increases, despite continuing consumption of goods. Spirits are generally high and only very few think further and realize that the level of the DS is not all that counts: How will a growing amount of meat, fish and wild vegetables make up for the dwindling supply of milk and flour?

All the work groups report to the committee on Wednesday. The reports show a high degree of ingenuity.

The "Egg Brigade," as they have dubbed themselves, has come up with the possibility to increase the number of chickens and eggs. They suggest keeping the egg consumption low until the number of chickens has been increased. They are planning to solve the feeding problem by collecting a winter stock of bugs, worms, and seeds. This should guarantee a large output of eggs and even some meat for the coming year.

With the help of the XP's archives, the "Milk Brigade" has come up with a way to raise caribou and use them as animals for milk. This will also require a large amount of labor, especially when it comes to the production and erection of fencing. The small supply of barbed wire will make it necessary to stick to wooden fences, and since there is no sawmill, they will have to be produced solely with the few chainsaws.

The Salt Brigade's report sounds especially promising: Simple methods should make it possible to turn the road salt into table salt. This should allow for an unlimited supply.

The Vegetable Brigade has identified an uncountable number of edible plants, including wild leech, nettles, dandelions, and wild turnips. They have also compiled information on the optimal time for harvest of each vegetable. They also suggest digging out an artificial ice cave for preserving meat and vegetables. They have come up with an even more revolutionary idea: to use the tunnel leading to the underground transformer gallery of the plant as an indoor growing facility. The tunnel is 2.5 km long, twenty meters wide and equipped with fluorescent lighting that produces a spectrum similar to that of sunlight. It is always well heated by the heat given off from the generators, and could be heated up even further by sending large amounts of electricity through the water pipes that lie underneath. This would also provide warm water. By creating a thirty cm deep layer of soil, they hope to create a huge greenhouse. Every resident would be granted a plot of eighteen by forty meters. There is still a large quantity of seeds for several vegetables.

When it comes to potatoes, it will be a similar procedure as with the eggs: it will be necessary to do without them for some time. Each resident would have to decide for himself if he should eat his four kg ration or turn it into a 400 kg ration in the coming year. It will be hard work getting the soil in there, but the fact that the tunnel is on an 8% gradient will definitely make the whole job easier.

The news from the Sugar Brigade is less promising. There are hardly any wild bees in the area, so no substantial honey production is in sight, especially if they don't want to completely exploit the beehives at this point. Due to the short blooming period, the Labrador bee can only produce honey necessary for its own survival. Maple syrup and boiled sap of other trees seem to be the only substitutes for sugar. And even that will be problematic because the surrounding woods consist mostly of pine trees.

The Flour Brigade has been even less fortunate. However, they have managed to produce a mix of ground hazelnuts and acorns, which could theoretically be used to bake pies and cookies. No real substitute for rice and flour seems to be in sight. No wild tubers similar to potatoes grow in Labrador. The spare growth of wild thistle is not a substantial substitute either: it took every single forager about an hour to collect 100 grams. The thistles may be tasty, but this will never amount to more than a hobby.

The Fruit and Berry Brigade sounds more hopeful: there is a huge amount of edible berries out there. Of course they all ripen in the fall, which will entail a very large harvesting effort. Even the children could help here. Should there ever be school again, they would have to move their holidays back a month. Certain mushrooms could be collected earlier than that to be dried for the winter. It sounds especially cheerful that some of the berries, such as juniper, can be turned into wine and spirits.

As the reports of the individual workgroups continue, it becomes clear that the archives of the XPs are still able to provide immensely important knowledge. Now it is time to calculate which of the suggested projects can be carried out and on what scale.

The results are sobering: assuming a thirty-five hour work week and eating habits which barely reach sustenance level, 1300 adult workers would be necessary to start all the different projects. And even if they could all be started, they would still need 700 workers (twice what they have) to feed the population.

It seems a given fact that to survive in this climate requires help from the outside.

"We'll have to accept that our diet will consist mostly of meat, fish, wild vegetables, and salt, accompanied by berries, mushrooms and hazelnuts," Newmoser explains. "Different kinds of tea will be our primary beverage. Sweets will be a real luxury. To be able to have the occasional glass of berry-wine or egg, we would have to increase working hours to forty per week. Other projects, like raising caribou and planting vegetables in the tunnel will have to be carried out during leisure time. As a community project, this doesn't seem to be a reasonable sacrifice. I'm really sorry, but that's the way it's going to be. I would now suggest having another vote to decide if we should proceed like that. If I don't have your trust, I will resign. I am really trying to do my best here."

There are several groans and unhappy faces, but eventually most residents raise their hands. Newmoser's threat to resign seems to have influenced their decision.

But Newmoser does not fail to notice that none of the group of teachers has raised their hand.

"Thank you for your trust. We will get through this somehow. I want you to know that the committee has decided to allow for a little snooping around in the form of a reconnaissance mission. With a sound mind and a clear conscience, I am convinced that all these measures will not stand longer than one year."

When the gathering is just about to dissolve, two men rush into the theater. They are the ones that took the snowplow to Goose Bay to look around.

Everyone returns to his or her seat to eagerly await the report.

"It took us two days to get there. We really had to work our way through. It was real tough. The rivers have washed the street away in some places so we had to push dirt in to be able to cross. When we were twenty km away from Goose Bay, we hid the plow and continued with the ATRV we brought with us. We were very careful not to be noticed and left the ATRV behind before we reached the first houses."

"Well, to sum it all up, when we arrived there on Tuesday, it was already chaos. Apparently, they had been without electricity since the breakdown. Just like us, they're completely cut off from the rest of the world. Remember what Frank told us about that frigate? It really did show up on Monday and picked up about 100 people. But for some reason, most of the locals preferred to stay in Goose Bay and hope for the best. We stayed in an abandoned house and had another look around the next day. All I can say is, we're much better off here. No one seems to have taken control over there. We watched them loot that one big supermarket next to the Labrador Inn. The situation is really out of control there. So we came straight back and made sure to make the streets impassable behind us. There's no reason to worry that anyone will come here from Goose Bay and give us trouble."

One of the teachers raises his hand and Newmoser gives him the floor. "But the people in Goose Bay have snowplows as well. Why wouldn't they be able to fix the road again? Also, I think that we shouldn't cut ourselves off completely. If they really want to, they'll find a way to get here, won't they?"

The two men look at Newmoser quizzically. After all, he asked them not to give certain details away. But now, he shrugs his shoulders and throws them a gesture to continue.

"No, there won't be a way to get here," the younger plowman continues, "not even in the winter. Not with a plow, not with an ATRV, and not with a snowmobile. The only way they could theoretically make it here would be upstream with a motorboat, but that would take a huge amount of fuel. As a matter of fact, you know the big bridge 120 km between here and Goose Bay, the one that crosses the canyon? There's no way you can drive around it. We followed Newmoser's orders and blew it up. There is simply no land connection anymore."

Murmurs and whispers go through the crowd. Some of the residents admire Newmoser for his foresight, others wonder about his cold- bloodedness, while still others are shocked that one of the only two ways out of here no longer exists. They do not yet know that Newmoser has also arranged to blow up the bridges leading to Labrador City, even though, with some effort, it would be possible to circumvent them...

Instinctively, Newmoser reacts correctly: he doesn't try to explain or defend his decision. Instead, he exclaims, "Thank you gentlemen for your great effort and for the important information. Now we know that our precautions were just and necessary. Give these guys a hand!"

Newmoser starts clapping and more and more residents follow his example. Whatever reservations there may be towards Newmoser, those two men did a good job. There is no doubt about that.

In the Executive Committee meeting that directly follows the general one, Fred asks in astonishment, "You could've told us about your plan for the bridge..."

Newmoser interrupts him and looks at him sharply. "You know very well that I had already sent those two off before we even had our first Executive Committee meeting, so how could I have asked you? Of course I would've done so otherwise. But sorry, I interrupted you. Was there anything else you wanted to tell us?"

Fred continues hesitantly, "Well, I only wanted to know if you have any other new information. About what you said.... that you're sure that we'll be 'better off in a year?'"

"I never said anything like that," Newmoser answers, "All I said was that those measures would stand for a year at the most. What I meant was that they'll become much more unpleasant if we don't have any support from outside by then. Don't forget, though we still have a lot of supplies at the moment, at some point we'll run out of ammunition and gas for the ATRVs, motorboats, and chainsaws. And we'll run out of diesel for the plow eventually, too. I could go on and on. Even though we presently don't have a problem with the meat and fish supplies, we'll eventually fish out the nearby lakes and it'll be tough to shoot deer with bow and arrow. 600 people will take their toll. Remember, there's a reason why the Eskimos were nomads.

They always moved to other hunting grounds. I really think we'll have to ask people to be more careful about how much they consume. We might have made a mistake with the DSs. We should also have raised the price for rare goods. Have you noticed how many of these clowns drove to the meeting with their ATRVs? It's beautiful weather outside and none of them would have to walk longer than fifteen minutes to get here. Do you know how much that gas costs us? But on the other hand, we all heard their complaints today. Maybe we just can't tighten the belt further until the shortages become imminent."

Churchill Falls, Two month after the breakdown
August 8, 2080

Two months have passed since the breakdown. The village is still cut off from the rest of the world. The situation has become slowly but steadily worse. Flour has become an extremely scarce commodity and this has led to some very questionable arrangements: for seventeen-year-old Julia, for example, the only way to get flour is to visit Jim, who has apparently hoarded flour. She provides her "service" for a while in order to get a tiny bag of the precious white powder. She refused sex once; she also left without flour. Jim told her never to come back again. Only after she repeatedly apologized and promised to be a "good girl" was she allowed to come back. But Julia is not Jim's only "servant"; Roberta visits him almost every day. Once, he arranged a nice evening for both of them but neither of the girls thought of the evening as "nice," even though they said it was and encouraged Jim.

Both Fred and Newmoser make similar use of their dwindling supplies from the cafeteria. Newmoser has never experienced such a level of female attention, not even from his wife. He is even happy that she is not here with him. Still, he hopes that she and their daughter are better off than him.

Newmoser cannot even begin to know how hard the summertime is in the Arizona desert without air conditioning and almost any food or water. It has been a struggle to survive and only very few have made it. Only those who have withdrawn to a reservoir with a stash of hoarded goods and have been defending themselves against intruders made it through the summer. But even some of those "defenders". have died from a disease contracted from unburied corpses. Newmoser cannot know that he has been a widower for a month and that his only daughter begged for her end before being shot dead.

The first uprising against the Executive Committee of Churchill Falls takes place on August 8th. Ironically, it occurs when the last roll of toilet paper is sold at the supermarket. All kinds of paper have become scarce now. When Newmoser is confronted with this problem at a meeting, he snaps, "We have more important problems to discuss."

Angrily, Walter Crane, the history teacher, jumps up. "Yeah, we know that you executives have more important things to deal with, like seducing our wives and daughters. We know that you still have goods at the cafeteria that weren't included in the inventory. And what about that survival chamber that you used to be so proud of in the good old days? We know that you have supplies there for almost three years. You guys are having a ball while we have almost forgotten what coffee and butter taste like. And the best thing is that you are all self-appointed. But those days are over. I will now nominate a new committee." He picks up a megaphone and reads out eight names. Among these are the names of some of the most popular people in the community, like the gas station guy, the owner of the restaurant, the owner of the sports park, the manager of the library, and the postmaster.

"All in favor of this committee say 'aye,'" calls out Crane. A resounding "aye" thunders from the crowd. Newmoser quickly turns to Fred. "Quick. Make sure that the supermarket, the liquor store, cafeteria, the gas station, the icehouse, and our private houses are guarded from intruders. None of those traitors will have any access to our supplies until we've regained control. According to the plant regulations, which everyone here has signed, we can even shoot at attackers and intruders. I'll try to delay them here."

"So the old committee is dissolved," the teacher announces triumphantly. "The new committee will now find out how much we really have left. They will also try to clarify three questions:

what can toilet paper be replaced with, how can we repair our appliances, and what can we use in place of soap."

Newmoser turns his microphone up as loud as it will go. "You seem to have forgotten that this entire village, and everything in it, belongs to the plant. And you are also forgetting that I am the manager of this plant. That's the reason why I'm the one who gives the orders around here. I've never tried to be a dictator; I always tried to get a consensus. Go ahead and appoint your own committee, but I intend to keep control over the plant and all the other institutions thereof. Until everything's back to normal again, no one shall have access to the supplies. Let me also point out that you've all signed the plant's regulations." Newmoser takes out a copy of the regulations and reads paragraph eighteen aloud, "*Anyone who causes trouble or refuses to recognize the authority of the plant's management shall be terminated and will leave the settlement within two hours.* Walter, my friend," he addresses the teacher, "may I ask you publicly if you still recognize my authority as Plant Manager, or do you not?"

"Those regulations were written a long time ago, in a different world. They're not valid anymore. We're a group of people here fighting for survival. We don't need over-privileged leaders."

"Walter, Walter, let me ask you one more time. If you don't give me a 'yes,' I'll take your answer as a 'no.'"

"You're canned, Newmoser. Let's take this place, folks," Crane shouts through the megaphone.

Newmoser nods to Richard, Fred's other security officer, who has positioned himself at the light switches. Richard flips the bank of switches and complete darkness descends on the theater. Suddenly there is complete silence. Then Newmoser speaks out, even louder than before. "Walter, you're fired. If you're still here in two hours, we'll force you out of town. There'll be no more supplies until the teachers send a delegation with a personal apology to me."

Now Newmoser's emergency plan proves efficient: The Inner Circle gets together at the plant. Their houses and all the shops remain under strict surveillance. It comes in handy that the security forces have just been given additional arms on the pretext that there is an increasing danger of attack from the outside.

Newmoser disappears through a rear exit and is long gone by the time the lights go back on again.

Walter, who seems to have nothing more to lose, takes control. "Let's take over the warehouse first!" But there is limited enthusiasm for this idea. Most of the residents leave the theater in embarrassment. On their way home, most of them notice that the windows of all the shops are shuttered and stationed with armed guards.

Some of Walter's friends and colleagues follow his call. They get their hunting rifles together and meet by the chapel. From there, the twenty or so wildly convinced men and women, including all of the teachers, approach the supermarket from different sides. They find an unguarded spot, break a window, and climb inside. The sound of the broken window attracts a guard.

"Put down your weapons and come out of there with your hands up. Otherwise, you and your families will be expelled from Churchill Falls, as per paragraph eighteen!"

The rebels answer quickly with a lethal shot to the chest of the guard.

Those inside the supermarket are shocked: 'Who shot the guard?' they all wonder. 'That wasn't in the plan.' They all take something from the shelves, climb out of the window and run away as fast as possible. But when they begin to get shot at, they return the fire. Eleven rebels escape but seven rebels and two guards are killed.

When Walter arrives back at his house, his wife runs towards him. "There's no more electricity! What have you done, you fool!"

"I just wanted to free us from that tyrant. Everyone was on my side, but he's just too strong. We gotta get out of here. We're packed, right?"

They take their ATRV down to the water outlet of the plant, encountering no further obstructions. There they meet all the survivors from the uprising, including mostly members of the "new committee." With six more families joining them, the group consists of twenty-two adults and twenty-four children.

They quickly board their motorboats and leave in the direction of Goose Bay.

None of those forty-six people will ever arrive in Goose Bay. Just outside of Goose Bay, a rope stretched across the river stops their boats. They are mercilessly robbed and killed. Even the robber barons of medieval Europe treated other humans with more dignity.

The plant security reports to the Committee on the skirmish with the rebels. One of the killed guards was unmarried, and the other married, but without children. Newmoser decides to take care of the widow. He takes her to the plant, gives her two glasses of wine and a nice dinner before he tells her about her husband's "heroic death:" "You're one of us now," he says, pouring her another glass of wine, "I'm terribly sorry about what happened."

Not used to alcohol, the woman disregards these words and continues to wail for some time about the injustice in the world and the emptiness of life without love. She carries on in this manner for some time and finally passes out on the table.

The following night, Newmoser has everything taken out of the newly deserted houses. Anything useful or usable is added to the community inventory.

The next morning, Newmoser receives a delegation of the residents. It disassociates itself from the "mutineers" and begs the Committee to keep up the good work.

The new inventory list and the fact that the population has dropped from 589 to 532 triples the individual DS. In addition, broken appliances can now be replaced with working ones. When Newmoser announces this to the public at the first meeting after the uprising, he receives a storm of applause.

Churchill Falls, winter, 2080-2081

The winter is as severe as usual. For weeks it is minus forty degrees or below. But despite the monotonous diet of caribou, no one is ever truly hungry and the electric lights of the Christmas trees glimmer with their usual cheerful sparkle. The presents are a bit simpler this year, but the executive committee found a way to spice them up: because there is hardly anything to buy anymore, they have started a Christmas exchange between families who don't have much contact with one another. This ensures that new books and games find their way into peoples' houses.

They also organize a community Christmas dinner where the first hothouse potatoes are served. All the residents agree that these taste much better than the ever-present caribou steak and caribou stew. They also finish eighty of the 200 liters of the freshly processed berry wine, which everyone is delighted with. Despite the growing shortages, like light bulbs, gasoline and flour, a certain Christmas atmosphere prevails.

The rest of the winter is bitter. More and more people try to break into the village from the Labrador City side. Most of them come on skis or snowmobiles. On two occasions there are serious gun battles. Once, one of the intruders is left behind, severely wounded. The doctor is sure he would have been able to save the man's life if he'd still had antibiotics. The repeated encroachments make the people more and more nervous. All efforts to seal off the entrance roads fail. Towards the end of the winter, the village sees fewer and fewer interlopers. Newmoser surmises that there might not be many people left alive in Labrador.

Churchill Falls, August 2081, fourteen months after the breakdown

The hard winter has taken its toll and now swarms of mosquitoes and horseflies plague the village. No more insecticide is left and the few mosquito nets have more and more holes in them. Then comes the big day.

August 10th, 2081 will be a day to remember for everyone. In the waning light, a Moller suddenly appears above the village. It circles above for a while, having seemingly noticed the settlement. Like castaways, the residents start to wave and light signal fires, but to no avail. The Moller disappears into the clouds. Two days later, they make out another even bigger Moller, but again there is no contact made.

How could the residents know that these are discovery flights from the slowly rising empire of the Master of Masters. These are carried out because the relay stations for the empire's drones in Goose Bay and Labrador City have broken down.

At the next general meeting, Newmoser makes a terrible mistake. "You have all seen those Mollers. This can only mean that civilization in more temperate regions is beginning to stabilize again. So we won't have to wait much longer before we can leave our isolation behind and live our lives like we used to. So there's reason to cheer up!"

Newmoser expected this to be an encouraging speech, but the consequences are terrible: most of the residents abandon all concern about their DS because they feel they are sure to be saved soon. Others disappear in the direction of Labrador City, some of them secretly, others not, and hope to reach Quebec or Nova Scotia on the roads or the train tracks East of them. To arrive in a real city and to eat an apple, a few cherries, or even a pizza seems like a dream.

Much earlier than usual, winter comes back with all her might at the end of September. Only 124 people are left in the fifty-four inhabited houses in Churchill Falls. Most of the other houses have been destroyed to gain new spare parts. They still have electricity, heat, light and even some functioning luxuries like Holoplayers, electric shavers, and hair dryers. Theoretically, even the indoor swimming pool at the Donald Gordon Center could be used but for the lack of chlorine and antibacterial cleaner. Furs increasingly replace tattered shoes and clothes.

When spring 2082 finally arrives, nearly half of the remaining population decides to leave for the South to find the civilization that seems to have forgotten about them. In the summer, the now seventy strong group faces two more misfortunes: first, the doctor is found to have disappeared one morning, and, only two weeks later, the last remaining XP breaks down for good. There are no more fuel cells and no way to replace them. All of a sudden, those useful helpers that had warned of an approaching bear and poisonous mushrooms, or had given so much technical advice are gone. The summer also sees the last of the ammunition fired. It's back to bows and arrows.

On the other hand, the vegetable hothouse is flourishing and they even manage to domesticate caribou: after two years they finally taste milk and butter again. By now the population of chickens has exceeded that of humans. And there have also been efforts to keep up some sort of entertainment: Fred, Jim, and Richard successfully turn the indoor pool into a warm waterfall.

Despite the coming winter, and the fact that the residents of Churchill Falls can now hardly be distinguished from furry animals, Newmoser believes that for the first time the group has stabilized. But he is also sure of another thing: should the turbines or the transformers ever fail, then God help them!

5 The Flight to Alberta

Newfoundland Peninsula
Shortly after the breakdown, June 11-13, 2080

Greg's frigate leaves Goose Bay on the evening of June 10th. On board are his wife Felitsa, his brother Frank, Frank's wife Melissa, and Frank's son and daughter. Altogether, the frigate houses 102 "refugees" and a crew of forty-two men. In the waning light of the evening, they glide through the long bay until they reach the straight, located between the two small villages of Rigolet and Henrietta, where the bay opens into the sea. The steep cliffs fall directly into the water, causing large swells, even in the calm, clear weather. When they reach the open sea, the crew breathes a sigh of relief. In the meantime, the moon has risen in the starry sky, allowing for good visibility. This is important because several icebergs appear ahead of them, rising from the black sea like fantastic bluish towers. Time and again they sight huge whales, which exhale fountains of steamy breath. They go almost directly south, with the land always at a safe distance to the west. Normally they would be able to see the lights of the little fishing villages, but only occasionally do they spy the flickering flames of an onshore fire. Fortunately, many of the lighthouses are still operating their rotating lights. Apparently, the batteries have not run out yet.

They have a rich dinner. Greg has no reason to conserve because they will soon have to leave the ship and won't be able to take all the supplies, anyway.

In the early afternoon of June 11th, they reach Lewisport, eighty km away from Gander on the northern shore of the main island. The water is too shallow to allow a landing there, so they have to anchor further out. With surprise, Greg can see through his binoculars that his recommendations for the refugees have been carried out: he and the captains of the other two frigates, which were docked in St. John's harbor, agreed that he would pick up the people in Labrador while they would provide camps for them and other refugees.

For Greg, this was a good excuse to pick up his brother's family there. Even though Greg hoped that the two captains would be able to build the camp, he secretly doubted their determination and chances of success. But he is pleasantly surprised to see that they have kept their word and were able to make the necessary preparations, even without the normal communication devices[17]. Several transport vehicles, mostly ATRVs, are waiting at the harbor. It will be no problem to drive all the refugees to the camp. Greg can also see a large Coast Guard boat approaching them, apparently to pick up the refugees. Greg is impressed, and surprised, but also a bit worried about the fact that this issue enjoys such a high priority.

The Coast Guard ship anchors next to the frigate. They start to board the refugees and get them to land. When the captain of the Coast Guard ship boards the frigate, he happily welcomes Greg in a surprisingly obsequious manner. Greg is handed an envelope. It contains important documents that Greg skims quickly. Now he understands, but his worries have not faded: the two other officers, Anthony and Edward, forcefully occupied the government building and announced a state of emergency just after Greg left there on June 9th. They overthrew the government and installed a triumvirate consisting of themselves and Greg as an emergency government.

Among the documents, Greg finds the official announcement making him the leader of government and the note that he should meet up with the other two officers immediately. He also finds an impressive certificate stating that he has absolute command over the entire population of Newfoundland until the end of the state of emergency. This includes the freedom to use force at any time. In addition, he finds several flyers with orders and regulations that have apparently been distributed to the population. Greg does not yet understand how they managed to inform the population in the first place.

---

[17] Communication between the villages on the main island could only be maintained because of Newfoundland's traditional fishermen, who always refused to give up their small boats that are independent of computer navigation.

Greg pretends not to be surprised. The captain of the Coast Guard ship informs Greg that communications within Newfoundland are mostly maintained by eight Coast Guard ships that continue to distribute public service flyers and posters. In addition, a system of individuals who carry this information further inland already exists. From there, the very few people who can still read distribute the news. This system guarantees keeping at least a minimum of information flowing throughout the province.

Greg is growing more and more uneasy. He knows that he will soon have to meet the other officers. Once again, the captain of the coast guard boat guarantees the safety of the refugees before Greg leaves.

Near the coast, there are still several small motorboats that can be steered manually. However, on his way back to the frigate, Greg avoids contact with other vessels. He wants to avoid any discussions or responsibilities that could endanger his flight to Alberta.

Greg discusses the new situation with his brother. "I don't trust those two, especially Anthony. He always seemed very egocentric and power hungry. I agree that the military order that they are keeping up will help us to avoid chaos; nevertheless, it would've been much more logical and reasonable to support the existing government instead of starting a dictatorship. After all, they were elected democratically. I know that they didn't include me out of sympathy. They knew that the three of us were the highest ranked soldiers on the island and have equal authority. Whether I want to or not, I have to go to St. John's now. But you stick to the original plan: you meet up with Old George and prepare everything for the flight. Depart on June 13th at 11:30 p.m., no matter if I'm back with you by then or not. I'll then try to get together with you some other way. I've already thought about some alternatives."

Greg allows no dissent, not even from Felitsa, who does not want to be separated from him. Finally, Greg takes out the certificate of empowerment and shows it to his family with a smile. "No more time for discussion. I have to go to St. John's now. They may need me there. I'll get through somehow. You guys are in danger here, and Felitsa is pregnant, so that's an order!" This is how Frank and Melissa find out Felitsa and Greg are expecting.

Because of lowered visibility, the frigate sails slowly the whole night. On the afternoon of the next day, they reach Grace Harbor, fifty km northwest of St. John's. This is the point where Greg's family will have to disembark, in spite of their complaints. Greg gives them final instructions. "Frank, you know how to get to Old George's, right? Here's a letter for him; it should explain everything. He may be old, but he is still fit and young at heart. You can trust and rely on him. He'll get you to Alberta safely. But now you have to go. See you soon."

Greg does not allow any sentimentality. He quickly hugs everybody good-bye. He waits until the dinghy is several hundred meters away then orders full steam ahead in the direction of St. John's. For a long time he follows the dinghy through his binoculars. Even though he didn't say so, he is not sure if Old George will be able to get them to Alberta. But now he uneasily begins to prepare for the meeting with his fellow "dictators".

At 5:00 p.m., the frigate reaches the entrance to St. John's harbor. The tide has risen and a stiff wind is blowing. Navigating the frigate through the straight is a true challenge without navigational devices. Miraculously, nothing goes wrong. Once they have passed through the narrows, the water is very calm. On their right lies Signal Hill, a big rock famous for receiving the first radio message from Europe in 1901[18]. In the middle of Signal Hill, Greg can see the Battery Hotel, which makes a very grim impression in the light of the coming thunderstorm. Suddenly the signal horns of the two docked

---

[18] The message was sent by Marconi from Cornwall, Great Britain. It had long been thought impossible to broadcast over the Atlantic because of the curvature of the Earth. Finally, the physicist Heaviside proved the existence of the ionized reflective layer of the atmosphere that made the transmission possible. The layer has since been called Heaviside's layer.

frigates sound. Apparently, Greg's boat has been noticed. But this is simply a welcome.

Once the frigate has docked and gangway lowered, a young petty officer named Keith rushes on board. In an almost unpleasantly humble manner, he gives Greg the news that the other two "commanders" are waiting for him in the Battery Hotel. Keith asks Greg for permission to accompany him there. In a truck that has been luxuriously furnished, Greg is driven from the harbor to the Battery. The People in the streets quickly hide or disappear when they see the truck.

"Why are they all running away from us?" Greg wants to know.

"They just want to make room for the government vehicle. They all admire the government, you know."

"I'm not sure I understand. It almost seems as if they're afraid." Greg wants to know more about that but Keith doesn't seem to be comfortable with the topic.

When they arrive at the eerie Battery-Hotel, the receptionist jumps up when she sees Greg and guides him to the bar. She withdraws instantly while Anthony and Edward heartily welcome Greg. Except for the three commanders, the bar is completely empty. A fire crackles in the fireplace. Once the formalities have been dispensed with, Anthony and Edward lead Greg into a niche overlooking the entire bay.

After some small talk, Greg becomes more serious. "Is it true that we're the government now?"

"Ooooooh, yeah!" They both laugh.

While the waitress pours them champagne, Edward explains, "Yes, we're the government. We take care of our citizens now. We don't want to come up short here too." They both seem to have had a lot to drink, so it takes a while before Greg can get a clear picture of the situation: the elected local government is in prison.

"We confiscated the Battery and now it serves the new government and its friends," he continues.

"And our girlfriends!" Anthony roars boisterously."

93

"We've managed to secure the basic needs of all Newfoundlanders. It was a lot of work and we had to be pretty tough sometimes. We felt that we should introduce a reward system. Anyone who wears a badge like this—" Edward takes one from his pocket, "is a Class I citizen, which means that he has many privileges. There are also Class II citizens, who have fewer, but still have more rights than people without a badge."

They order more champagne, caviar, and several bottles of vodka. They make rude jokes about the waitresses, who try to get in and out of the room as quickly as possible.

It dawns on Greg that Anthony and Edward are genuine, drunken, egomaniacal tyrants. He'll have to assess the situation himself. But how will he be able to get away without them noticing? He understands now why heavily armed soldiers were standing in the hallway, and why the people were so scared and humble before.

When Greg has to go to the toilet, he makes sure to take an empty vodka bottle with him and fill it up with water before he goes back. He serves Anthony and Edward vodka while secretly sticking to water himself. It seems to take forever, but finally the two become almost unconscious and don't notice Greg's departure.

At the reception desk Greg asks for the "government car," which is at his service shortly afterwards. Keith is still at work. He looks very tired. "What are my orders, commander sir?"

It's hard for Greg to get used to this title but he plays along and gives the driver directions. While they are trying to find the right way through St.John's, they do not notice that a motorcyclist is following them.

Finally they reach their goal: a little house on the outskirts of the city belonging to Greg's now retired former boss, Captain Samuel Reed. Greg is sure that Captain Reed will be able to give him a more precise picture of the situation. He rings the doorbell but it takes forever for the door to open.

"It's so good to see you back! I just had to check, you know, times are rough. Come on in."

"What's the matter, Sam? You look worried."

94

Sam looks at Greg skeptically for a long time. He wants to know why he, the third commander, was not in St. John's for the past few days. Greg tells him about his recent arrival and about his first scary meeting with his two colleagues. Sam's face brightens. "I think I can trust you after all. You know I've always believed in you, but when you were announced as one of the commanders, and when you seemed to just go along with the others, I really began to question your personality."

"Going along with what? Is there anything I should've stood up against?"

"Well I should say so! First they removed the government and threw them in prison, where they still are. And do you know what happened to the policemen who didn't want to play along? They declared them traitors and executed them by firing squad after a short show trial. And those were not the only ones. Your government buddies, especially Anthony, behave like medieval despots. They think they can do whatever they want, no matter if it's in line with human rights or not. And that whole Class I and Class II citizenship thing? That's just to guarantee that everyone is an accomplice."

Greg is shocked. The situation is worse than he could have ever imagined. They have a long conversation before they go into the basement to pack several objects into a backpack. They also type up a rescue plan for Newfoundland with an ancient fuel cell driven Compaq Prolinea 466. Sam explains it was his grandfather's, and that it was second hand even then.

"But Sam, what if something goes wrong? They'd just shoot you too. You should definitely come to Alberta with us."

But Sam declines, "I'm an old man. Now I see a chance to overthrow those two. It won't be easy, not least because of the Class system they've imposed, and even if we get the old government reinstated again, we'll still need help from the outside."

After saying their farewells, Greg leaves the house with the rucksack. He tells Keith to take him to the prison. The motorcycle continues to follow them.

At the prison, Greg demands to see the warden, even though it means waking him up. A couple of minutes later, the warden wellcomes him humbly and Greg orders him to take him to the imprisoned members of the government. He also orders the warden to hand him a master key to the prison. The warden makes no fuss and hands him a wand, which will open all the doors in the complex. More and more guards seem to be following Greg and the warden to the cell. He finds the prisoners in good condition but when they see Greg, they run to the bars of the cell and begin shouting all at once, "This is wholly illegal! You and the other two commanders will be tried for this! The longer you have us imprisoned, and the more crimes you commit, the more severe your punishment will be!" exclaims the ex-prime minister.

The warden becomes more and more uneasy, even though he seems to share the prime minister's opinion. For a moment, Greg even considers letting him in on the plan, but then he notices that the warden is a Class II citizen which would make everything too risky, so Greg decides to send him and the guards away. "I have to speak with the former government alone. I will lock the doors behind me."

The warden and the guards hesitate before they finally leave. When they are finally out of sight, Greg explains the plan to reinstall them. It takes him a while to convince them of his honesty and the feasibility of the plan. Before he leaves, he takes the weapons out of his backpack and hands them to the ministers, together with the master key. He makes sure that they do not plan to do anything before tomorrow night. "At 9:30 p.m. tomorrow, everything should be prepared. You should be safe with Captain Sam's help, and with the police on our side. Greg leaves the prison and tells the guards to go back and lock the doors because he has forgotten to.

He is taken back to the hotel and only has a few hours to sleep before he has to begin a very strenuous day.

When Greg has been asleep for three hours, his family starts to prepare for the nocturnal adventure. They have met with George, who has explained the hazardous plan to get to Alberta. For days he has been working on an old cargo plane of 2030 vintage. At that time, people were not yet dependent on integrated navigational systems. The plane is located in a hangar at the nearby military base. The repairs were authorized by the military. It seems George is the best chance for the family because he repaired and can pilot the plane. George estimated officially that the plane should be ready to go on June 16th if he worked hard.

In fact, the plane is already flyable and partially loaded. There is enough room in the plane to allow a small group of people to survive for some time.

At 3:00 a.m., the "refugees" drive to the base. They have to hide under a tarp in a trailer being towed behind a tractor. They can only bring a few of their personal belongings, including the ham radio. When they reach the entrance to the base, George has to have a few words with a guard. Fortunately, he is too tired to check the tractor and the trailer. George drives straight into the hangar. They quickly enter the cargo space. They arrange the loaded cargo so they will not be seen if the plane is inspected.

"You should try to get some sleep now," suggests George, pointing to some cots. "You know, you'll have to stay in there without making any noise until Greg joins us. I'm going to drive home now. I'm afraid I'll have to lock you in. Some people might come to the hangar tomorrow morning, so please try your best to be quiet. I'll come a little later with more stuff and then I'll stay with you."

They all nod. They are so tired that despite the uncomfortable beds and their uncertain future, they fall asleep immediately.

It's about 7:00 a.m. when Melissa wakes Frank.

"Wha...what's the matter?" he whispers, frightened.

"There's nothing to worry about, hon, you were just snoring so loud. Someone outside the plane, heck, the hangar, could've heard you," Melissa whispers, barely able to contain her laughter.

Greg gets up very early the next morning. There is a lot to do and he wants to avoid Anthony and Edward at breakfast.

Keith drives Greg down to the harbor. When they arrive, Greg gets out and tells Keith to go directly to the military base. "Ask for Old George. Give him my regards and ask him how the repair work is coming along. Then go back to the Battery and tell them that I'm out here trying to get an idea of the situation. I suggest all the commanders meet at 1900 hours for dinner. Tell them that I'm bringing a very special bottle of champagne for toasting the triumvirate. If they don't have any plans for you, then return here immediately, please."

This is the first time that Keith has heard the word "please" from one of the new commanders. He looks at Greg strangely. "I'll be back here as soon as possible."

On the way to the base, Keith again fails to notice that a motorcycle is following him.

Once on board his ship, Greg lets his first officer in on the plan. He knows that he can trust him as a soldier and as a friend. The first officer reacts with shock and disbelief. Without wasting time, Greg gets right to the point. "Are you willing to play the part I have planned for you when we try to get the old government back in power? I know it's a risk, but don't we all have to take risks in these difficult days?"

"Of course I'm with you. Of course I will. But what's your deal in the whole thing?"

Even though the question is not unexpected, Greg finds it hard to answer. "Now I'm going to try to prepare everything for tonight. From now on, you're in command of the ship. Here are all the documents you'll need. I won't be back. I plan to fly to Alberta tonight together with my family. We should be safe there. I have to take care of my family, you see?"

"So you're the first one to leave the sinking ship?" the first officer reacts reproachfully.

Greg nods slowly and looks his friend directly in the eye. "Trust me. This was the hardest decision of my life. My wife is pregnant and my brother is there too with his wife and kids. I really don't have a choice. You're young, free and single. You can stay here and play the hero. I know this isn't going to be easy. I had my XP carry out a simulation of what will happen if electricity, gas, transportation, and communication aren't back to normal soon. It'll be no picnic. There'll be rebellions and lootings everywhere. We are presently losing valuable days that we should be spending on rebuilding the infrastructure. That's why it's listed as a first priority in the rescue plan to maintain the legitimate administration. It's necessary for organizing the reconstruction of the power plants. If we don't get that done before the winter, people will simply freeze to death."

"With all the things on this frigate, you should have a better chance than the people ashore. At worst, you'll have to get as many people out of here fast. Maybe you can make it down south to a milder climate. But you know the continent as well as I do. Florida would be the only safe bet during the winter. My XP predicts that people will soon start wandering down south, and that the southern states will have a problem with that. Personally, I think I have to save my family first, but your place is here aboard the ship."

"But how are you going to make it across the continent all the way to Alberta?"

"A friend of mine had an old airplane repaired. It'll fly without a navigation system."

The face of the first officer reddens in anger. "So you're just going to take the plane away from us? Don't you know how important that could be for the people around here?"

Greg sighs. "That plane is only going to make it for 10,000 km and can probably be restarted three times at the most. So I suppose it wouldn't be of any great help to you. But I'll make up for that and leave you my ham radio. You should know how to use it by now, considering how much flack you always gave me about it. That way we'll be able to stay in touch. I'll keep you informed about what's going on out there. My brother has one too, you see?"

Now the first officer regrets his harsh words. He should've known that Greg would handle the situation responsibly.

The two of them discuss some details for quite some time, then they say good-bye.

When Greg leaves the frigate for the last time, Keith is already waiting for him. "George says everything is under control. He sends his regards."

Greg breathes a sigh of relief, but then he is reminded by his XP about the many things that are still on today's list. They meet with several people in St. John's. Everyone is willing to help reinstate the former government and give the rescue plan a realistic chance. By now, Greg knows for sure that Keith would also be more than willing to get rid of Anthony and Edward. Time is scarce, so Greg decides to tell him about the plans to overthrow the commanders tonight. Keith is jubilant.

But Greg dampens his excitement. "You'll have two important jobs to do in this. They may be dangerous. First I want you to convince one of the waitresses to slip this sleeping powder I am giving you into Anthony and Edward's drinks at 9:30 tonight. It's guaranteed they won't taste it."

Keith nods.

"And afterwards, I'll need you and the car at the lower exit of the hotel at 10:30. Will you be able to do that?"

"I'm pretty sure I can. And let me say sir, I'm really proud to help free Newfoundland." It's such a hokey sentence that even Greg has to grin.

Back at the Battery, Greg joins his "colleagues" with his special bottle of champagne. They are already back drinking in the niche again. They are very eager to hear how Greg has spent the day.   Greg tells them about the rescue plan without mentioning that they will not be a part of it. He also tells them about his plan to start the computer systems again by using the ships' generators, about the rationing measures, about potential substitute products, etc.

His colleagues wave him off. "Just look at that! We really seem to have an idealist and a dreamer among us! Ha ha ha ha ha ha ha ha!"

"I know a lot of this won't work. But we should at least try, shouldn't we? What's your plan?"

"We'll just try to keep everything in order here and decentralize the responsibilities to the mayors and community representatives. We've already initiated a class system in order to create two elites. A lot of people will have something to lose, so they won't try to get us out of the way. I think we're pretty safe. Good idea, right?"

Greg nods and Anthony continues.

"Without any additional means of transportation and communication, that's all we can really do. But still, you won't be able to have the government car for yourself every day. Besides that, we'll just try to have a good time–Cheers! And in the worst case, we'll just grab a bunch of pretty waitresses or whatever girls we can find, load them onto our ships and head south. We'll reach the Caribbean eventually, so we won't have to freeze."

Greg is agitated: so, just like him, they have already planned their escape. Is he really morally superior? On the other hand, he becomes aware of a much bigger problem. This kind of regionalization, which Frank had already mentioned in respect to Churchill Falls, is very likely to be happening all over the world. He wonders about the complex system that has now broken down completely because it was too global and too intertwined. But on the other hand, there has to be some kind of a network to create a high technology based standard of living for such a great number of people. Such a network cannot be developed through regionalization and segregation, so what kind of compromise might work?

After this moment of philosophy, Greg is back with his colleagues. All they can think of is booze, grub, and snatch. Anthony forces a waitress onto his lap against her will, kisses her, and slips his hand into her blouse. She tries to defend herself and bites his upper lip. Anthony wipes the blood off and excitedly calls two of his soldiers. "That little bitch just bit me! Hold her down. I'll teach her a lesson."

The two men take the girl and bend her over. Anthony lifts up her skirt, removes her slip, takes his belt off, and whips her naked buttocks. The waitress screams in pain. Before Anthony can hit her a second time, Greg stops his arm.

"Stop that. Now."

Anthony shoots him a menacing look, but then calms down again. "Yeah, I guess you're right. This isn't the right time or place. Then he turns to his soldiers. "Take her into the gym. Tie her up and keep an eye on her. I'll have plenty of fun with her later on. If I forget about her, you boys go ahead and punish her."

The drinking continues. Around 9:00 p.m., Greg pretends to be very tired and very drunk. Once he even trips and falls. He gets up and slurs an apology. "I'm tired, I gotta hit the sack." He burps, yawns, then stumbles off.

Once outside the bar, he goes straight to the gym. "I'll do the punishing", he tells the two guards and sends them away.

"I've come to get you out of here," he whispers to the girl and starts untying her. "Is there another exit?"

She nods and shows Greg the way out by the swimming pool. "Thanks for your help, sir, but that won't solve my problems. It'll just make them even angrier. I think I better go and apologize. Maybe they won't punish me as bad as they did with the last girl."

"So you aren't the first one? What's your name?"

"I'm Mandy, I'm definitely not the first. There must've been dozens."

"Is your family here in St. John's?"

"No, I'm from Edmonton. I'm a biology student, or I was. I only came here for this summer job. I study botany.

"Some of us are flying to Alberta today. Though we're not going to Edmonton, we are going to Calgary. We have a place where we are pretty sure we'll be safe. Do you want to come along? It's no more dangerous than staying here and maybe your knowledge will come in handy."

Mandy agrees without hesitation.

They hide in the corner by the exit. Keith is supposed to be here at 10:30, still an hour away. Greg hopes that he can make it here earlier.

The waitress that Keith convinced to help them isn't able to mix the sleeping powder into the commanders' drinks until 9:45. From now, it will take about thirty minutes until they are rendered unconscious for several hours. At 10:00 p.m. the top guards who were supposed to have punished Mandy storm in with the messenger that was following on the motorcycle. Before they can speak, Anthony, already drunk again, wants to know about something else. "How was it with the girl?"

"But we thought Commander Greg was going to take care of her."

It takes a while for this news to sink in. "But he left, drunk as hell. Was he just acting? Something's not right with that guy," Anthony grumbles loudly.

Now the messenger can't hold back any longer. "That's what I've been trying to tell you, sir. I've been following Commander Greg, and he's definitely planning something."

This quickly sobers the two commanders up. The sleeping powder hasn't kicked in yet.

The messenger tells them about Greg's visit to the prison and that he now has a passkey for the prison. He thinks that's how the prisoners were able to escape twenty minutes ago. "I followed them. They're on board his frigate now."

"Is Greg there too?" Anthony asks with a thick tongue.

"I'm not sure. All I know is that his driver was at the military base today asking questions about the airplane."

Anthony and Edward look at each other: 'Is he trying to get away with the airplane that old man is repairing?' Despite the increasing effects of the sleeping powder, Anthony and Edward are both enough the officer to give precise orders. After having blocked the narrows with another one of the ships, Edward orders the navy men there to get a group together to take over Greg's frigate. Anthony orders the messenger to drive to the military base and hand over the following note: *Commander Greg is a traitor. He is to be arrested immediately and kept at the base.*

"If Greg is arrested, I'll promote you to a Class I citizen."

The messenger is elated. From now on he will be treated specially and might even be among the elite. He leaves immediately.

At 10:30 sharp, Anthony and Edward, who have just disappeared into their rooms, are arrested by Greg's men and the police. The legitimate government's decree has had the desired effect.

The harbor is peaceful. More than half an hour ago, the crews of all three frigates stated their allegiance to Greg. The police have a list of all Class I and Class II citizens and will collect their badges over the next few hours. The rescue plan has been initiated: Flyers are being printed on board, but it will take days for the whole island to receive the news.

Keith arrives at the hotel right on time. Greg and Mandy get into the "government car" and, shortly before 11:00 p.m., they reach the military base.

Within seconds, the car is surrounded by dozens of soldiers, their weapons drawn. Keith and Mandy are pulled roughly from the car and forced into a room. "You are traitors. We have orders to arrest you."

The messenger can now leave the base and eagerly await his promotion. He is looking forward to reporting the arrest and telling the base commander that he'll be back with new orders in no more than forty-five minutes. If everything works out the way Greg has planned it, the messenger won't return. But maybe it will all be too late; George has strict orders to start the plane in thirty minutes.

Greg tries hard to convince his guards that the other two commanders have been imprisoned and that the legitimate government has been reinstalled. No one seems to believe this, but at least the guards become more insecure. But Greg doesn't stop and is finally forbidden to speak. They even threaten to gag him. "We'll know very soon where we really stand," says one of the guards.

Time has been passing slowly for George and the five refugees inside their plane. They were happy to hear the news from Greg, but very irritated about the evildoings of the other two commanders. The clock continues to tick and there is still no sign of Greg.

The situation is becoming more and more uneasy. At 11:31, George can no longer wait. "I'm afraid something went wrong. I have strict orders to start the plane now. I have to do this."

Frank does not want to believe that his brother would leave his pregnant wife behind like this, and, after more and more pleading, George is forced to draw his pistol. "I'm warning you Frank–all of you–it's not the right time to lose your heads. Greg knows what he's doing. If he doesn't come then it could mean that the plan has been exposed and they'll soon try to stop us by force."

After carefully opening the gate of the hangar, George starts the jet engines and slowly taxis the plane out. The plane rolls across the tarmac, passing the main gate of the base and some of the guardhouses. Light is still coming through some of the windows. This, even in normal times, would be strange at such a late hour. Driven by a spontaneous inspiration, George slows the plane, opens the cargo bay hatch and lets the jets roar.

For more than half an hour, Greg, Keith, and Mandy have been sitting in the little room on the ground floor of the guardhouse, watched over by two men who seem to be getting more and more tired. Several more guards stand outside the door. But because of the warm June night, one of the guards has opened up a window in the back of the room that looks out to the runway. The three prisoners all know that this window could be the only way out of here.

Greg keeps checking his watch: it is now 11:31 p.m. and nothing can be heard. Those engines are really loud. Why hasn't he heard anything? But suddenly, there is a light roar coming closer and closer. And soon the shadow of a rolling plane appears in the darkness. When the jet engines start screaming, the guards are taken by surprise. Greg nods to the other prisoners. Then he gets up and creeps out of the window. Mandy follows. When Keith tries to do the same, the guards finally notice. "Stop!" But it is too late to draw their weapons. Then they make another mistake: instead of taking care of the plane, they run to the back window to track down the prisoners. By now, however, Greg, Keith, and Mandy have run around to the other side of the building and are approaching the open hatch of the plane. When the guards get back to the front of the building, they can see their prisoners climbing the rope ladder into the plane, which is now speeding up for take off.

Greg is the first inside, and before Frank realizes what is going on, Greg has already helped the other two in as well.

"Close the hatch!" screams George as he increases the speed of the plane.

A group of soldiers are following them in the "government car" and starts shooting. They miss and lose more and more ground to the accelerating jet.

George gives the O.K. for take off. The engines roar even louder before the plane finally lifts itself off the ground. He is overcome with relief: all this was very risky without a dry run, but he hadn't wanted to admit it to the others. They quickly gain altitude and soon reach 10,000 meters while George monitors the compass, the altimeter, the artificial horizon, and the air pressure gauge. Everything seems to be holding together. "They still knew how to build back then," George comments half seriously.

The tension slowly ebbs.

"How long are we going to fly?" Frank's daughter wants to know.

"About thirteen hours, with this wind," George answers.

"Why so long?" his brother chimes in.

"This is a jet cargo plane. It wasn't built to reach high speeds but to be fuel-efficient. It can only make about 500 km/h. It's about 4800 km to Alberta. If we can average 400 km/h, which is the most we can do with this wind, then that makes it about thirteen hours. But the plane is so good on gas that it can almost make 20,000 km without refueling. Its landing speed is only 120 km/h. That'll come in handy if we can't land at an airport."

Keith, who has come along without much consideration, wants more details. "You're not planning to land this at an airport?"

"That's not very realistic. The ranch we are aiming for is located in the foothills behind Bragg Creek. There is a big parking lot there that should be big enough if it's empty, but there will probably be some Mollers, and anyway, it's kind of far away from the ranch. We'll probably have to make do with a field. There's a big one right by the ranger's station. But I'm not sure if it'd be wise to land right in front of the ranger's door."

They all seem to be calm now and the kids try to get some sleep. They fly over Halifax, the capital of Nova Scotia, around 1:00 a.m. No lights can be seen and Frank doesn't receive any radio messages at first. Then he decides to switch to Greg's frequency. Frank is surprised to reach someone at this late hour, but Greg's first officer is still up and gives them the good news about the reinstallation of the legitimate government and update on the state of the rescue plan.

Melissa decides to send a telememo to her brother Alex in Alberta. *"We're all O.K. We're flying over Nova Scotia and should be with you in less than twelve hours."* Alex will be able to receive this through his Mindcaller and foreword it on to his father in Greece.

General Paul Kalkias is relieved to receive this important information. It is around noon in Greece on this June 14th and everything seems to be running smoothly. But the bad news from Athens has not arrived yet.

6 Alberta

On the way to the ranch
June 14, 2080

Some three hours after taking off from the base in St. John's, the plane passes over the nation's capital, Ottawa. Nothing seems to be going on down there.

The Prime Minister of Canada is woken up abruptly at 2:00 a.m. "Sir, a jet airplane is approaching us from the east. Apparently they do not plan to land here. How shall we respond?"

A few minutes later, the Prime Minister is wide awake and meeting with some of the members of his cabinet, all of whom have withdrawn to this comfortable emergency facility with their families. "It's good to know that there are still airplanes out there," the prime minister begins.

The rest nods. The past few days have been frustrating.

In the beginning they tried hard to keep the country under control, but even communicating with nearby cities proved practically impossible. The military was not much help either: their whole intranet broke down as well. They were left with simple vehicles on the ground, which only allowed for travel of 100 km at the most, and with some small boats that allow manual navigation. The situation in the air was especially dramatic: only some very old models could still be flown. Like most other governments, the one in Ottawa cursed the fact that they had allowed Moller, Inc. to have such a monopoly in North America.

The army managed to get their hands on a few ham radio systems from amateurs and museums. However, there was little success in contacting other military bases. Finally, they got a connection to the Toronto and Calgary Air Bases, but not to Winnipeg. When they realized Canada was no longer governable, they tried to find new ways of keeping people informed. Throwing flyers out of the few still operable aircraft proved to be the most efficient, despite the fact that a high

109

percentage of the population can no longer read or write[19]. The message on the flyers was simple: the federal government is trying to work out a new basis of communication and transportation. In the meantime, the local authorities have complete authority.

So now, for the first time, there is an unidentified aircraft over Ottawa, and he, the PM, has to make a decision. "There's not much we can do," he speculates, "We can shoot flares or start a signal fire at one of the airports to invite them to come down to land. I guess we could also start one of our airplanes, but to what end? If they don't want to land, should we shoot them down? That wouldn't make sense. Let's try to contact them somehow. If we're lucky, they'll have some kind of radio system on board. They could have important information. They're coming from the east, so maybe they know what's going on in Newfoundland and P.E.I.[20] If they don't then good luck to them.

Suddenly the ham radio crackles to life. It's the prime minister's office. They tell each other what they know and it's a sobering experience for both parties. Apparently the breakdown occurred all over North America. Greg informs them about the new situation in Newfoundland and explains that they're on their way to Alberta, and that the condition of the plane won't allow an additional landing. After several farewells, both parties agree to try to contact each other again soon. But Greg has one favor to ask: the government password for today, just in case.

It takes the government a while to consider this. "This is a highly unusual favor to ask because you don't appear to be on an official navy mission. But these are strange times and we'll make an exception."

After the prime minister gives him the code, Greg promises not to abuse it and to keep in touch. Frank is worried. Apparently even the federal government is now in favor of regionalization and segregation. How will they ever return to normal?

---

[19] In 2050, reading and writing were downgraded to elective subjects in all Canadian public schools.

[20] Prince Edward Island: the smallest province in Canada.

The flight continues north of Toronto towards Winnipeg. This is a very deserted area so the four hours bring no new surprises. Greg decides to take a nap while Frank joins George in the cockpit. George is showing no signs of fatigue.

When the sun rises, they are able to make out Lake Winnipeg below them. Frank is overwhelmed by memories: five years ago, he spent a romantic week down there in a little hut with Greta. He especially remembers the day it rained ceaselessly. What a day for lovers. They had no reason even to get out of bed, except for once when they were driven by hunger to eat some soup on a rocky old table. But after a few more glasses of wine and a few chapters of the book they were both reading, they crawled back into bed and continued where they had left off. 'Why is there still so much love and melancholy inside me when I think about Greta?' Frank thinks reproachfully. 'We haven't spoken in three years and Melissa has forgiven me for the love affair. I couldn't even imagine a better partner than Melissa. God, I'll never be able to forget Greta. But how can she treat me like this? How can she not want to even read my e-mails?'

Suddenly, George interrupts Frank's self-pity, "Maybe you should go and wake Greg up. I don't like what I'm seeing here." Now Frank can also see two black dots in the sky approaching them, and the lines of warning flares rising from the ground. This is a definite signal to land. Frank tries to communicate with the ground and the two planes but to no avail.

He wakes up Greg and explains the situation, "What should we do?"

Greg remains calm. It takes him less than a minute to make a decision. "George, change course due south and give the signal that we understand and respect the warning. Please show me how to use the lights on this thing. I'll try to Morse code them something."

By now, the two fighter jets are very close and one starts to shoot over the plane with its machine guns. Greg's Morse message includes the government password, but even that has no effect. "I don't understand it!"

But soon Greg understands and sends a different message. Both fighters change their course, tilt their wings, and one of them fires a green flare. The second plane discharges an orange flare. Greg laughs and insists that George answers them in the same way.

After George changes course to the west again, Frank demands an explanation, "What was that all about?"

"Well, first I morsed today's government code and I was baffled when they didn't accept it. But then I realized that they haven't had any contact with Ottawa since the breakdown so I morsed them the code from the day the breakdown happened and that worked. Green flare for 'Keep flying,' orange flare for 'Sorry, all the best.'"

"We still have four hours until we reach Calgary. Maybe you should get some rest, Frank. You need to be fit for the landing."

When they reach the border with Alberta, they all get up and have a bite to eat. The sky has clouded up and George has to decrease his altitude. When they reach 1500 meters, there is still thick fog and George gets a little uneasy. But suddenly the fog is gone and they have a spectacular view: still over the prairie, they can already make out the city of Calgary directly ahead of them. They can see the little Husky Tower surrounded by giant skyscrapers, the foothills to the west, and the snow capped Rocky Mountains beyond them. To the south, Mt. Assiniboine is piled up like a pyramid and the blue cloudless arc of a Chinook arch spreads across the mountains[21]. This can only mean that the temperature outside must be unusually cool for this time of year and that they can expect strong winds. George, who always tries to sound positive, explains that such a storm could even help them because it could lower their speed during the landing. He does not mention that most flat fields in the foothills run from south to north, which means that the wind will be coming from the side.

---

[21] The Chinook arch is normally a phenomenon of the winter. It comes about when damp sea air rises on the western side of the mountains, shedding meters of snow on the Western slopes of the Rockies. The air warms up again when it falls, and then blows across the prairies. A sudden increase of temperature from 40 degrees below to above freezing is not unheard of in Calgary.

"How strong is the wind?" George asks Frank eagerly. But Frank's XP answers faster than its owner, "Wind speed: ninety km/h, gusty, but not on even ground." But the turbulence shaking the aircraft doesn't seem to confirm this statement.

Suddenly, a fighter appears next to them. With tracer rounds, they demand an immediate landing. Again, Greg morses first the old and then the new government codes. Suddenly the radio reports, "CJ 103, land immediately."

Greg and the ground station have some intense but short communication, but none of his arguments can change their minds. "We can talk about this once you've landed."

Greg tries to draw out the conversation. When Cochrane, the nearest big settlement west of Calgary, appears ahead of them, Greg starts to pretend that the connection is failing. Then he turns the radio off completely. As an answer to that, the fighters start shooting at them.

"Quick, George, turn north and get back into the clouds. We'll have to make them believe we're on our way to Red Deer or Edmonton. They can't see in the clouds any more than we can, so once we're out of sight, we'll change course to the southwest again and go back down near Bragg Creek."

"And how do you want me to do that without being able to see?" grumbles George.

"Because you're good, George, that's why."

Before they can get out of sight, George tries hard to stay on a northern course without being an easy target. The plane is hit several times but without taking much damage.

"Up now! Go up!" Greg orders when the attacking jets get too close.

George pulls up the plane and becomes "invisible." First he makes a steep curve to the west and then another to the south. He is worried about getting too close to the higher mountains. For one moment, a hole in the clouds shows Devil's Thumb Mountain, helping his orientation. Suddenly, they emerge completely from the clouds to see the Yamnuaska, Calgary's most famous climbing spot. Only a few kilometers to the west, they cross the beginning of the Kannanaskis Valley before flying over the Sibbald Flats. George would have liked to cross the upper part of the Elbow River, but the clouds are too low. He has to make his way into the larger Bow Valley before he can take a sharp curve southwest into the mountains. They now have the Bragg Creek parking lot directly below them. On a normal weekday, it would be filled with thousands of Mollers owned by Calgarians traveling to the Elbow Waterfalls by rented ATRVs. Today there are only a few Mollers in the parking lot. Apparently some tourists who were on vacation at one of the nearby lodges were surprised by the breakdown and had to leave their vehicles behind. But even those few Mollers make a landing here impossible.

Melissa sends a telememo to Alex telling him that they are trying to find a suitable field for landing near the ranger's house.

Alex was expecting Melissa's memo. It comes in clearly, but he feels helpless; if only he could send a message back telling them to find a field further back in the valley where there are no roads for ATRVs. There are just so many dubious characters out there in the foothills, and some of them are armed with hunting rifles. Here, they are still within ATRV range of Calgary, and groups of young people have formed gangs and are abusing the situation to rob and molest others.

George steers the plane to follow the Elbow River upstream. The water below them glimmers like crystal.

But soon, too soon, the beaver ponds below the ranger station come into sight. The field they expected to use should be right there. Greg looks at George quizzically. But George shakes his head: The crosswind is too strong here. The situation is getting critical now: Soon the valley will narrow, which will make it impossible to turn around, but if they have to pull up, they will enter the impenetrable fog shrouding the mountains. They can now see Moose Mountain to their right. This is where the street leads down to the Elbow the last time before reaching the waterfalls. Here a smaller valley leads off to the right. It is narrow at the beginning, but where it gets wider, there is enough room for a farm: Alex's farm.

Frank, who knows the area well, starts to direct George. "Before we reach that next valley, you have to fly upslope and to the west. There are some meadows up there."

114

"I really hope we can land a plane in those meadows," mumbles George. "If this is getting too steep, we won't be able to pull up or turn out of here in time."

When George turns the plane westward into the wind with landing gear and flaps down, the plane seems to stand still. "The wind is so strong that we're only going thirty km/h relative to the ground." Soon a meadow lies below them. "Don't take that one," shouts Frank, "there's a better one coming up."

George accepts this reluctantly. The slope is getting steeper now and is overgrown with Scots pine and spruce. George is forced to increase the throttle in order to gain altitude. They are only a few dozen meters above the treetops. They all remain silent while the jets roar and the wind howls around them.

"There!" shouts Frank, pointing to a small clearing ahead of them.

George seems satisfied. He banks the plane over and starts to descend. But he doesn't land it yet.

"Land, for Christ's sake, land this goddamn thing!" screams Frank.

"Leave me be, greenhorn," George almost whispers. He does not touch the ground until he reaches the last third of the clearing. The strong headwind has decreased the landing speed to below thirty km/h and the uphill slope slows the plane down even further. George rolls the plane to the end of the clearing and then shocks everyone by speeding up one more time, rolling into the brushwood, and turning the plane 180 degrees, so the nose points downhill and back into the valley. This stops the plane completely.

"What did you do that for?" Frank asks unbelievingly.

"Well first of all, I wanted to hide the plane a little. There were quite a few ATRVs down there, and I don't really trust people any more, especially in times like these. Second, I wanted to have the plane in a position that would allow me to fly away again, just in case. I don't see why I shouldn't be able to start the engines one more time unless the wind is too strong. I still have fuel enough for almost 15,000 kilometers. Who knows what we'll need to do later."

Greg and frank are surprised at George's foresight. In the meantime, Felitsa and Melissa have telememoed Alex about their location. Now they'll have to start finding their way to the ranch that should take them at least four hours in this difficult terrain. They'll have to leave a lot of valuable equipment behind for now.

George inspects the airplane. There are some dents from the bullets, but no holes. The landing gear is not damaged either. "I'm pretty sure that I'll be able to fly this bird one more time if I have to. George insists on covering the plane with spruce boughs, which will not rot for a long time and will stay green, and attaches a sign to the plane reading, '*Danger! Do not Enter!*' Then he carefully locks all the doors.

Carrying backpacks, the little caravan starts the hike. Frank, Melissa, and the children walk in front followed by Greg, Felitsa, Keith, and Mandy, who seem to be getting along well. George takes up the rear. "I really hope Alex will find us soon and give us a hand. I'm not sure if we can make it down the steep cliffs between here and the ranch.

After a one-hour hike they reach the cliffs. It is soon obvious that only an experienced climber would be able to make his way down. "I'll go alone and try to get help. You stay here. It'll probably get cold later, but I hope to be back within five hours. I should meet Alex pretty soon if he received that telememo," Frank explains.

"Don't you think that you might pass Alex without even noticing him in this thick forest?" Keith asks.

"Nope. There's only one way down into the valley and to the ranch."

"I think Frank really knows his way around here. Let's make some tea and soup and relax under that rock overhang. It could start raining. I think we'll be all right here, Frank. Just come back soon," says Melissa, as she lovingly embraces her husband.

Only thirty minutes later, he runs across Alex and his friends. "It's great to see you! It's amazing that you could make it all the way over here from Newfoundland. Good job!"

Frank explains that it was actually Greg who worked out the plan.

"But how could you get here so quickly from the ranch? It should've taken you three hours to walk here."

"You forgot about the horses. We left them a bit further down. We're also expecting a couple of ATRVs for those of us who may not be comfortable riding anymore."

"But how did you know..."

"That she's pregnant? That's telepathy for you! I know a lot more about you than you know about me, you know," Alex says, grinning. "But enough of this. Let's go get the others now. I want to see my sister. They're already preparing a feast at the ranch."

A few hours later, the whole group reaches the ranch. There is no end to the embraces and greetings everyone exchanges. "Let me introduce you to some of our guests who have been stranded here since the breakdown. They're waiting by the fireplace. Let's all get inside and toast to our future."

When they enter the living room, Frank's heart seems to stop for a moment: 'Is that her? Is that Greta? And is that, could that be... her son, what's his name... Clemens?'

Greta is equally surprised and pales like a ghost.

With all the warm welcomes, no one notices the absurdity of the situation. Frank and Greta formally introduce themselves to one another as Mr. Schangl and Mrs. Weiser. But Alex cannot have that and insists that they all use first names. Frank is relieved that Greta didn't use her maiden name, which insures that Melissa will not find out that this very woman is the one who almost destroyed their marriage.

They have a ranch style barbecue, but Greta and Frank remain distant. Frank drinks more than usual. Melissa is glad to see that he is loosening up. She is sure that the difficulties of the last few days are the reason for her husband's uptightness.

Frank spends the first night tossing and turning in bed. His head seems to be exploding: 'Why is she here? Where is her husband? Did they break up? She's still as pretty as she used to be, maybe even prettier, and more mature and interesting with it. How will we be able to live together over the coming weeks, or months in such a close environment? Should I tell Melissa?'

Frank doesn't want to hurt or lose Melissa, but he also wants to be with Greta. He wants to embrace her. Greta's presence makes him unhappy and happy at the same time.

At the Ranch in Alberta
June 15, 2080

"What's the matter, honey?" Melissa asks Frank when he arrives at breakfast. "What was troubling you last night?"

"Sorry if I woke you up. There was so much going through my head at the moment, and I might be coming down with a cold, too."

Melissa looks at him with a slightly worried look on her face. "I hope you'll be O.K. You don't have to worry about us anymore. We should be pretty safe here with Alex. By the way, he says he wants to explain the situation to us "newcomers" after breakfast."

Soon afterwards, Alex arrives, arm-in-arm with Greta. Frank feels a sting when he sees the two of them together. Alex is cheerful as usual. "It took me years to get over my wife's death. But I've been better for quite some time now and eventually I ran into this pretty girl in Edmonton." He embraces and kisses Greta. "We get along very well. This is her third time here, you know. Maybe it's destiny that she was stranded here after the breakdown. But... we don't have any definite plans yet. We haven't yet discussed if we want to stay together. There'll be enough time for that, right Greta?"

Alex smiles at her, pulling her back towards him. Greta smiles back.

"Just a minute," Melissa interrupts. "As your sister, I should be allowed to ask one or two questions here. That little boy who was with you yesterday, is he yours, Greta?"

Greta nods.

"And is Alex the father?"

"No," says Great, almost embarrassed. But then she answers very openly, "I'm married and my husband is Clemens' father. My husband and I have drifted apart, and a year or so ago, we decided to take a break from the marriage. He's a Mennonite and

118

he's back with his brothers on the farm. I agree with what Alex just said: We get along very well, but it's too early to make any big decisions yet."

Frank feels that Alex is not too happy about her being equally reserved about the situation, but he seems to swallow it and moves on to another topic. "I think we all understand the general situation. It's pretty bad, apart from a few exceptions. *We* are an exception, but I'll get into that later. There have been lootings, robberies and gang warfare in Calgary. Those gangs' territory seems to extend as far as the foothills. On the other hand, we're dealing with a kind of castle mentality: Groups of civilians, mostly those who were living in safe settlements before, have formed paramilitary groups and don't let any strangers come near them. This is actually what we're doing, but we seem to be better equipped and much safer here than most people."

Alex lets this sink in for a moment before continuing. "As you all know, there's only one way to come here: straight up the gorge. Some smaller ravines also have to be crossed to get up here. We blew up all the bridges leading over those, but we still have some light metal bridges that can be assembled and dissembled very quickly if necessary. Here on the ranch we have cattle, goats, sheep, pigs, and poultry. We have enough grazing land for the cattle and big enough potato fields to feed us and the pigs." He smiles. "We have a small field of barley, which can be used to bake at least a little bread. We also have some vegetables and fruits–well, at least what will grow here in this harsh climate. Actually, we only grow small grabapples and pears, but there're several types of berries here in the fall. We're on the border of the national park, and there are also hazelnuts and mushrooms around, as well as trout and lots of venison. In short, we won't have much to worry about, food-wise."

"We have a small hydroelectric plant, enough ammunition to last years, a well-equipped workshop, and a vast multimedia library. We have clean drinking water, canned food, rice and chocolate stored in large quantities. We also have horses and ATRVs for transportation, and a good supply of fuel to run them. I think that, just like my father, I've always prepared for the worst, which now seems to have arrived with the growing chaos around us. In case of emergency, we'll have to defend this valley against intruders. We've been trying to prepare for such a case. What we really lack is good medical supplies. We should also be prepared for cabin fever in the winter, but, physically speaking, we should be well set. Together with my father's people, which now also includes my sister Christina and her husband, this group should be one of the best equipped around except for heads of government in well equipped nuclear-safe retreats."

"How long do you think we'll have to stay here, Alex?" Mandy wants to know. "My parents are in Edmonton. I know they can't be as well off there as we are here, but I think I should try to get through to them somehow."

Alex looks at Mandy for a long time. "If your parents don't have a safe haven and adequate supplies, they'll soon be in trouble."

"They have a big piece of land with a vacation house, or maybe a manor would be a better description. It's near Nordegg. It even has an underground bunker. I'm sure they've already gone there. My father always said that it wouldn't be a problem to survive there for six or maybe even eight months. Do you think that'll do it?"

Alex tries to answer very carefully. "That's more than most of them out there'll have. Sounds like they might be able to make it until spring. It'll all depend on if they're attacked and overrun. But you also wanted to know how long we'll have to stay here: according to some of my XP's simulations, only 2% of Alberta's original population will still live here after the winter. And most of those who *do* survive and *do* stay will be desperate enough to do just about anything. After another winter, there'll be no more real settlements, only nests of humanity who had a good plan or were brutal enough.

A shocked silence falls over the group: no one has ever articulated the potential vastness of the catastrophe before. But Mandy insists on knowing more. "Are you saying that everyone else will die, starve or freeze to death?"

"I'm afraid a lot of them will. A lot of them will also try to make their way down south. It'll be easier to survive in warmer climates, except for deserts. But there's yet another unknown quantity..." Alex doesn't seem to be comfortable going on.

"What're you talking about? Keep talking!"

"According to my XP, there is a 98% probability that the breakdown was caused deliberately. There is a 96% probability that whoever did it knew what they were doing. However menacing such a group may be, it's pretty likely that it made good plans for itself, and will probably have further plans that have yet to be initiated, and could change everything."

"What kind of plans?" they ask, almost in unison.

Alex waves them off. "I don't want to speculate on that at this point, but back to Mandy's question: it's very likely that there'll be so few people around here in two years that it won't be a problem for us to leave the ranch then. But until then, I consider it too dangerous. But enough of that now. I'd like to show something to Frank and Greg while you others take a look around the ranch."

Alex asks Frank and Greg to prepare for a short climbing tour. They are eager to find out what Alex has in store for them as they leave to ride downstream on horseback. They ride until they reach Poison Gas Valley[22]. They reach the point where the public footpath used to leave for the ice caves. This path is on Alex's property, and now, since the destruction of the bridges, can only be reached from the ranch. They leave their horses behind and climb across a scree slope to the entrance of the cave and then turn right along the wall of a cliff. When they reach a hardly noticeable groove, Alex stops, and points upward. "We have to get up there."

Roped together through climbing harnesses, they slowly make their way up, piton-by-piton, together. After a little more than half an hour, they arrive at a narrow ledge. Spruces grow directly from the rock here. Alex makes his way through the growth. His friends follow him in anticipation. He bends over and produces a

---

[22] Poison Gas Valley is home to the only well-known ice caves near Calgary. For 150 years, people have been warned about the poisonous gas coming from underground pockets.

pair of helmets and flashlights from a bush. But only a slit in the rock is visible. "Welcome to the entrance to my cave."

They find it hard to get in at first. But soon the entrance becomes wider. There is no ground. Instead, with legs akimbo, they have to traverse a deep crevasse that narrows as it descends into the rock. Greg has an uneasy feeling about walking over it: If they were to slip now, they would fall and might get stuck so hard they'd probably never get out again. But twenty meters later, the crevasse leads into a cave with a soft sandy floor. It seems to widen deep into the rock. They can hear water dripping somewhere. When Alex reaches into the wall at a specific spot, the whole cave lights up so it's almost as bright as daylight.

Frank and Greg feel as if they are in Ali Baba's cave. In the new light, a cavern the size of a football field appears in front of them. Many niches become visible. Some of them have almost been furnished like living rooms, while others resemble storehouses. Alex laughs at his brothers-in-law's astonishment. "Did Christina tell you that my father also has a cave in the mountains of Konitsa? The 'last refuge-idea' seems to be within the family. All this is equipped for 2000 human-days, and seven people could live here for almost a year without ever having to leave the place. I'm sure you've also noticed the dripping in the background. Well, there's a little creek back there. Good drinking water. And there's also a turbine that produces electricity for light, heating, and cooking. And better yet, there's a huge block of ice that makes a great refrigerator. Basically, everything necessary should be here. This book contains an inventory list. Now you have to promise me you'll only tell your families. Should it ever be necessary, all of us can find refuge here. The remote location, and especially the narrow crevasse leading in here makes this place more or less attack proof."

The longer they inspect the cave, the more Frank and Greg marvel. "Just one question," asks Greg, finally. "The climb up here and the crevasse, that can't be done by children or unpracticed climbers. How're they supposed to get in here?"

Alex smiles. "Finally somebody asks. There is a very comfortable transport system that can be let down from here. Just look at it! Actually, only one person has to climb up here and all the others have it easy. But let's go back now. I just wanted to impress you a little bit. Let's hope that none of us will ever need this cave."

The group returns quietly. After lunch, they all discuss how each individual can be useful to the group. Alex lets everyone pick one or more field of activity. They all enjoy the feeling of taking over important responsibilities. Frank seems to feel better too, but it hurts him again when he sees Alex and Greta disappear into Alex's bedroom. Frank curses his irrational jealousy: He himself had suggested that Greta find herself someone else instead of forcing a decision from him. So why does he have these strong feelings?

June 21, 2080

The "Newfis" have been on the ranch for a whole week now. Today is the first day when everyone has a job to do outside. This is Frank's first opportunity to talk to Greta.

"Greta, I think you know that I loved you very much and that I still do. I'm terribly sorry that I let you go, but why did you cut yourself off from me? Why didn't you even let me write you an e-mail once in a while? Didn't we spend happy years together? How can you just try to erase those from your life?"

Greta looks at Frank for a long time. "Frank, I know you loved me in your own way and maybe you still do. But you never lived up to that. You never did what you should've done. You had the chance again last week, but you just ignored it. After you arrived here, if you'd said in front of everybody, 'Greta, you're the woman I want to spend the rest of my life with. I'm sorry I have to hurt other people, but you're just too important to me...' I'd have fallen into your arms. But once again, you did nothing. You just suffered for a week and you let me suffer too. And now here you are telling me that you love me. Will you say the same thing when the others are back here? Will you be able to do that to your beloved Melissa? The way you're looking at me now convinces me that the answer is no.2

"So what do you want from me? I loved you like I never loved anybody before. I was prepared to give everything up for you. Yes, maybe this would've been easier for me than for you, but you always kept me at arm's length; to show off, for a nice conversation, a trip or two, and for bed, of course. I was good enough for those things, but not good enough for a real relationship. That just wasn't enough for me. When I got to know my husband, everything was so different: he was there just for me. He may have his bad sides, but so do you. More importantly, he really belongs to me. Please understand, I didn't want any contact with you because I didn't love you, but because I loved you too much. I just didn't want to be reminded all the time about what I had lost: the caring, the caressing, the travel, and the love. There were just so many places everywhere that reminded me of you against my will."

"And I was so angry when you were trying to force yourself back into my life without being there. I thought so much about you. I learned and saw so much because of you. There were things I wouldn't have done otherwise, and that I did just for you. All in all, I haven't been able to forget you, like in *Dr. Zhivago*, remember? But time heals all wounds, I guess, and even though I was still thinking about you a lot, I eventually started to feel better. The sting of memory became rarer, and I slowly became satisfied with my life again.

"And it's the same now: Alex and I were really happy before you showed up. I still wasn't sure whether I belonged to Alex or to my husband, a conservative, loyal, hearty, and yes, imaginative man. And then there you were again, forcing me back into a maelstrom of feelings. I just can't take that any more. Maybe I should thank you, because now I know where I belong. I belong to my husband. And in case you still don't understand, you *were* the love of my life but it's too late now."

"You won't have to suffer much longer: three days ago, Clemens, Mandy, Keith, and I decided to ride north. We think we can reach Mandy's parents in two days. After that, Keith will accompany me to my husband at his brothers' farm. The Mennonites have never needed technology, so they won't find it hard to get through this crisis, even if they have to use weapons for the first time to defend their lifestyle. Clemens is looking forward to seeing his father again. The Mennonites lead very simple communal lives, which is probably even better than here. Keith will then return to Mandy, but if her parents' don't accept that, they'll try to make it back here. So you'll never see me again. And never try to force yourself into my life again. The Mennonites have never had Internet and all letters are read publicly, so don't even think about it. Maybe there will be a time someday when we'll be able to think about one another without having to suffer. I know this isn't possible now, not for you, and not for me." Greta laughs. "Don't look so shocked. You knew, didn't you? You just wanted to hear it from me, didn't you? All the best."

Greta bends over to Frank, kisses him on the mouth, and lets a tear roll down her cheek. "I hope this is the last tear I shed for you. Don't forget, we made each other both happy and sad. Let's try to forget the sad."

When the four leave for Mandy's parents the next day, both Alex and Frank watch them go for a long time. "You knew her before me, right?" asks Alex. "She's an unusual woman, and I guess neither of us deserved her. Yes, dear brother-in-law, we're very similar–what do you say? Frank looks at Alex until Alex continues, "It's good that Melissa hasn't really followed the whole story. And to change the subject: I hope that Keith can stay with Mandy."

7 The Master of Masters

Near Nacodoches, Texas
June 28, 2080, 8:30 a.m. Central Standard Time

The little sleepy town of Nacodoches is situated on the upper end of the Sam Rayburn Reservoir, about 230 km southeast of Dallas. If you travel twenty km east from there, toward the Toledo Bend Reservoir, the low hills sink one more time and you find yourself in a subtropical basin covered mostly in bushes and open to the south. The valley flows into the higher landscape to the north like a bay.

Since 2066, 400 square kilometers of this basin have been privately owned. One third of the basin has been deforested and is now used for agricultural purposes. Mostly corn is grown on this reclaimed land, but in addition to the grazing Longhorn cattle, it is also home to an unusually large variety of crops and other animals. At its periphery, the area is well protected: the airspace has been deemed Moller-free apart from the usual special permits.

At the north of the basin lies a modern ghost town: a huge settlement of modern, well-maintained houses, built partly underground and providing space for hundreds of thousands of people. Only a very small section of the town is occupied. Huge halls are located on the eastern side, but due to their flat construction and color, they are only noticeable at a second glance. At the town's northernmost point, where it melts into the hills, there lies a huge, extended palace-like construction: this is the headquarters of the Church of the Chosen (the COC). Only the forty rows of houses bordering the frontcourt of the palace are occupied: forty rows of houses, fifty houses per row, housing a total of 5000 people. Half of the population consists of so-called students, while the other half has reached the rank of apprentice. Only those who have reached the status of Master live in the palace extensions with their families.

This "ghost town" is actually quite busy near the palace. Many people drive their ATRVs to the factories, and children run around or ride their bicycles; the atmosphere is cheerful and relaxed. Everyone is talking about the heat. How long will it continue?

Everyone here agrees that they are well off compared to the unbelievers "outside" who are paying for their sins until they are *perhaps* redeemed by the COC. Here they are, on their way to their friendly, air conditioned workspaces, looking forward to the evening's festivities where the Master of Masters (MoM) is going to speak. Unlike all over the rest of the world, there is no desperation here; instead, there is a feeling of euphoria. The "worldwide" breakdown of net technology hasn't happened here. The computers and the factories operate just as they always have. MoM's Mollers are rolling off the assembly lines, XPs are being systematically adapted in huge workshops, and people are sitting at their desks controlling agricultural machines.

The Master of Masters, or MoM, as his followers like to call him, is content. He and his petite, charming Japanese F1[23] are relaxing in a whirlpool. She lovingly massages him and he continually leads her hand to the places he likes touched the most. At the same time, his tall, long-legged F2 serves him breakfast. F3, who MoM especially appreciates because of her objectivity, intelligence, humor, and fantasy, and who has already reached Master status, informs the others of the news: as predicted, the drones[24] have discovered the whole world is falling apart.

'Oh how stupid they are out there,' MoM thinks. 'Instead of grouping together to find a way out of the crisis, they fight and rob each other, and waste the time they will need to secure their survival.'

Even regional attempts at stabilization do not seem to be making much of difference. It amuses MoM that an old general is trying to maintain "normality" in northern Greece, and that the governor of an obscure Austrian province is still trying (with a large degree of success) to care for his fellow Styrians, even after

---

[23] MoM tends to number his "playmates" according to his current preference.
[24] Miniature unmanned spy planes that carry cameras and microphones. Normally they are controlled remotely by satellite communication. Due to the breakdown of the net, MoM uses an alternative: drones, which send their discoveries via a series of wireless relays to headquarters.

three weeks without net technology. He notices that groups all over the world are withdrawing to easily defendable places where they have carefully stored supplies. Even those who foresaw catastrophe will still face serious problems within the next twelve months. He is not surprised to hear that government and military leaders all over the world have made sure that they are safe... or so they think.

'But for how long?' MoM wonders. It has been confirmed that many people are abusing the vacuum of power, either as well-meaning dictators, or as malevolent gang leaders who simply take whatever they want. His prediction that catastrophes will also break out in regions rich in natural resources has yet to be confirmed.

However, there are signs that the lack of technology is already starting to bother the population there as well. It is a fact that no central power has managed to survive the first three weeks, and that no one has control over more than a small region. Most governments have given up control voluntarily, and very few places continue to show any sign of coordinated activity. This is due more to a lack of communication than transportation, but most vehicles (particularly the ubiquitous Mollers which depend on global navigation systems) have broken down too. Islands and countries with many waterways seem to be a bit better off because smaller boats have been affected much less than was expected.

Finally, MoM stops F3. Nothing really new seems to have happened.

MoM is irritated because the ATRVs and a larger than expected number of ham radios are still fighting a truly complete breakdown. On the other hand, he is pleased that the previously unknown number of Mindcallers seems to be very low. These artifacts, which allow high quality communication, could have endangered his plan. One of MoMs technical teams is trying to alter its own Mindcaller to eavesdrop on the others.

MoM is baffled about the situation in Newfoundland. He is very surprised that one of North America's largest hydroelectric plants is still operating. At the moment, this doesn't seem to be playing a big roll because its electricity can only be used locally.

But if they manage to repair the distribution devices, large parts of Northeast America would suddenly have electricity again. This would be a bummer: humans will only join the COC if they die and suffer, and he must rule America before he can control the rest of the world. He will have to keep an eye on Churchill Falls. He decides not to save anyone there as a punishment.

Newfoundland's main island is also developing atypically: at first, two self-proclaimed regents seemed to be doing a "good" job, but then, suddenly, a glorified sailor and his brother from Churchill Falls somehow managed to get the legitimate government back into office, and even to work out some kind of a rescue plan. He might have to move a sabotage group in there. The two brothers and their families later disappeared westwards in an old airplane. They seem to be dangerously over ambitious: MoM will have to find them and get rid of them.

But these are small problems. MoM is convinced that nobody will doubt his holy calling after having predicted the whole catastrophe.

He smiles to himself. 'Yes, I knew, or perhaps predicted is a better word, that this near-complete breakdown would start exactly on the 8th and 9th of June 2080.' His missionaries are concentrated mostly in the USA right now. Only a few of them have been sent into other parts of the world in order to recruit new missionaries.

His missionaries warned the population about the breakdown. They explained to the world that the only way to survive the coming Armageddon was to join the COC, but these warnings fell mostly on deaf ears. MoM repeatedly announced that the situation was going to change dramatically after the breakdown. And so it did: suddenly all his missionaries are reporting a change of attitude and want to know how to handle it.

After breakfast MoM starts to prepare for tonight's speech: he will announce that the missionaries can now start to recruit new disciples. According to recently gathered information, a huge number of people now want to join the COC, if only to get necessary supplies. The MOM knows most of them won't join because of devotion, but because they want to save their own lives. However, he is convinced that the wisdom of the Chosen will soon reach the hearts of the unbelievers.

He formulates this to all the Masters, those high-ranking men and women of the COC who will have to carry out the training of the Apprentices. It's almost every COC member's dream to reach the status of Master. Masters have special privileges: they are the only ones who are allowed to have servants, and they have the right to choose their partners freely and for as long (or short) a time as they want. A careful selection process is applied to Apprentices. Only some of them are capable of proceeding to the rank of Master. The majority become missionaries. A small group is secluded and trained as saboteurs. Only the Masters are informed about the saboteurs, whose job it is to "lead the people on the right track" through depravation. Similarly, only the Masters know that some of the technically gifted Apprentices are being secluded, never to be seen again. Only MoM knows their purpose. Mentioning these saboteurs and doubting MoM's holiness and infallibility are strictly forbidden.

As usual, during his meetings with the Masters, MoM reads from his *Scripture of Enlightenment*. Today he again mentions certain details that are not explicitly mentioned in the *Scripture*, especially new enlightenments that he experienced during his last pilgrimage to the COC's stately manor in Truth and Consequences, New Mexico. As is the case for most houses in this small town, its basement floor is only gravel with hot mineral water pouring from the ground creating a natural hot swimming pool. In the past, this house was used by MoM and other Masters for "ritual communal relaxation exercises". It's very well equipped for that purpose: the relaxation area is located directly above the hot pool and is equipped with comfortable cots and other devices.

MoM keeps talking about his last pilgrimage. He has very satisfying memories, mostly due to the fact that F1, F2 and F3 accompanied him.

F1 and F2 went through some of the purifying rituals with MoM. As a Master, F3 read out all the rituals MoM picked out, step by step. It was also her duty to supervise F1 and F2 if they

131

hesitated or tried to circumvent one of the orders. She had to interfere and punish F2 twice in order to show her the way. MoM was so pleased about F3's ceremonial skills that he even allowed her to choose her own ritual to carry out with the Apprentices.

In order to help F2, who apparently still needed to learn a lot, F3 decided to pick a rather profound and difficult ritual. This famous Ritual 13 increases in difficulty step by step. F2 was already having obedience problems by step 6, which needed to be corrected several times by F1. There is no doubt that MoM and F1 enjoyed F2s devotion, and that F3 trembled with delight. Afterwards F2 was so grateful for the experience that F3 decided another ritual would not be necessary that day. As usual, the two Masters involved in the ritual withdrew afterwards to carry out some exercises together. At this opportunity, F3 dared to ask MoM if he would allow her to carry out rituals in the Masters' ritual room with people of her own choosing. Generously, MoM agreed to that.

Two days later the big day arrived. F3 had picked three powerful men and two women who appeared to be somewhat shy. Rituals for two men and three women were rare, so MoM was very curious about the selection of the ritual. F3 surprised him: She had taken advantage of a Master's privilege to add one new ritual per year to the Book of Rituals. MoM could hardly believe what F3's imagination had created to purify the participants. Step by step, MoM carefully went through the ritual, making sure that every point was carried out precisely. Several times he had to interfere with a warning or a punishment. Four times, rituals had to be repeated until they were done perfectly.

At the debriefing F3 insisted on getting MoM's opinion on every individual step. "As soon as F1's month is over, you shall be my new F1," MoM promised.

F3 beamed. "I think I'm the first Master who has been granted this honor. In return I am willing to submit to any Novice rituals just for you."

"Any? Do you know them all?"

"I think I do. And I shall submit to any one of them."

These memories, which date back more than three weeks now, and the looks that F3 threw at him today have the following effect: "I think I will relax in another ritual before this evening."

The gathering of the Masters dissolves but F3 is in no hurry to leave. Finally, the MoM approaches her. "Do you remember your offer?"

"Of course. Are you thinking about carrying it out now?"

The MoM nods and makes her follow him. For the first time, F3 enters the MoM's ritual chamber.

"Only the two of us? No one leading the ritual?" F3 wants to know.

"Yes, the screen will be leading us." MoM opens the book of rituals and finds the chapter called "Ritual for Novices without a Leader" and starts to go over the short descriptions of the rituals while F3 sits with him. F3 always considered this chapter too simple and never took a close look at it. But now she begins to suspect that she has a difficult ritual ahead of her.

MoM begins, "What's most unusual about this ritual is that it has no element of surprise. First the Novice must read out the individual steps that must be carried out, and later she has to explain them in her own words. You're good with words; you won't find this very difficult."

As F3 reads the steps out loud, she gets stuck here and there. When she's done with all the steps, MoM dryly notes, "This will purify you for a long time."

F3 nods devoutly.

Now the ritual can start. F3 kneels down and starts with the usual prayer for a Novice. "Oh God of the Church of the Chosen, please give me the power necessary not to disappoint the Master, who allows me this ritual. I vow to carry out every step, which will purify me further. I shall appreciate every step and be grateful to the Master, who allows me to carry it out. Give me the strength to bring the ritual to a close without hesitation. May my will reign over my body or my unworthy body shall be punished. Amen."

MoM gazes into F3's eyes. "Let the ritual begin."

F3 is more dedicated than any other novice before her. She is proud to master even the most difficult steps and she notices how

133

much she's learning through them. 'Yes, this is the right way to purify a Novice,' she thinks, already looking forward to carrying this out herself to help other novices.

During the analysis, MoM is very content. "You were excellent. I hope this purified and relaxed you like it relaxed me."

"I think my devotion and religious fervor really showed in some spots, didn't it?"

"Yes, you're an asset to the COC, and I hope vice versa. Once you're my F1, you will help me to guide the Novices through their rituals. I'm looking forward to that."

After the ritual MoM decides to visit his most secret underlings: As usual he carefully passes through the high security entrance before taking the elevator deep into the earth. When he gets out, he enters a different world: a thirty-five square mile cave appears in front of him. They were already starting to develop it before the settlement was erected. It is now a self-sustaining bio-system of several levels. Some are cooler; others are warmer, and in addition to humidity and temperature control, the duration and intensity of light are altered according to the time of day and seasons. This produces rich flora and fauna.

800 computer specialists live here, some with their partners, some without, in the lap of luxury. They are the true basis of MoM's success. Their lives may be better and richer than those of most other people, but there is one important limitation: they know the outside world only through three dimensional computer simulations, a la the Holodeck of Star Trek's *Enterprise*. Only on very rare occasions may they leave their 'continent', and even then they must have their memories erased.

This is the place responsible for the worldwide breakdown. It carries the almost cynical name "Newstart Central." For almost ten years, a very inconspicuous virus created here has been planted into all of the world's computer systems. The virus was programmed to start its destructive effects on June 8th, 2080 at 11:34 a.m. CST, sharp. In many cases, the distribution of such a virus was easy: for decades, the most widely used computer system had security weaknesses that allowed the implantation of viruses and worms.

However, MoM decided to go a different route: he smuggled one of his underlings into every single large computer company in order to make sure the virus left together with all the latest software. This also assured the infection of computers that were not attached to the net (even parts of SR Inc.'s secret XP software).

Over the years, computers have turned more and more into embedded systems, into steering computers that can be found in almost all devices from simple doors, to vehicles, to even more complex devices. Considering this, MoM was almost disappointed when not all devices broke down right away. In hospitals, for example, some emergency generators still worked, as well as simple appliances such as washing machines, which should have broken down immediately. However, MoM estimated that there would be certain "failures" and, after all, he has other things to worry about, like the entire logistics for the time after the breakdown.

While MoM is walking through Newstart Central, he has the occasional friendly word with one of his staff. It is his dearest wish that the future plan will work just as well as the plan for the breakdown did. When he reaches a waterfall, MoM sits down to watch the play of the dragonflies. He starts daydreaming, falling back into the past:

He grew up the only spoiled and well-educated son of the rich Texas Muriel family. His father, the politician Oswald Muriel, and his mother decided on a lark to name him Muriel O. Muriel[25], the O. standing for Oswald. One day his mother ran off with a lover and he never heard from her again. His father took good care of him, even though his job as Senator for Texas took up most of his time. When Muriel O. Muriel finished high school, his father was running for president. Muriel O. Muriel, or MoM as he was already known, traveled from gathering to gathering with

---

[25] His father always hated it when people didn't know whether Oliver or Muriel was his first name. By calling his son Muriel O. Muriel, he hoped to spare his son that problem.

his father, his great idol. But soon he had to watch his father be killed by a lunatic.

The days after the murder were like an evil dream for MoM. At the funeral the priest said a few words that Muriel would never be able to forget: "Like every other death, this death is very sad. But we may not forget that humanity is like a tree. A tree can lose its leaves and we may be sad about that. But even when it loses all its leaves in the fall, the tree remains strong and will grow strong, new leaves only months later."

This interpretation of death would influence MoM for the rest of his life. But it could not ease the pain of the ensuing weeks. Then suddenly, in the middle of one of his many sleepless nights, MoM had a vision that seemed to show it all clearly: He would have to lead humanity, not just in the USA, but also worldwide. He would have to make them happy and make sure that wars, hatred and murder disappear from the planet. He would have to be the redeemer.

A flood of thoughts and emotions flowed through his brain (or were they produced by it?). For days following the vision, MoM wrote all those thoughts down into what he would call The Book of Enlightenment. He realized that he was the chosen one who would have to lead others. He could feel the mission and that it could only be carried out within a hierarchical organization founded on the cornerstone of his vision. (Later it was unclear how many of those rules had been part of the original vision, or had been invented pragmatically afterwards: was it part of the vision that he would be the Master of Masters, and that only some people would become Masters with special privileges, and that there would be Apprentices and missionaries who would carry the message and widen the influence of the church? Were all those rituals that turn humans into Apprentices and Masters invented or received?)

From then on, MoM had the meaning "Master of Masters". Very pragmatically, MoM tried to find the right way to fulfill his quest and win leadership over humanity. He was sure that he would have to convince the people that he had been appointed by God. But how would he prove that? With a spoken prophesy that would then be fulfilled. But how many Armageddon's had *already been predicted without coming to pass?   But his breakdown would happen. He would make sure of that.*

No one was supposed to know that MoM himself was responsible. The fact that almost all humans would have to die because of this breakdown never seemed to worry him: the tree would remain healthy and grow new leaves. The survivors would see him as a prophet and a savior and they would follow his visions and his rules. This would create a better humanity and the fewer survivors there were, the better. Hadn't they always said that the world was overpopulated? He would only be able to save the survivors if not too many existed.

MoM systematically developed his plan, risking his entire paternal heritage. He first bought a huge but rather worthless piece of land 100 km southeast of Tyler and fifty km north of Beaumont[26]. This unfriendly hot and humid bush land in Texas would be perfect for his ends. He also considered buying a piece of land west of Karlsbad, one with even better caves, but with much drier land above.

He soon began to build the palace to found the Church of the Chosen and to build the city for those people he would later choose to save. He recruited computer freaks and locked them in their golden cage. He violently suppressed troubles but made sure a balance between the sexes existed. The unique atmosphere of the cave was an important reason for most of its inhabitant's ready acceptance of their new world. He fired those who were not content there, but made sure they soon disappeared. Scruples were one thing he was not guilty of. For him, a human was only a leaf on the tree of humanity. That's how the Celts had seen it too, that's how they justified human sacrifice.

His first followers were convinced of the catastrophe with a piece of land and their own house, which would be theirs should the breakdown not occur. He also paid them well for producing and storing supplies, and building new houses and machines, which would also function without computers. He produced a fleet of Mollers that didn't require satellite navigation systems to

---

[26] The town where the first big oil field in Texas, Spindletop, was found in 1901.

be operated, and would be able to fly after the breakdown. He modified hundreds of thousands of XPs in order to make sure they would be able to communicate through a series of relay stations, and he built super safe, fully automatic production centers for sugar, paper, fuels, synthetic fibers and other basic necessities.

For months everything has been running in top gear: slowly, he is now able to supply his missionaries with goods that have become rare "out there." This is what he will announce tonight. But still, he will have to be very careful. New members of the COC will only be supplied when they are "out there." They will not be allowed to come to the headquarters until they have passed several long tests. MoM is worried that some military institutions could still be functional enough to attack him. But of course, he has also taken precautions for such eventualities: he even has three nuclear bombs in his arsenal.

Suddenly a young female programmer sits down next to him, tearing him out of his daydream. "Highest Master, is it true that our programs have put many people in serious trouble?"

MoM penetrates her with his sparkling blue eyes. "That is true. But at the same time, the programs that all of you write make sure that we can produce everything that is needed to save those people and to make them aware of the truth of the COC. Continue to do good, my dear." He blesses her and quickly rushes back to the elevator after this uneasy moment. He is worried that there is still communication between here and "out there." He hopes that information will only flow inward because otherwise his prophecy could turn into a huge boomerang.

The evening's party is in full swing. There is a large variety of food and entertainment. Beer, wine, whiskey, and tequila flow in an endless river of intoxication. But suddenly there is silence.

The MoM appears on the screens and declares in his soothing voice:

"Dearest friends of the COC, while we are living here in luxury, the world around us is beginning to suffer severely due to the breakdown I prophesied. Over the entire world[27], our missionaries warned non-believers about the catastrophe, but only

---

[27] He is exaggerating here.

138

a few have converted to the true church, and they are now secure with us here. Now that the breakdown has come to pass, they all want to join us."

The MoM pauses to let the thought of billions of people swarming over this paradise like biblical locusts sink into their minds.

"We cannot allow this. But we do not want to let the new believers starve or freeze to death. Starting tomorrow, we will begin to ship aid packages. Later, those who prove most loyal to the COC will be allowed to join us and to help rebuild the world outside. But for now the existence of this place has to be hidden from the public. This is why none of you will be allowed to leave for now. Please understand the necessity of this measure."

MoM's speech continues, and becomes a riveting sermon. After he is finished, he allows the party to continue.

Near Nacodoches, Texas
Mid-June 2080 to May 20, 2081

Indeed, the MoM and his missionaries try their best over the following months to provide the new believers with the most necessary goods. MoM knows that he must be very careful not to give away the origin of the supplies. This turns out to be much more difficult than he expected: on the first day, two of MoM's Mollers are ordered by USAF Mollers to land. MoM has given strict orders for such a scenario: no one must be taken alive because the military would definitely try to squeeze out the missionaries' identities. So on the first day of the operation, the Chosen Ones are immediately forced to bring down an air force Moller: Surprise is on their side.

The MoM hadn't expected the American military to still have functioning Mollers. His hopes that the air force only has a very few are dashed over the next few days. Despite the repeated shooting down of more USAF Mollers, they continue to appear in the sky.

MoM tries hard to disguise his Mollers' base: for example, he has some Mollers fly up to the Canadian border under cover of darkness so they can begin their deliveries from there the next morning. But when they return north in the evening, they are discovered and followed by a fighter, which manages to shoot down several Mollers before being hit itself.

MoM has to accept the fact that he will not be able to fly out as many goods as he planned. Without their knowledge, the military is responsible for people starving and freezing to death. Even though MoM is not really concerned about these casualties, he realizes that this continues to worsen the atmosphere on the base. There are more and more calls for the church to make itself and its intentions known to everyone so it can help the world with its full strength.

Naturally, MoM cannot give in to those calls. Instead, he puts more and more effort into finding out where the military keeps its Mollers and jets. His continent-wide system of drones proves very effective here, and the MoM congratulates himself for having conceived of it. Of course, some relay stations break down eventually, and those can only be repaired if a trustworthy missionary is nearby. The MoM had expected breakdowns in remote areas like Labrador, but he never thought a whole group of stations could possibly break down around a big city like Calgary. This is suspicious and he knows that he will have to investigate it eventually. But now there are more important issues to deal with.

In early May 2081 the MoM knows enough: all the military's functional Mollers and airplanes are stationed at one of four locations: Brooks AFB near San Antonio, a high security base in southern Colorado, Washington, and Boston. All other military bases are practically nonfunctional. The MoM plans an assault on all four bases to destroy their aircraft.

But this has to be postponed for the time being. The military has been able to capture several church missionaries and play them against each other to get information about the location of the COC's headquarters and their air base. They soon assume that the breakdown was triggered there. Nobody seems to believe the prophecy theory.

This is why the President of the United States orders a concentrated air attack on the COC headquarters followed by a ground invasion by the remnants of the US infantry and Marine Corps. This seems to be his only option after the last eleven terrible months, which have cost so many lives and have put the country under a constant threat of civil war.

At dawn on May 20th the majority of the world is not aware of the fact that the military is launching an air attack in a remote part of Texas. 850 US aircraft face about 1000 Mollers. Even though the MoM possesses more Mollers than that, he does not have the necessary trained personnel for a larger force. The MoM knows that his Mollers would never have a chance against fully operative fighters, but soon he realizes the planes are only making a path for the following wave of Mollers to bomb the base.

Over the modified XPs he gives the order for 100 of his Mollers to destroy Brooks Air Force Base. But when his palace is hit by a bomb which causes a short power outage, MoM's hatred no longer knows any boundaries: he orders three Mollers equipped with nuclear bombs to go straight to Washington, Boston, and the base in Southern Colorado.

When the military bombardment fades, almost half of the MoM's Mollers have crashed or been shot down, and his headquarters has suffered severe damage. Several bombs hit the rear of the palace, opening up the entrance to the top-secret caves. This is a serious setback, but MoM is prepared for such an event. With a remote control he triggers an immense underground explosion, causing the entire cave system to collapse, burying everything and everyone within under yards of rubble. Without any feelings for the people he has just murdered, MoM can now be certain that no one will ever be able to prove that he was responsible for the breakdown. This guarantees that he will remain to be seen as the great prophet that he is.

Or so he thinks; there have always been members of the programming group who did not trust MoM. These "traitors" wrote a second virus into many of the programs, and unless someone orders the virus to self-destruct, it will announce the truth over all functioning computers and XPs on October 17th, 2083.

In stoical silence, the MoM watches the explosion of the first nuclear bomb over Washington, DC: The expanding mushroom cloud does not give away the bomb's devastating effect.

The USAF pilots cannot believe the news about the bomb at first. They take a direct course to San Antonio only to find a destroyed base on which they can barely land. They soon hear about the bombs over Boston and Colorado, and realize the US government no longer exists. There is no longer any authority to give orders to the military.

MoM congratulates the returning pilots. He is the only one who knows about the nuclear bombs. Later on, he will lay the blame on foreign powers.

"I deeply regret that we had to lose so many of our friends, and that we had to fight our own countrymen. But we didn't throw the first stone, they did. We have suffered great losses, but we'll have to make the best of it. First, we'll rebuild this city, then we'll continue our aid efforts."

For the first time in twenty years, MoM finds himself slightly uneasy. He knows that the dead computer specialists would have been very useful in rebuilding the automatic production facilities. He knows that there will be shortages, even here at the headquarters, and that the aid efforts to the outside will start more slowly than planned.

MoM decides to adapt his plans to the new situation. This is what he's really good at: Planning. His empire, the COC, will continue to rise; perhaps not as quickly as he originally hoped, but it will rise!

8 Order and Chaos

The Ranch in Alberta
November 2080

Finally, Felitsa goes into labor. All precautions were made a long time ago. Felitsa has gone through dozens of multimedia lectures and a daily regime of birthing exercises. Since there is no doctor at hand, these preparations will have to suffice.

There are no complications. A feeling of relief spreads through the house when Felitsa delivers a healthy boy only four hours into labor. In honor of his grandfather, they name him Paul. The General is proud of his new grandson and elated when he hears about the birth.

Two weeks later, the General is careless enough to telememo some disappointment. *"It's good to see Paul II over the Mindcaller, but will I ever be able to lift him up and hold him."* A slight shadow descends upon the ranch.

Alex is hiding some sorrow from the others: as well equipped as his medicine chest may be, he has no sera for vaccinations to protect the baby. He just never considered the possibility.

March to mid-May 2081

The winter is not over yet in Alberta. Groups of heavily armed messengers dispatched by Alex confirm his worst fears: Bragg Creek is deserted. There are traces of looting and fighting everywhere. Calgary, which was a booming city only a year ago is now a pile of rubble. Every single shop has been broken into and cleaned out. There are hardly any people to be seen. The office buildings that have not been destroyed by fire are completely empty. 'But why?' thinks Alex. 'How many people are still alive around here?'

Alex thinks back to what he has heard about the Black Death that plagued Europe in the fourteenth century: After this devastating disease had killed about one third of the population of Europe, the only way to find out how many people were still alive was to count the chimneys that were still smoking. Alex decides to send scouts to the city to carry out a similar census with the XP's infrared sensors. Their findings are disconcerting: Less that 3% of all houses are still occupied, and the people still alive are suffering terribly.

The news shocks the people on the ranch and cause many guilty consciences. While they were worrying and complaining about the lack of freedom and privacy, hundreds of thousands were dying out there, and are still dying now.

Compared to this, the news from Greece, where the almond trees are already in bloom, seems almost harmless: every large Greek city already experienced a mass exodus before the winter, and even though the city dwellers were not warmly welcomed by the country folks, there were fewer fights and far fewer casualties than in Alberta. In his district, General Kalkias has managed to keep order and the supplies lines relatively good condition, but what can they to do in western Canada? It is impossible to help everyone in need. "Normality" will very likely never be reached again, so it would be wise not to give away any of their stock of goods.

The group is torn between a desire to help and the instinct to survive. They decide, finally, and mostly to ease their guilty consciences, to start at least one rescue operation. They decide to find out what happened to Keith, Mandy, Greta, and her son, who left for the Mennonite colony and Nordegg almost a year ago. It was Keith's original plan to come back here but he never returned. They assume that he must have stayed with Mandy and her parents in Nordegg, and assume their supplies must be very low by now. The three leaders quietly agree that Greg should run the rescue operation. It will also be his goal to find out about Greta and the Mennonites' situation. Due to their delicate relationships with Greta, both Alex and Frank decide not to engage in this second operation.

On March 15th Greg leaves with an armed group of six men and fourteen horses. He is expected to be back in no more than six days.

When only two men return on March 21st, the community is shocked at first. But soon the situation becomes clear: The supplies in Nordegg already almost ran out two months ago. The four people they wanted to rescue are nearly wasted away, especially Mandy's parents, who are in an extremely bad condition. It will take at least one or two weeks before they can be transported, mainly because they have to wait for warmer weather. A larger group leaves the ranch to deliver more food and medicine to Nordegg. The whole group is expected back by April 15th.

As expected, Greg and ten of the twelve men return to the ranch on a warm and clear April 15th. They have Keith, Mandy, and her parents with them, but they all look frightful. They were attacked several times between Nordegg and the ranch. If it weren't for Greg's leadership, more than just two of their men would've been killed.

"It was terrible," explains Greg. "The people are so hopeless, even heavy fire couldn't stop masses of them from trying to attack us. We must've killed dozens of them. They were just like a pack of hungry wolves. The only thing that kept them at bay was throwing them a sack of food. They tore that up like nobody's business."

Greg breaks into tears for a moment, then continues, "If the news about how well off we are off here spreads, then we'll be facing an invasion that we won't be able to stop. We have to take more, many more precautions here."

Despite the two casualties, the rescue operation is considered a moral success. Everyone is happy to have Keith and Mandy back at the ranch. They are also glad to hear that the Mennonites seem to be better off than most. They had to protect their community with huge barbed wire fences and guard dogs. Mandy's parents are bursting with gratitude, and once they are back in good shape, they prove to be of great value to the community: all their lives, they have been learning to trick vegetables and fruits into growing in the cold climate. For example, the group learns that you have to pile up snow against the trunk of a fruit tree in order to prevent it from blooming before a late frost. They also learn how to plant certain types of vegetables indoors before planting them outside and how to protect themselves from mice and other parasites.

The reports from the rest of the world get more and more frightening: The General has news about terrible conditions in almost all big cities worldwide. Those in the colder climate zones, or in overpopulated countries like India, are suffering the most. The situation seems to be a bit better in the subtropical zones around the Mediterranean Sea, in parts of Australia and New Zealand, and on the Pacific Islands. But even Hawaii, especially Honolulu, is facing serious problems. Not even small islands seem to be safe from unusual problems. "My brother Takis thought himself lucky at first at the resort in Tonga, but he keeps sending more and more sinister pictures. I'm beginning to worry about him."

Only six weeks after their last census, the number of occupied houses has dropped from 3% to 2%! However, the situation in Alberta seems to be getting better due to the warmer weather.

George and Frank have become very good friends. They continue to scout the area and are soon pretty sure that the improvement of the situation has only come about because the cattle herds have been greatly diminished through rustling and mass slaughter. This may be a relief at the moment but what will that mean for the coming winter and after?

The Ranch in Alberta
May 20-25, 2081, almost twelve months after the breakdown

On May 20th there is more news from General Kalkias. For the first time since the breakdown, he sounds desperate, and not just about the general situation, but also about his own. The radio station they were so proud of and which was the spine of morale was completely destroyed by vandals. In the repeated question "Why, why, why?" Melissa and Felitsa can sense their father's frustration.

Christina, who has made her reputation as "the Angel of Konitsa," is at her wits' end because she has just used up her last dose of antibiotics. Now, their Uncle Takis' life seems to be in danger in Tonga: like Christina, he was able to help heal many people, but now that he has run out of medicine, they are accusing him of letting people suffer and die.

That evening, they all sit together to discuss the situation. In the middle of the discussion, George asks, "How many antibiotics do we have left here at the ranch?"

Alex waves him off. "We have more than we could possibly ever use ourselves, I think. Why do you–"

He is interrupted by General Kalkias trying to contact them over the Mindcaller. Alex asks the Mindcaller to switch to projection mode and surround sound. The mysterious artifact[28] complies.

Suddenly the General seems to be standing in the middle of the room and is able to see the group. As usual, the seventy-year-old man is glowing with energy and warmth, but today he is also giving off an aura of sorrow and horror.

"You won't believe this. I just found out who's responsible for the breakdown. It's a group called "The Church of the Chosen." Their leader calls himself MoM, the Master of Masters. He claims to be able to communicate with God and to have written down the whole truth in his 'Book of Enlightenment.' For years he's been prophesizing the end of the old world order on the 8th and 9th of June 2080, and that his "Reich of the Chosen" will then become a reality. I've always suspected something behind those prophecies, but I was never sure if that was just religious bullshit or something more dangerous. I guess it was the latter. No matter if this MoM was following a calling or not, it must've taken him years to plan and execute the breakdown like that."

"Because of this prophecy, the church is now being overrun by followers. Apparently, MoM has sent missionaries all over North America, and even further. Whatever was left of the American government has tried to gain control over his huge stockpile of resources. They attacked his headquarters and that was a mistake. This very morning nuclear bombs destroyed Washington, Boston, and a military base in Colorado where the remainder of the US government was holding out. Apparently MoM is now trying to systematically widen his empire. So far this is only a territory of 400 square kilometers in Texas, parts of which have been

---

[28] See " Xperts: The Paracommunicator."

destroyed in battle. There are rumors that everyone who submits to him and the rule of his church will be accepted there as a novice "student," guaranteeing all necessities in return for doing work for the church. But once you've joined the Church of the Chosen, any criticism of it is punishable by death."

"People who don't want to join the church now won't have another chance for a long time. Apparently this MoM waited a whole year to scare the people, and then to prepare them for himself, the savior. It's also easier for him now because he's no longer dealing with twelve billion people, but just a small fraction of that. His first goal seems to gain complete control over North America, which, according to my XP, only has eleven million inhabitants left. You seem to be far away still from his headquarters in Texas, but sooner or later you'll be in trouble as well. It looks like Europe will be a safer place for quite a while. By the way, this transmission is being carried out at the highest level of security. If this MoM heard this, we'd all be on his blacklist."

The hologram of the General flickers and for a moment the sound is down too. But soon the General is back, with a much paler face than seconds before. "This fellow seems to have a jamming transmitter that he can use against the Mindcaller."

Now Alex jumps up. "No, Dad, it's even worse than that. He has a Mindcaller too and is trying to intercept the conversation! We can't communicate like this any longer. My Mindcaller is sure that he is listening. From now on we can only use coded language and text in both directions. You'll have to put an XP in between. I hope your experts–"

The connection is broken. Alex asks his Mindcaller, 'Was he able to locate us?'

'No. I made sure he couldn't. But from now on, we have to do as you said and use codes. This MoM must've manipulated his Mindcaller; it wouldn't work against humanity otherwise. I'll contact other Mindcallers to find a way to switch off the one he has. But you have to be careful, MoM is prepared for many eventualities.'

The group is paralyzed: Nuclear weapons! A religious nut caused all this! Again religion has endangered this planet. Everybody in the room thinks, 'To hell with religion!'

Greg is the first to find words for this. "I'm furious that we can't help Paul or Christina or Uncle Takis. But I think that Paul is a bit too pessimistic about our situation here. Do you really think that this MoM could hurt us here in this remote corner?"

George answers thoughtfully, "It all depends on how much the MoM was damaged by the attack. Just think about it; this guy managed to infect all the different computer systems with viruses. That must've taken him years of planning and tons of cash. I'm sure he didn't fail to plan for the time after the breakdown: He must have functioning factories, transportation, and communications systems. I'm especially worried about the communications system. Let me show you what I got with my shotgun near Bragg Creek a couple of days ago."

George pulls a dead bird from his pants and lays it on the table. Despite the tension in the room, George can't help laughing a little. "That's not a bird you suckers, it's a drone: a little airplane with cameras instead of eyes, and microphones instead of ears. Frank had a close look at it. Go ahead and tell them about it."

Frank takes the "bird" in his hand. "This drone was produced by somebody who knew that the net was going to break down. It has an unalterable memory chip that is completely safe from viruses. It doesn't send the information it collects to a receiver via satellite as one might expect, but rather to the nearest relay station, which then passes it on to the next, and the next, and the next, and so on. Judging by this, I suspect that MoM is observing large parts of the world with drones like this one. I'm sure they are covering all of North America, but I'm not so sure he has discovered our ranch yet. If he has, then he knows where to send his "missionaries" for supplies. If he hasn't, then we've been really lucky. Anyway, George and I destroyed the relay station in Bragg Creek, and Cochrane, and a bigger one in Calgary. But to be honest, I'm not so sure anymore if that was such a great idea; they might notice it and send someone to find out what's going on."

149

The group remains quiet for some time before ninety-five year-old George speaks up again, "I'm pretty sure that the MoM has more important things to worry about right now, but sooner or later, he could become dangerous to us. That's why I've decided to take a trip to help three people who so far I've only been able to meet indirectly through the rest of you. Everyone who wants to come along is very welcome."

No one knows what to think of this. "Could you be a little more clear there, George?"

"I want to rescue Uncle Takis, bring Christina some Antibiotics, and help the general repair his radio station." George smiles when he sees the astonished faces. "You look like you've forgotten that we still have a transport plane. It seems to have survived the winter and still has enough fuel to make it to Tonga. I'll pick up Takis there and then fly on to the General's. Who wants to join me?"

"But you said that the plane could only make about 10,000 more miles and that it could only take off three more times, maximum. Now you want to take a trip around the world?" Greg asks in disbelief.

George shrugs his shoulders. "Of course the plane isn't new any more, but if you don't fly too fast, it should be able to withstand a lot more. Actually, the landing gear seems to be the weakest part. If I told you that in Newfoundland, we'd still be sitting there because you wouldn't have wanted to withhold a useful plane from your friends."

George pauses before he continues. "I'm serious. The flight to Tonga shouldn't be a problem. We can only hope that the airport is still OK there, and that they have some fuel left over there. My XP gives it a 70% chance: even though the airport was in perfect condition and had large stores of fuel before the breakdown, according to the flight schedules, a large passenger plane was landing during the breakdown. If it did not get down safely, there's a very good chance that it crashed near the airport and caused severe damage. But 70% isn't that bad. Why don't you ask your XPs about the probability that we'll still be alive in three years if we stay here?"

Frank enters this problem into his XP and it calculates a probability of 76%.

"Told ya! Not much of a difference, huh?" George crows. By comparing apples to oranges he managed to take them by surprise. If they had asked their XPs about the probability that they would still be alive in three years if they follow George's plan, it would have been far below 50%.

"And how do you plan to pay for the fuel in Vava'u?" Frank interrupts.

"First of all with medicine which they don't seem to have, right? We have a lot of that around here, don't we, Alex?"

"Yes, but a lot of it will soon expire, or already have."

"Ahh, you can't take those expiration dates seriously. They only make those up to sell new medicine and to protect the pharmaceutical companies from lawsuits. Some medications can be stored forever and have an expiration date nonetheless. Just ask your XP. So that's one good way to make money, especially if the Tongans have more fuel than they need. Those fuel tanks were built for large airplanes. They have enough to feed their little generators and motorboats forever. I'm sure we'll come up with more things that we can trade. I bet you that no Tongan has seen any milk or butter for months."

George's excitement infects the others as he continues, "Just think about how great it would be to surprise the General. It's been forever since he last embraced his grandchildren, and you've all seen how much he would like to see Paul II. If you all decide to come along, and if we take those young Canadian Greeks who work on the ranch, then we could leave a huge amount of supplies to Keith, Mandy, their parents, and the Canadian ranchers. We couldn't take all this with us anyway. But we won't just take consumer goods with us, we'll take a lot of important tools: an ATRV, guns, ammunition, and much more. So who's with me?"

In order to provide for an easier loading of the plane, they append metal ladders to the cliff that separates the ranch from the meadow. The beautiful spring weather makes the operation easier. As George predicted, those who remain at the ranch are left with more supplies than the twelve passengers can take with them. In addition to Frank's family, the group consists of Alex,

Felitsa, Greg, their baby, two young Greek men, and one Greek woman from the ranch, and George, of course, who is supervising the loading of the plane. He also makes sure that part of the meadow in front of the plane is evened out.

On May 25th Alex takes a last walk across his ranch and asks Keith to come with him. Alex tells Keith about the secret ice cave. Keith and Alex exchange a sincere handshake.

"We won't have a lot of space during the flight. We can only take what we really need. This means that we'll have to do with the six cots that we used on the way here, so we'll be sleeping in shifts," explains George. "It'll be about a twenty hour flight to Tonga. For reasons of security and orientation, we'll have to take a little detour via Hawaii."

George has designated May 26th as the perfect day for departure. But the days till then seem to pass much too quickly.

When Alex hands over the keys of the ranch to Keith at 3:30 a.m., tears well up in his eyes. "This place is yours until I get back," he says, even though he is sure he'll never see the ranch again. George urges them to go quickly. The day begins to dawn and the light morning wind blowing up from the valley will make the take off easier. After short good-byes, the doors of the airplane shut. It is now 3:50 a.m. With a calculated twenty-one hour flight they should be able to reach their goal in daylight, which is the most critical factor for orientation and landing. Because of the International Date Line, it will be May 27th by then.

The Flight
May 26 to June 4, 2081

Without hesitation George starts the jets. The plane rolls down the slope faster and faster before it takes off heavily. After one more tilt of the wings at those on the ground, George follows the Elbow Valley out.

Constantly gaining altitude, they soon reach the wider Bow Valley. Here George switches to a westerly course. He reaches the planned 10000-meter altitude shortly before Banff.

With a mixture of reverence and melancholy, Alex, who is sitting next to George in the cockpit, can't help admiring the beautiful mountain world in the early morning light. Mt. Assiniboine is to the south, and the Cascades are right below them. Soon they'll be able to see the deep, green waters of the Moraine Lakes, the icy flank of Mt. Temple which he has climbed three times, and after that, all the way through Larch Valley, the glaciers behind Lake Louise, and finally, the waterfalls splashing down to the Lake O'Hara Lodge. They soon reach the Kicking Horse Pass and from there proceed south across the mountains less well known to Alex. An hour later, Mt. Rainier appears ahead of them just as they reach Seattle, the Olympic Peninsula, and finally the open Pacific.

The weather is on their side but the flight across the ocean seems to be endless. Around noon George makes out the Hawaiian Islands and the incomparable 4000 meter high Mauna Kea through his binoculars. He breathes a sigh of relief. The dead reckoning navigation is so imprecise that this fixed point was most important. From here they fly an even more direct southerly route towards the Palmyra Islands, which he describes to Alex:

"You should be able to spot them in about two and a half hours. Just stay on course and we'll reach Samoa in another six or seven hours. I should be back by then, but now I need a nap. Once we're over Samoa it's only ninety more minutes to Vava'u, the northernmost inhabited island group of Tonga."

"Are there any Tongan islands north of that?"

"Yes, there is a volcanic island. But it's not completely uninhabited. The Malau birds thrive there...and only there," grins George.

"What's so funny about those birds?"

"They look like unremarkable, little brown and gray chickens, but they have a special quality: They're the laziest animals in the world. They don't even keep their own eggs warm, but just bury them in the volcanic ash."

"You're kidding!"

"No, there are a lot of strange phenomena here in the Pacific. But I'm too tired now to tell you stories. See you later. If anything unusual happens like the jets starts to sound funny or we encounter thick clouds, make sure to wake me up right away."

By the time they are flying over Samoa, George has taken the pilot's seat again. The sun stands low on the horizon. Even though George sped up, a strong trade wind has cost them some time. When they spot the small smoky island of Kao the sun is already setting. They are flying very low now. Everyone is very nervous.

"Don't be scared. We're practically there. Buckle up. We're going to start our descent. The next big group of islands is Vava'u. We have to find Neiafu Airport. Let's hope that we can land there. And now let's do as we discussed earlier."

They find the airport easily but the surface does not look promising: apparently a large aircraft crashed here, as they feared. It must've caused a huge fire. But the runway seems to be intact, and George manages to land his baby as though he'd been doing it every day. He rolls the airplane near the burnt-out airport building and parks it with the tail against a doorless side of a hangar. This means that they are safe from the back and could take off at a moment's notice. But without additional fuel, they could only make it another 1000 km, either back to Samoa or to Fiji.

Greg, Alex, and the two Greek men jump out of the plane with loaded weapons in hand. Frank and one of his sons roll the ATRV down the ramp. They hope to find Takis still at the Vava'u Beach Resort.

In order to get to the resort, they have to drive through Neiafu village. Their nerves are too strained to appreciate the beautiful avenues of breadfruit trees, the charming sound of the cicadas, and the various pleasant scents of the tropical island. Despite the late hour, many people are still out in the streets enjoying the pleasantly warm evening air. But maybe those people were just attracted by the landing of their plane.

They are struck by quizzical and hostile looks. When a group tries to block their way, Frank's son makes sure to show his rifle. That's enough for the moment. They roll down a gradual slope until they reach a tongue of land. Here a little wooden bridge leads to the resort. They hear the sound of a motor before they spot a couple of low buildings where lights are burning, and from where what they realize is the sound of a generator is coming from. When they reach the buildings, they can see a man leaning on his rifle next to a cone of light produced by one of the lamps. The man looks to be Caucasian; this must be Dieter Eyck!

Frank kills the engine. They leave their rifle in the ATRV and walk towards the man. "You must be Dieter Eyck," shouts Frank. We're relatives of your guest, Takis. We've come to pick him up."

Dieter Eyck is so surprised that he almost drops his rifle before he stutters, "But that's not possible. Was that your plane? You may have arrived just in time to help us fight..."

It takes a while before they have exchanged the most important information. Frank is not surprised to hear about the situation from Dieter. It is in line with the last report from the General: half a dozen Neiafu locals are suffering from pneumonia and varieties of SARS, which first hit the island seventy-five years ago. The victims can only be saved by special antibiotics. Dr. Takis was still able to cure such cases several weeks ago, but without medicine, he can't help them. The locals are accusing him of letting people die in order to save the medicine for himself. Eyck and his team have taken Takis' side and are now expecting an attack.

"I think we can help you, Dieter. Go and get Takis. We have plenty of antibiotics and other pharmaceuticals that he could administer right away. The condition of the affected people should then improve very quickly. But we need help too. We need fuel for the plane in exchange for the antibiotics and the syringes. Would that be all right with you?"

Dieter shakes his head regretfully. "I'm sure you've seen the consequences of the plane crash. All the fuel tanks burned out. We have no fuel left, but we have more diesel than we could possibly ever need for the two small generators on the island."

Frank is relieved. "But...that's great! We have a slow cargo plane. It flies on diesel, not gas."

From now on, everything develops quickly and without problems. Takis is elated to see Frank and his son. He can't believe that he will soon be able to fly to his brother, together

155

with all his other relatives. As soon as the affected locals have received the injections, the atmosphere takes a turn for the better. The "visitors from Canada" give Dieter food that he hasn't seen in a long time. In return, he invites them all to a late dinner cooked by his brother, just like in the good old days. They all sleep long into the next day in the comfortable beds of the Vava'u beach resort.

Only George gets up early to organize filling up the plane. The rest of the day is almost like a holiday. They decide to have a big party the same evening, and Alex supplies an entire Alberta cow's worth of meat, which is cooked together with the local poi dish and with rhizom, the root of the taro plant, and garnished with the plant's leaves, along with coconut milk and fruit. The visitors enjoy an idyllic south Pacific evening. 'Should we maybe stay here?', they all think at least once. But it is clear that the quality of life is suffering here too due to the lack of trade and it will soon get worse. How long will the medicine last? Who will care for a covetous tooth? When will the generators stop working? When will the last of the cloth be turned into a colorful skirt?

Alex offers to take their new friends with them, but as expected, both Dieter Eyck and Takis' girlfriend, who has been withdrawing over the last couple of months, decline the invitation. Even Mary, the computer specialist who was with Takis on the boat during the breakdown, declines. She heard the news from the USA. "I'll stay in Vava'u. You know, Boston... my home was in Boston." She breaks out in tears.

On May 29th a fully tanked airplane leaves with only ten people on board: against all warnings, the three Greeks have decided to stay on Vava'u. The elders of the island have agreed to their decision. They have thirty-seven hours of continuous flying ahead of them: this will be no piece of cake.

While they are flying over a widely extinct Japan, Alex and the general contact one another over their Mindcallers, using code as they agreed. Again the General explains his worries about Takis, who he hasn't heard from for many days.

"You don't need to worry about him. I contacted him not long ago. His problems have vanished, but he is resting now and will contact you within the next twenty-four hours. What are your plans for today and tomorrow?" Alex asks his father.

"Well, they need me here of course, why do you ask?"

"Just because. By the way, is that landing strip on the small military airport north of your property still useable?"

"I don't understand why you would want to know that. You've been asking strange questions for days now. I hope you're not going crazy, son. If you must know, we try to keep the landing strip free at all times. You never know..."

Alex can hardly hold back. 'You're right there, father, you never know.'

After this conversation, the General's Mindcaller speaks to the General telepathically: 'I think you should know that the position of Alex's Mindcaller has changed dramatically over the last couple of days.'

'What do you mean by that?' The General is surprised by the Mindcaller's initiative.

'You know Alex was in Alberta the last couple of years. But he left Canada on May 26th. He traveled to the south Pacific first, spent a couple of days on Vava'u, and is presently flying over Japan. If he stays on course, then his route will take him directly to Greece.'

The General freezes. He asks for additional information, evaluates it, and finally can see only one explanation: somehow, his son must have hijacked an airplane, saved Takis, and is now on the way here. That would explain why he wanted to know about the landing strip. The information from the Mindcaller allows the General to calculate their time of landing to within a one-hour time frame. Now the surprise will be on theirs. Christina's family, his wife, and himself will be by the landing strip to welcome them.

After taking the shortest route across Siberia, they fly over Saloniki from the northeast. Again, Alex's Mindcaller contacts the General to make sure that he is not too far away from the landing strip.

But the General is already there and the Mindcaller which seems to be enjoying this as well, regularly informs the General telepathically. 'Alex is crossing Mt. Olympus at the moment. He'll be here in fifteen minutes at the most.'

The atmosphere in the plane is very cheerful: finally, there seems to be an end to the everlasting flight. Just before they land the plane, George and Alex make out a group of people and a couple of vehicles on the side of the airstrip. This is suspicious, but it is too late now to change plans. All they can do is land. After the airplane has come to a stop, a group of people rush towards them. George opens the door hesitantly and climbs down. The General is surprised to see someone he doesn't know, but before he can find an explanation, Alex rushes down from the cockpit.

The General is pleased to see the baffled expression on his son's face. "So now the advantage of surprise is mine!" roars the General happily.

But he realizes that he is not completely correct when both his daughters climb from the plane as well. Felitsa embraces first her mother, then her sister, Christina, and finally her father. Before the General can speak, he is holding the baby in his arms. "That's Paul II, dad. He came all the way to see you," says Felitsa, breaking into tears.

Almost three years after the breakdown
February 20, 2083

Canada is facing one of the coldest winters in decades. This may also be the reason why the last operating turbine at Churchill Falls begins running hot and finally burns out. Fourteen of the surviving thirty-three inhabitants, including Newmoser, the long-term leader, are killed fighting over the survival chamber. Of the nineteen left, ten make it into the chamber while the others are locked out. Those ten survive for only forty days. Apparently, Newmoser and his associates have already used up more than half the supplies.

158

March 2, 2083

In Vienna and Lower Austria, the hunger has reached its peak. There is more and more pressure at the defense lines at the Semmering and Wechsel passes. Due to the resourceful leadership of Governor Stoeger, Styria is now known generally as "the promised land." Thousands of people from Linz and Prague stream through the Enns Valley and over Eisenerz into Styria. The Styrian troops can barely hold their posts at the Praebichl Pass.

Slovenian troops have joined in. They help Styria protect itself against the hoards coming from Budapest. But when the troops at Radstadt can no longer hold back the Bavarian hoards, the bastion of Styria falls at last. Small groups withdraw to well-equipped hideouts. The villages of Radmer and Johnsbach, which are connected by a saddle, decide to cut themselves off completely from the outside by blocking the canyons with stone avalanches. This was a recipe for success in 1800 when Napoleon marched from Graz to Upper Austria via Eisenerz and Hieflau.

April 10, 2083

A typhoon roars across Tonga. Miraculously, it passes without anyone getting killed. But the Vava'u Beach Resort no longer exists. The storage buildings have been carried away; the hotel and its generator have been destroyed. Due to the missing machines and building materials, no reconstruction is possible. The Tongans stoically start to build new huts from wood, tree bark, and banana leaves. Life will go on, but the storm has erased the last signs of a technological civilization. More than a year ago, they threw away their XPs that had become useless after the fuel cells gave out.

April 30, 2083

Desperate survivors in Calgary have heard about a "treasure in the mountains": a huge store of food and even luxury items reminiscent of the good old days. They try to reach the ranch through the canyon. While the remaining rancheros are doing their best to defend the canyon, Keith, Mandy, their baby, and Mandy's parents withdraw into the ice cave. Keith leaves the pulley system down until one of the rancheros convinces him that there is no one else coming. Here they will be safe for several months, but what then?

From the exit of the cave, Keith observes what's happening down in the valley: wild hoards of people throw themselves on the house and the storage sheds, fighting for food and tools. Many things are destroyed. Suddenly, flames shoot from the house. It's made of solid stone but it is soon reduced to just a burnt-out shell.

When it begins to snow heavily at the end of April, not an uncommon occurrence in the foothills, Keith knows at least one thing: should Mandy look down there tomorrow, she will only see a snow-covered house, but won't know that no one will ever live there again.

June 4, 2083

"It doesn't look good. A great mass of armed men is approaching our castle. You, my son, my daughters, and your men must escape to the cave. George and Johann's family are going too!" orders the General.

George protests, "I'm an old man. I'll stay here and help defend the castle." Alex insists on staying too. The General accepts their requests but remains strict about the others. They walk down the Vikos Gorge and ascend the long trail on the other side. They only get as far as the bivouac hut on the first day, and reach the cave on the second. It would be comfortable here, but for Alex, George, and the General's fear. Two days later, Alex appears at the cave. "You can come back down again. We managed to push back the aggressors. This group will not come again." The castle was hardly touched, but two questions remain: "How often will we have to hide and will there be no return one day?"

Three days later, the General dies from a heart attack. At least he does not have to see his castle fall. However, he also does not have the satisfaction to see that the families of his children survive in 'his' cave safely, and can come back to his castle and eek out a simple but satisfying life in a world almost devoid of a substantial population.

Sunday, October 17, 2083

The MoM's plans are bearing fruit: almost all of what was once known as Texas and Louisiana has by now converted to the COC, and worship the MoM as the great prophet, the enlightened messenger of God. The MoM's empire knows no hunger. Except for the Master of Masters himself, and his fellow Masters, all individuals have the same rights and live a strictly regulated life that is simpler than before the breakdown. There is less freedom maybe, but it is still a paradise compared to the rest of the world; a paradise created by the MoM, the prophet and the savior.

The MoM enjoys great power but also great thankfulness. After all, he is on his way to guiding the entire human race onto the right track. There is even radio and television again, but the latter only on Sunday, the day of the MoM. The COC stretches out its arms further and further into North America. Several islands of believers have come around and are being supported.

At noon Central Standard Time, the virus, which was written into every computerized device by the now dead programmers, activates. They suspected that MoM could not be trusted. The XPs become messengers from the past. It was true: he could not be trusted. The programmers take a late revenge.

But the XPs don't only tell them about their murder; the prophet is proven to be a deceiver. The breakdown is explained as nothing but a manipulation to help MoM to power. The MoM is nothing but an egomaniac who was willing to accept the deaths of billions of people for his own benefit.

Nobody regrets that the MoM does not survive these allegations. But the emerging anger of the people leads to the persecution of all Masters, and preachers, and to the destruction of most of the church's production plants. When the anger subsides, the smarter survivors realize that they have just destroyed the only remaining functional organization on the planet, no matter what shameful fundamentals it was built on. Humanity has gone back into a pre-technological era, and with one additional handicap: in this situation they can no longer rely on the knowledge of their parents and grandparents: They have been thrown back into the Stone Age.

9 What Now?

Great Barrier Island
*December 12, 2020... some sixty years **before** the breakdown*

At this point the supercomputer Atlantis stops its simulation of the years 2080 through 2083.

Atlantis is an heir from the time of the Ancient Ones. It helps humans as much as it can, but due to the Galactic Laws, it may not take a leading role in lesser-developed cultures such as that on Earth. It could otherwise make humans dependent on itself and suffocate the urge and the ability for research.

On Great Barrier Island, a large, barely developed island just off the coast from Auckland, six paraskilled people and the Prime Minister (PM) of New Zealand are sitting in SR Inc.'s holo-room. They are still under the spell of this intense simulation of the future.

The six people are the telekinetic Marcus, the leader of the group, his wife Maria, who is a paraseer, their son Stephan, who can give orders to animals and even sense some of their emotions, Klaus Baumgartner, the parascout who can locate other paraskilled people, and his partner Cynthia, who can erase parts of a person's memory. The sixth is Aroha, who found half of a Mindcaller in the Waitakere Hills near Auckland. Mindcallers were the first discovered traces of a culture that lived on Earth long before humans, but left the planet for unknown reasons. This culture left the Mindcallers and black pellets behind in the event that another culture would arise. These artifacts are supercomputers that possess unusual capabilities.

They all stare at the supercomputer Atlantis, a black pellet that is only the size of a chestnut. Atlantis has just simulated a terrible scenario. It did it so realistically that the audience "almost forgot about their own existence," as Herb, Aroha's boyfriend, put it so eloquently.

Marcus is the first to find words. "Atlantis, will what you just showed us really happen? What about the people we just saw? Will they live and die just like that or are they just invented characters like in a movie?"

"Marcus," answers Atlantis, "the truth lies somewhere in between. But what you've just seen is not simply an arbitrarily conceived scenario. Something like this will occur almost to the letter if nobody interferes dramatically. What you've just experienced was not just invented like that. It will happen in one of the possible futures with all the details that I showed you and all the details I left out. As you know, I am a friend of humanity. I considered it my duty to warn you. I wanted you to see where the current course of humanity will lead if nothing substantial is undertaken to change it."

The PM interferes. "Thank you Atlantis, for this warning. So far we've always taken your warnings[29] to heart. You have always proven correct. We won't take this lightly either. From now on, I'll take all legal measures at my disposal to ensure that we won't make ourselves more dependent on technology in the future."

"That will not do," Atlantis, answers succinctly. "Even you, the PM of New Zealand, don't have enough influence to stem the power of the corporations and the indifference of the majority of the human race."

"So what do you suggest?" Klaus throws in.

"You know that I may not suggest solutions. I have already reached my limits by showing you those simulations and by commenting on some of your ideas. It could very well be that the Ancient Ones will decide to extinguish me, or will have to extinguish me when they find out how much support I have already given you. But please stop pushing me to my limits all the time."

Atlantis does not react to any further questions; even Klaus' apologies cannot change this.

The young Stephan comments without respect, "Atlantis is pissed off at us."

Aroha observes quietly, "Atlantis is extremely concerned because we're not searching for a solution with enough imagination. I think we should all go into ourselves and reflect on what he has just shown us."

---

[29] E.g. the earthquake warning, see "Xperts: The Para-Warriors"

"She's right," says Marcus approvingly, "Let's analyze what we've just seen. Aroha, has your Mindcaller recorded all this?"

"I'm sure it has," Aroha answers.

"All right. Klaus and I will type out a summary of what we think we could learn from this simulation. All of you can add your ideas to that. Can we have the Mindcaller for a couple of hours?"

Aroha does not like to give her artifact away so easily. The Mindcaller is more than just a computer for her. It strengthens her and her partner Herb's senses. It also strengthens those senses that people wouldn't even be aware of otherwise. With the Mindcaller, Aroha experiences the world in a completely different way than she would without it. She hesitates before she hands the Mindcaller over to Marcus, who knows what's going on inside her.

"You'll have it back in two hours," he promises.

The PM has to go back to Wellington. "Marcus keep me abreast of all the developments. I'm very curious about what you'll come up with this time."

Before the group parts, Maria addresses her husband Marcus. "Would you mind if I did some research into which parts of what we've seen are fact and fiction? Do the city and caves east of Nacodoches really exist? And what about this canyon near Bragg Creek and the ice cave there? Maybe we should try to find it now we have the description."

"We can be pretty sure that the Vava'u beach resort exists, but what about those stone avalanches in Styria? Did they really do that to protect themselves from Napoleon? Is the farm really there near Wildon? How about the Dragon Lakes in Greece with the strange cave nearby, and were those accurate descriptions of Labrador? There were just so many details, and I'd really like to know what's reality and what Atlantis has made up. I think I should invest some energy in that."

Marcus agrees. "Yes, I like your idea. I'm very curious about what you'll find."

After the meeting Marcus and Klaus go through the simulation one more time step by step in fast forward and take notes. Before they start to discuss their notes, they return the Mindcaller to Aroha.

"Marcus, you're better with summaries than I am, so why don't you start and tell me what you think we can learn from this simulation," Klaus suggests.

Marcus nods. "Well, first of all, there's something that strikes me that almost seems to be a contradiction. The reason for this catastrophe is that the world is entirely interconnected by a single very powerful communication net. And the world is so based on the division of labor that groups of people who don't have access to any resources because they're so far from anything can barely survive. That's actually a point that anti-globalization advocates have been making for quite a while now.

Of course, these advocates argue mostly against the exploitation of the poorer parts of the world by the rich, leading to greater disparity. So on the onehand, we could see the simulation as a plea against globalization. But on the other hand, we could see that it was mostly a separation of groups that led to the negative effects: people working against, rather than with each other. This Frank keeps warning that an increasing regionalization will lead to disaster. However, it gets even more complicated because we can see how groups that have prepared for such circumstances have a realistic chance of surviving for quite some time, as long as no outside forces interfere. Take this Alex and his ranch, for example, the group around the General, or my home province of Styria; they could've survived much longer if they hadn't been attacked from the outside."

Klaus interrupts, smiling. "So we should note this. No group and no country in this world is stable if other groups or countries nearby are much worse off than they are. So there we have that old argument again that says that an unjust distribution of wealth cannot remain that way for the long term. That's not a moral point, that's a pragmatic point."

Marcus nods. "So I guess we're fully in line with those anti-globalization folks. Globalization supports dependence and enriches the rich at the expense of the poor. That's simply an unstable condition. But what we are experiencing now seems to go even further: a high level of regionalization is not the solution.

166

I think we could generally say that globalization is a good thing as long as it's not taken to the extreme, and the same is true for regionalization. So this world would be better off if there was regionalization wherever it's possible, and globalization wherever it's necessary."

"That's too abstract for me. Just give me an example."

"I think the two of us could come up with a lot of those. Let's start with a subject that we've seen several times: supply of electricity. Did you notice that that was one of the main problems? That little village in Labrador was able to survive for years, even though it's situated in one of the most unfriendly climates on the planet, just because they were privy to unlimited electricity. Even though their leader was begging God to keep the turbine running, he didn't take any precautions. Why didn't he just maintain the other turbines the whole time? Churchill Falls wouldn't have experienced such a sad ending if he had."

"Just take completely contrasting situations like that on the ranch in Alberta and the resort in Vava'u: both locations have local electricity supplies. Only when that typhoon destroyed the generators in Vava'u did their lives revert to what it was like before Europeans arrived there in the seventeenth century. I think the importance of electricity stands out very clearly here: if all ATRVs had electric motors instead of fuel motors, and if those XPs were rechargeable, instead of having those fuel cells, then they could run forever."

Klaus is getting very thoughtful now. "You know, we're just about to equip our e-helpers[30] with disposable fuel cells instead of rechargeable batteries... so I guess Atlantis was dropping a hint here. We have to change our plans."

"Whoa! So Atlantis does show us the way sometimes. So that's why he's so worried about those Galactic Laws. But back to the idea of electrical supply; I think it would make sense to

---

[30] E-helpers are so-called do-it-all devices. They are produced by SR, Inc. and are forerunners of the XPs described in the simulation. Together with communication glasses (see " Xperts : The Paradoppelganger"), they play an important role in the XPERTS books. SR Inc. belongs to Marcus and Maria. It allows them to conceal their abilities, as well as sponsor their para-research and other activities.

compromise here between far-reaching electricity networks and local supplies. Why doesn't every house have solar cells or heat pumps? That would guarantee at least some kind of basic supply that would normally be supported by the network. And similarly, regional power plants could be supported by larger ones that are further away."

"I'm not sure what advantage such a step-by-step supply would have. Why shouldn't we just do everything locally in the first place?" Klaus throws in.

"Because that's just not realistic. In a normal situation the local supply would only be enough to support the lights, simple household devices, local computers, XPs, stoves, and warm water. But it wouldn't be sufficient to get ovens going, heat an entire house, keep a whirlpool hot, etc. That would require more electricity than could be produced locally. So a breakdown would have consequences, but not really serious ones: People would just have to grill strips of turkey on the stove instead of baking the whole bird in the oven."

"You would have to do without your whirlpool, and you wouldn't heat the entire house, just one room. If the local power plant were still running, you could have even more luxury than that. But in order to have all the comfort you're used to, the entire network would have to be running. I just told my e-helper to carry out some calculations. They show that an average of 20-30% of electricity consumption can be produced locally, which would suffice for a moderately comfortable life. There are large differences from place to place, but it shows that regional power plants are very reliable because they don't need any complicated transformers or distribution systems. So theoretically, they could actually supply an additional 30-40% of the total normal electrical output. So in order to have the "full luxury," you would only need to import 30-50% of what is transported now. Fare thee well, new high voltage lines!"

"Speaking of heating houses, don't forget, Marcus, that in the beginning we could see a city where most of the people were living in houses underground: aesthetically beautiful, warm in the winter, and cool in the summer. Perfect! It would be a great step if it were possible to replace normal windows with virtual windows. That would save a lot of energy and provide more security. And then, if you could have your own underground biotope, not quite as big of course as the one we saw at the COC's headquarters, then that would be really something. Wouldn't it be great to enter your own little underground garden directly from your underground house? I'm afraid Atlantis has given us more ideas than he should've, but it looks like those underground houses can only be realized in the distant future. All right. Let's forget about electricity for now. That's only one aspect of this situation. What about the others?"

"Well, let's talk about transportation then. One thing seems to be clear. There should always be navigational systems that run without satellite or remote control. Today's Mollers have an override mode. We can use them to fly forbidden routes. But of course this can lead to accidents and complaints. There have been many attempts to forbid this mode by law. But as we have just seen, that would be a dangerous law. So we'll have to stand up against it. But there is an alternative to that. It would be possible to program the override mode in a way that it switches into it automatically only when satellite or remote navigation systems collapse. Or even..." Marcus is getting excited. "Why hasn't anyone thought about this yet? We don't even need satellites and radio systems to figure out your exact position. We can use our e-helpers for that!"

"What're you talking about, Marcus?"

"OK. This is how I see it: The camera built into the e-helper can see wavelengths that are invisible to the human eye. So it is able to scan the sky in daytime at night and in any weather. So that way it can always give, for example, the exact position of *Ursa Major* in the northern hemisphere or the Southern Cross in the southern at any time. If you know your exact time and horizon line, which you do when you have an e-helper, you can calculate your latitude and longitude. Let me just ask my e-helper now... just a second... there we go: we have at this time an accuracy of one tenth of a second that equals about three meters on the ground."

Klaus is astonished. "What a great idea. I'm sure we could improve the accuracy by a factor of five to ten. I'll tell my programmers to get to work on it right away. We should also check out if we can get this idea patented. The whole thing seems logical to me: after all, man has always navigated using the stars. Every space probe uses them too. The only place we don't use them is down here on dry land. I can hardly believe it. Satellites are just too expensive and too prone to error as navigational devices. They'll be a thing of the past very soon if your method works!"

Klaus continues, "This should solve every navigation problem for ships, airplanes, and Mollers. When it comes to earth-bound vehicles, navigation is less of a problem than fuel. But as you've said before, if all ATRVs were run on electricity[31], we'd have less noise, and less pollution. And if your ideas in respect to electricity supply can be carried out, they'd be catastrophe-proof."

Marcus laughs. "We're about to revolutionize the world, at least in our minds. But let's go on. How shall we keep up the communication between humans if there is a breakdown?"

Klaus thinks for a little while before he answers. "I think that Atlantis has already shown us some kind of solution. Due to their regenerating software, those XPs, which just seem to be further developed e-helpers, could prove to be very stable against computer viruses. But their communication components are not. We'll have to put some thought into that. I believe that the old John Von Neumann Principle is just not suitable anymore. It may have seemed a stroke of genius up to the end of the 20th Century because it treated data and programs similarly. But now, important parts of programs and data, especially those that deal with communications, have to be "write once": they have to be indestructible, which isn't really a problem, technically. This way, they are safe from Viruses, worms, Trojans, etc."

"All- right. That will protect us from errors within net connections, but what can you do against people like the MoM? He just smuggled his own people into companies so their basic software could be bugged and start dangerous actions at a specific point in time," counters Marcus.

---

[31] See the articles about the Mauto in "Xperts: The Beginning".

"You've got a point there. But isn't it really strange that there are worldwide agencies who control food, vehicles, and practically every device you can think of, but there are no such agencies that control computer programs. Obviously, we need a powerful organization to check every program according to its stability and safety. Can you explain to me why we don't have that already?"

"You'll never believe this," says Marcus, "but I did some research about computer history: there once was such an agency certifying "teleprograms" as they used to be called. All the programs that could be loaded onto your MUPID net-computer over the network (which was called BTX back then) were checked in Austria between 1983 and 1990. Unfortunately, this never caught on with the big corporations, and the idea never took off. But there is another problem: it's really difficult to test programs, and the bigger they get, the more difficult it is. But when they are only available in a computer-near code, it gets even more difficult. So, they should either only certify open-source programs, or at least demand that the source, the easily understandable version of a program, has to be submitted for approval. As a matter of fact, if you safeguard a device like the XP in such a way, then the communication network just can't break down any more, particularly if you used XPs as relay stations in the event there are no permanent relay stations nearby or if they collapse. That's how the MoM did it, remember?"

"This sounds as though it's very simple; I do get the basics, but I'm still not sure if I understand it all perfectly. I'm sure that we can work something like this out eventually. Anyway, it looks like we've already discussed some of the most important problems of the higher technical levels. But how about normal everyday technical devices? Remember when they ran out of light bulbs in Churchill Falls, and when the washing machines couldn't be repaired anymore? Even toilet paper became a problem for those people."

Marcus nods. "I don't think we can find solutions to all the problems a general system breakdown would cause right away. But don't forget, if they had only carried out what we've already discussed today, then they would've been much better off to

171

begin with. They would've been able to keep the communication going; electricity and water would've been available; the Mollers would've worked, just like their ATRVs, and have been completely independent from liquid fuels. That way, they could've kept up the transportation of food, replacement parts, and raw materials. That's because their production plants would've been functioning, which was not the case in the simulation due to the breakdown of the power plants and the computers. Except for what was produced in the factories and the headquarters of the COC, there were no supplies at all. In addition to all this, there seem to be two more important aspects that could guarantee a certain regional independence that both today's society and that of 2080 lack:

First, all our devices are becoming increasingly monolithic. If only one little part breaks inside a washing machine or a holo-projector, you often have to replace the entire device. It's true what they've been saying since 2005. Remember the jingle:

Repairing parts? Just let that be!
However small, however wee!
Just throw all of the junk away
Do as I tell you, sure, I say
Just go and buy a new device
It works much better, it works nice!

It would make much more sense to start building modularly again. The other day all I needed was a short, thin piece of copper wire. I just couldn't get that. So I bought myself a small electronic toy car, took it apart, took the copper wire off the motor block and threw the rest of the car away. When I was a child, we still had Maerklin construction kits; we had Matador and Lego systems. With just those you could build almost anything. We would need systems like that for real applications, not just as toys. But it will be very difficult to convince the throwaway economy to jump on the bandwagon. The PM told us once how she thinks we could apply measures leading in that direction. But I can only vaguely remember two of them: raise the tax on raw goods, which would also help some of the poorer countries, and would at the same time make reusability and exchange of components more attractive. And second, introduce a "monolith tax": All devices must consist of replaceable parts. The tax is based on the cost of the most expensive component: the higher the price of that part, the higher the tax. This should make it more attractive to produce devices consisting of many replaceable parts. On the other hand, those little parts will become very simple and will be used for a lot of different devices. They can be produced regionally, which will make mass production cheaper. Then it'll also make sense to hold on to such parts for future repairs.

"She also said that it would make sense to grow a large variety of foods locally. That ranch in Alberta, and the indoor growing area in Churchill Falls are good examples of that. When I still lived in Austria, it really made me angry when I had to buy milk and butter from Holland instead of buying the products of Austrian farmers."

Klaus smiles. "You should've become a public speaker or a politician, Marcus. You just gave me an entire speech there. But how would you try to change the whole food industry? It's a fact that Holland can produce milk more cheaply than Austria. They have a longer growing season over there and the fields are simply flatter. No Austrian mountain farmer could ever possibly compete with that."

Marcus angrily interrupts him, "But that's exactly what's wrong. We have to change that."

"You're just full of hot air. What're you going to do?"

"I'm going on a mission for the PM to Brussels next year. I'm going to present one of her ideas that I strongly believe in: The distance tax."

"And what would that be?"

"It's simple. The farther a product has to be transported, the more tax is added to it. This would make milk from Holland more expensive, giving the Austrian farmers a chance to compete again, even without those EU subsidies, which are getting smaller and smaller anyway. Or take bananas, for example. They come from even further away. They wouldn't cost half the price of domestic apples, as they do now, but three times as much! It

173

should be like that for all products: in Austria you can buy strawberries throughout the year. But only in the summer can you buy the domestic kind. For the rest of the year they're imported from South Africa or elsewhere: even if they're not more expensive, they're certainly less tasty because they ripen during transport."

"And there's another thing: The taxes levied don't have to just support the consuming country; they could be split between the supplier and consumer countries proportional to the per capita GNP. So between Austria and Holland, having comparable GNPs, it would mean that the distance tax for Dutch butter would be split almost equally. But that wouldn't be a lot because Austrians wouldn't buy so much Dutch butter anymore. For bananas coming from the Congo, for example, the tax would be split at a ratio of 1:40 in favor of Congo, reflecting the per capita GNP. Congo will export fewer bananas but will have a much higher profit margin in line with an attempt at re-distribution of wealth. That's only a rough sketch but you have to admit that such measures would lead to greater regional independence, to healthier seasonal eating habits, and to a decrease in traffic. Furniture from Sweden would then be much more expensive than the furniture that a carpenter from New Zealand would make from local wood. Not bad, eh?"

Klaus nods thoughtfully.

"So what are your ideas, Klaus? What do you think we should learn from the simulation?"

"Well, in addition to what you've just said, there seems to be another very important point: First of all, I think that every family is well-advised to stock goods for emergency situations for, let's say, a period of two weeks. Checklists would make sense here. There have been several attempts to do that, but when the danger of war lessens in a certain region, then those recommendations just stop being taken seriously. People forget that, in addition to war, there are many other possible scenarios that cannot be predicted. Just think about the terrible situation after the nuclear bomb hit Washington: Hundreds of thousands were killed immediately without even knowing what happened. But there were also hundreds of thousands who were severely injured,

174

either physically or by radiation. Poor people. But how about those who weren't immediately harmed because they were further away and could no longer leave their apartments because of the radioactive ash? And what if a highly infectious, dangerous disease breaks out? There would only be one way to stop it: quarantine everyone in their homes for several weeks. What about the families who have not taken the precautions for that?"

Medical precautions are important too: Felitsa did not have any professional help in delivering her baby. Wouldn't it be sensible to make basic medical training a required subject in all schools instead of only teaching first aid? And speaking of that, shouldn't this simulation entice us to keep reading and writing a compulsory subject even though people keep bringing up arguments[32] against it? We could also see the problems they were having with medicine. The pharmaceutical industry should start producing medications with longer expiration periods. After all, it doesn't take a lot of space to stock a good supply of medicine. Of course, we're facing some interesting problems here, too: Many important medications require a prescription. How would people be able to stock any of those? Maybe we should introduce sealed boxes that have to be exchanged once a year and can only be opened in a crisis situation. I know all this is just speculation at the moment, but we should not forget this aspect."

"What we've seen should also not let us forget the danger of total surveillance by drones. Actually, in this area we seem to be the driving force[33] in this development. I really liked the idea about the Moller-free zones. The industry is growing and the problem is becoming increasingly urgent. The Moller Company still has almost a monopoly on their flying cars. Maybe that should be changed. Your distance tax could really help New Zealand to produce its own Mollers. There are some other minor points I thought of, but there's another important thing: what we've just seen, was that just a simulation, or was it some kind of a lecture program? When you think about what we've just come

---

[32] See "The End of Writing" in "Xperts: The Beginning".
[33] In "Xperts: The Paradoppelganger", SR Inc. uses e-hummingbirds. In "Xperts: The Parawarriros", it is already using surveillance drones.

up with, it's probably the latter. Man, we've already learned a lot. Do you think we should ask Atlantis about that?"

Marcus waves him off. "I think I know what Atlantis would say: A good simulation can very well transfer knowledge or entice a process of gaining knowledge. But didn't you want to mention something else?"

Klaus looks at Marcus seriously. "We have just discussed how the world *should* change, but we haven't discussed yet how we might bring such a change about."

10 The Plan

Great Barrier Island, New Zealand
December 13, 2020

Klaus and Marcus meet with the rest of the group the next day. The PM has to stay in Wellington: However, Aroha's friend Herb, whose parability allows him to slow processes down, is present. Klaus and Marcus give a short summary of their discussion yesterday. Before they address the main question of how they should proceed from here on, they ask the group to offer criticism on their findings.

After some members of the group have elaborated on certain issues, Aroha, who has remained silent so far, takes the floor. "When it comes to learning from the simulation, then we should all agree that only a just world can be a stable world. The way things run now, 80% of all resources are consumed by 20% of the world's population. Not only is this immoral, but it also leads to an unstable situation. During the simulation we saw how a religious egomaniac brought the human race to the brink of extinction. In reality this may as well be caused by a group of Africans or Asians who have been suppressed and exploited for so long that they decide to crush the rich man's world.

"We've already experienced bomb and terror attacks, but as of yet we have not had to deal with the most efficient method: the infection of all computers. The Third World could probably survive such a scenario, but the rich and network-dependent countries couldn't. So it should be one of our main goals to get rid of this inequality. It has been proven by scientists[34] that a simple redistribution of money is politically impossible. They've suggested continuing growth on an ecologically justifiable level, together with uneven growth that could lead to a fair equality of life standards within a maximum of 100 years. In fact, the steps of expansion the EU carried out were leading in that direction:

---

[34] Radermacher, F. J.: Balance or Destruction, Oekosoziales Forum Wien (2003)

poorer countries were integrated and helped to reach strong economic growth instead of simply supporting them financially. What happened was that formerly poorer countries like Ireland, Portugal, East Germany, and Slovenia were able to rapidly reduce the disparity between themselves and the richer countries. Even though such strategies continue to this day, they seem to be proceeding much too slowly because other rich countries, like the USA, did not follow Europe's example; Central America is still as poor as ever."

"So further measures will be necessary. We can only speculate on solutions here, just like Klaus and Marcus have done. Don't get me wrong, I think your ideas are really good, but how can we realize them? What I'm going to say will also be speculation: There are several measures that can only be carried out if the leading industrial nations and the leading corporations agree on them. Without them no radical changes could help the poor countries."

"First of all, goods from countries that do not agree to basic regulations should be heavily taxed. In addition, we'd need regulations banning child labor, enforcing a minimum wage, guaranteeing a fair amount of health and retirement insurance, democratic workplaces, and a maximum forty-five hour work week and adequate vacation time."

"This list is not complete of course. Those are just some of the basics. Countries that are not in line with those regulations will face heavy export taxes. That way, their goods will be so expensive that very few people will buy them. Hence those countries will be forced to implement adequate laws to allow their citizens a better standard of living. The goods will be more expensive, but will remain competitive. As long as Marcus' distance tax doesn't harm them too much! What difference would it make if a new computer or e-helper were a little more expensive because SR Inc. has to pay more to buy the chips? People will buy new models less often, which would be helpful with respect to the battle against the throw-away economy."

"Of course, such measures will have to be well-considered and well-defined. Maybe we should work out a detailed concept and present it to Atlantis. It is the only way we could get accurate calculations and see if they make sense or not."

"In addition, there are certain economic measures that should've been carried out long ago, but I'll only touch on these: Long before there was a Euro, European currencies were only allowed to vary within a certain range. It would be a blessing for the entire world if that were the case for all currencies. How can it be that businesses that have just started up and trained thousands of employees are forced to close because production has become more feasible in other countries due to currency devaluation? It's also not fair to introduce unlimited traffic for passengers and goods between countries that have completely different levels of income."

"I know subjects like this would be better presented by economists; I just wanted to make sure we take them into consideration."

Aroha, who is usually a very reserved person, continues vividly, "But all we've heard so far sounds like philosophy rather than action to me. Here we are, a group that believes it can make the world a better place, and all we do is talk, talk, talk. I think we should define serious concepts now and present them to Atlantis. We shouldn't try to make Atlantis our leader; we know that's not possible. He can only advise us on the feasibility of our concepts so that we know if we're on the right track. Do you know what I'm talking about? Atlantis isn't our leader, but he's the best oracle there ever was. He never fails, he gives us very well-calculated probabilities."

Aroha feels that the rest of the group is in line with her. Finally Marcus speaks for the group, "So Aroha, how do you think we should proceed to reach our goal, whatever that may be?"

Aroha hesitates. "In order to execute globally far-reaching changes, be it regionalization, distance tax, new navigational methods, or basic legal regulations for all countries, we'll have to wake up the entire human race. In order to do that, there seems to be only one way: We'll have to cause a breakdown of electricity and computer networks for a longer period of time; for at least two weeks."

179

Suddenly, the room is engulfed in a breathless silence. This suggestion is insane. It cannot be carried out. That would cost so many human lives, and if they found out who was behind it... Could something like normalcy ever be reinstated after such a breakdown? Didn't the simulation show that immense problems would occur as early as a couple of days after a global failure of communication and power? But on the other hand, is there another way to convince the human race that they have to change their way of thinking?

As usual, it is Marcus who is able to find words in such a situation. The rest of the group knows why: He sped up his individual time, which is one of his parabilities. This allowed him to consider Aroha's suggestion in greater detail.

"Thanks for this unusual and courageous suggestion, Aroha. What speaks for it the most is that we don't seem to have an alternative. As you've suggested, we'll have to consult Atlantis before we could begin such an operation. I think we should discuss every point that we can come up with, both pros and cons, to this operation. Anyone wants to start?"

Klaus clears his throat. "Well the first thing I can think of is that none of what we're saying here should ever go beyond this group. Maybe we can let the PM in on it, but that's about it. If we really let something like this get out, and they find out that we triggered it off, then we'd be victims of punishment that goes beyond any laws. Are you all aware of that? If anyone is against such an operation, then he'll have to get out now and Cynthia can erase their memory."

Marcus looks at Maria and she nods understandingly before speaking. "Stephan, you're still a minor. You're going on a trip tomorrow with your friend Raianda. I really think that you're still too young to be drawn into one of the most unusual projects of humanity. I ask you not to partake. It would be much better if you went on the trip with Raianda first, and moved to Delhi with her family for six months as you have planned. We'll make sure that you'll be safe there if there is a breakdown. India will not be affected as much as other regions because their computer networks aren't so sophisticated yet. Do you agree that it would be best to leave this conversation after Cynthia has erased your memory?"

Stephan hesitates but seems relieved a bit.

"Stephan," Marcus says, "I think we'll need you, but you can help us the most if you don't know about the plan. If necessary, we'll contact you, but if not, it would be best if you didn't get involved. We'll also send your sister to stay with your grandparents in Austria. If anyone suspects us of being involved in the breakdown, then at least the two of you'll be safe. Is that all right with you?"

Stephan nods. "I hope it all works out. I'm proud to be one of the group and I hope I'll always be. Maybe it's better to leave me out of this. But Cynthia, please don't erase any more of my memory than you have to."

Cynthia looks at him. It only takes a couple of seconds to erase parts of his memory. As usual, it is a very spooky procedure. All of a sudden, Stephan behaves completely different. A couple of seconds ago he was serious and reserved, but now he is cheerful and light-hearted.

"So I guess you don't need me here any more. I really think I should start packing for my trip tomorrow." He looks at the clock. "Geez, Raianda will be here in two hours! Bye!" he exclaims, and rushes out of the room.

"Anyone else?" asks Marcus. Herb speaks for the rest of them. "You won't get rid of us that easily. Let's do it. Aroha, why didn't you tell me about all this last night?"

"You were thinking about other things, remember? Not things that I minded either, tiger!" she says, laughing.

Klaus begins. "Please allow me to organize the discussion. I believe there are four main themes. If we are to carry something like this out, how can we do it without having any casualties? If we can't answer this first question, then we should stop there right away. But if we can, we should then try to protect ourselves: How can we technologically cause such a breakdown without arousing suspicion? Next question, how can we reach some sort of normalcy after the breakdown? And finally, if we succeed with all this, then how will we meet all of our goals, and what are these goals exactly?

"So let's start at the beginning. As we've seen in the simulation, 2800 airplanes crashed and thousands of boats were put into distress within ten minutes of the breakdown. We can't have that. But how can we avoid this?"

They all look at Aroha. "I think that this will actually be the most difficult question to answer. This will have to be prepared over the long term but I think there is a way."

"As you know, we are the only ones who have mini-drones, and I hope that nobody even has a clue that such things exist. We have often used these drones to help the PM to warn of terror attacks and capture terrorist groups. Since September, Atlantis has warned us of seven large earthquakes: one right here, others in the USA, Europe, China, and Japan. The accuracy of the predictions the PM made have always surprised the seismologists, but they have also saved thousands of lives. The same is true for the tornado warnings in the southeast of the USA, the typhoon warnings in Hawaii, and the tsunami off the California coast."

"Only weeks ago, the PM was able to point out a dangerous mistake in the mechanism of the newest Moller model. The company heeded the warning but they were shocked at how easily this mistake could have led to casualties. Another tip that she got from the drones enabled her to warn the Russian president of a dangerous uprising, etc. In short, by now the PM has a reputation of having the best scientists and the best secret service in the world. If she continues being so successful which is easily possible with Atlantis' help, then the world will take her warnings even more seriously. So if she warns the world of several attacks on airplanes ships and governmental organizations to be carried out on a specific day, every government will take all necessary precautions to keep the traffic down and the people at home. That should ensure a complete breakdown of computer networks, electricity supplies, and power plants, without causing immediate human casualties."

"I've tried to consider all preparations that we'll have to make, and it seems to me that we wouldn't be able to trigger the breakdown before mid-October 2021. Maybe the PM should also warn of a possible breakdown of the electricity supply network. There seem to be too many weapon depots on this planet in the first place. So maybe, after the PM has given out her warnings, some of those should "mysteriously" blow up, like we did in India and Pakistan. I know that this is very delicate because four of our friends lost their lives during that operation, but that was not our fault. That was due to the evil parabilitists who Justo managed to gather against us[35]. Something like this couldn't happen again, mainly because of the shielding devices Klaus has developed. Those weapon depots would definitely not be a great loss for humanity, and those "attacks" would only increase the believability of the PM's warnings."

"Of course, there will be certain accidents: People getting stuck in elevators, boats getting into distress, etc. But our worldwide network of drones would allow us to quickly intervene in such cases. We would also have to make sure that all hospitals are equipped with emergency generators. But all in all, a vast warning operation would protect everyone who will listen from immediate danger. I'm not deluding myself: Whatever precautions we take, there will be some casualties. But I'm sure Atlantis will be able to give us an estimate on that. But when it comes to making this world safer for everybody, we'll have to learn to live with such casualties, won't we?"

Cynthia is surprised at Aroha's cold-bloodedness. "You're talking about the deaths of innocent people as though they were leaves falling from the tree of humanity!"

Marcus turns soothingly to Cynthia. "I'm sure that Aroha has the same amount of sympathy for people as the rest of us. But Cynthia, what percent of the world's population do you reckon will really stay home for one day after such serious warnings?"

"I'm not really sure yet, but I'd guess at least 90%. Why is that so important?"

Marcus looks serious. "Because that would mean that there would also be 90% fewer traffic accidents. We have an average of 4000 worldwide traffic deaths per day. So on that day, some 3600 people who would otherwise die would not die. So to calculate this with cold, hard numbers, if less than 3600 people die on the first day because of the breakdown, then at the end of

---

[35] See " Xperts: The Para Warriors".

183

the day we'll have more people living because of the breakdown then otherwise." Marcus lifts his hand to calm the irritated murmurs. "I know that human lives and deaths shouldn't be calculated against each other like that, but let's not forget that there is an even bigger danger if we don't do anything at all. However skillful our operation is carried out, it will have certain lethal consequences here and there. By what I've just said means that we just can't allow ourselves to be overwhelmed by that."

Klaus tries to guide the discussion back into more quiet waters. "Aroha just mentioned that the breakdown should go on for at least two weeks. I agree with that. It wouldn't have any effect otherwise. But how long should it really last? Aren't we sure to see uprisings after five days, as we saw in the simulation?"

Again Aroha interjects, "No this is 2020, not 2080. The Mollers will still function and so will the e-helpers, so there will be communication within a certain range. Every Moller has an in-built radio and many people still have television and holo-vision independent from their e-helpers. It will be possible to inform and calm down the populations over radio stations that have generators. The military still runs a lot of those, whereas in 2080, you would only be able to find them in museums."

"It won't be possible to buy anything with an e-helper, but most people still have cash. The less developed the country, the more cash is circulating. In restaurants, shops, and gas stations, the proprietors will let customers run a tab as long as they know them. And don't forget, people will have been warned, so a lot of them will have stocked food and water, and maybe even gas for a camping stove or something. If the people can be sure that everything will be back to normal in about two weeks or so, which we would have to organize, of course, then they will get through this phase unharmed. But afterwards, we'll let them know that another breakdown could last several months, so I hope they'll realize that basic changes have to be made."

"It'll be a very difficult task to convince the PM of those necessary changes. She'll have to pass these ideas on to other governments, asking for the promise that they act quickly. I believe the PM should indicate that for now the worst could've

184

been avoided, but that there could be another attack within a year."

Everybody notices that Aroha has thought all this through very carefully. Marcus continues, "I believe we can close point one with the following: it should be possible to organize a breakdown without endangering too many people. We still have to consider how many people will be endangered and how we can save their lives. I believe that we can also close point four for now: it's very likely that such a breakdown would rattle governments and their citizens sufficiently to push through important changes just about anywhere. Points two and three remain: How can we cause such a breakdown without being discovered as the responsible party, and how can we guarantee a return to normalcy afterwards? Does anyone want to say something about this?"

They all remain silent, so Marcus notes, "I think it would be enough if we concentrate on taking care of a total breakdown in the USA, Canada, Japan, and Europe. Do you agree?"

After some consideration, they all nod.

"That should make it much easier for us," Marcus whispers to Klaus. Finally Marcus says, "Klaus and I believe that we could make all this possible, but we'll have a lot of thinking to do. And of course we'll have to talk this over with Harry, our super-hacker."

When Marcus realizes that not all of them know whom he is talking about, he explains, "I'm talking about the Harry who has already helped us to carry out the earthquake warning for Tauranga [36]. All this will be very complex and I'm afraid we'll have to make use of our parabilities a lot, especially yours, Cynthia. Each of us should reconsider points one and four to find the best way to present all this to the PM. Klaus and I will work on Points two and three, and we'll keep you informed, of course."

---

[36] See "Xperts:The Para Warriors".

Helen Milton of the *Washington Post* goes through the same
information again: How is it possible that a small group of
seismologists led by an unknown fellow named Simms all of a
sudden came up with better predictions than all his renowned
colleagues? Over the last couple of months, Simms has predicted
all of the grade seven earthquakes and the dangerous tsunamis.
More than twenty-four hours before each catastrophe, he gave out
information of great accuracy. And why is New Zealand's secret
service all of a sudden more efficient than the much larger ones
around the world?

'Something stinks,' she assures herself. And Helen's nose has
not failed her often. Something is going on in New Zealand.
Something unusual. She will get on the trail of that. She has
been waiting a long time for a great story.

The flight from Washington to Auckland is tiring and
extremely boring. Her first impression of Auckland is not very
exceptional: Just another modern city with a lot of average
houses. But she soon finds out that the sea makes this place more
interesting: Beautiful bays and beaches are almost everywhere
around it, with exceptional views of delightful islands. The
young woman from the car rental has deluged her with tips and
even insisted on writing some information down for her. Helen
appreciates her efforts and finds all the pubs and restaurants
above average. She wonders if that is just because she followed
the woman's advice.

Anawhata Bay is really worth visiting. It is just outside a
metropolis, but completely deserted, and with beautiful red
blooming trees that have an enormously long name[37] that she'll
never be able to remember. The little restaurant in Ponsonby was
just as good as the Red Fox Pub on the way to the volcanic Mt.

---

[37] Pohutukawa trees, which are in bloom when Helen arrives.

Eden, which she was forced to climb by an outgoing group of locals. The view over the harbor and the city was very impressive, even at night, and she didn't really mind being repeatedly embraced by her new friends. One thing seemed to be clear: The people here are much more open and friendly than she ever experienced in Washington.

Helen ends up falling into her bed exhausted. And that is only the first day. She sleeps too long and misses breakfast. Before she starts work, she takes a walk from the Hyatt hotel where she is staying down into the city to discover many nice shops, passageways, and uncountable friendly faces of every color. She soon starts to revise her first impression of this city. Then she takes Queen's Street back to Auckland's university, which is situated surprisingly near the city center, directly adjacent to the small, but nice Albert Park. Like daubs of paint, many students hang out on the beautiful lawns, shaded by canopies of leaves.

The university itself consists of English colonial buildings as well as ugly modern ones. Nobody seems to know where the seismological institute is, and nobody seems to have ever heard the name Simms. How can a man who has been able to save thousands of lives be completely unknown here?

When she finally finds his office, she is disappointed. She is shown an outdated laboratory. She cannot believe that this is the place where all the amazing research has been carried out. When she is introduced to Simms, she confronts him right away with his latest success story. Simms reacts with pride, but carefully. When Helen wants to know more details about the sources for his predictions, Simms reacts secretively. "I cannot give away my methods or my sources... my sources," he gurgles. Then he looks at his watch. "I haven't eaten anything today, young lady, and you've already kept me from doing so. Have a nice day."

But Helen is not so easily put off, especially not by this aging British immigrant. "Well, I haven't eaten anything either and I'd really like to invite you to dinner. What you've just told me is very interesting. All of my readers admire how you can make these accurate predictions with such modest means. I'm not so interested in the technical details; I'd like to know more about you as a person: Where you grew up, how you became the famous scientist you are, etc."

While Simms hesitates, Helen notices the redness and roundness of the professor's face. With sudden intuition, she adds, "I'd really love to share a bottle of California wine with you." This finally does the trick.

Simms is full of praise for the wine. They are already into the second bottle, and Simms has not noticed that Helen hasn't even finished her first glass yet. However, the professor seems to loosen up. By now they are calling each other by their first names, Helen and Arthur, and it soon becomes clear that Arthur's success is based on his cooperation with a company called SR, Inc. He is now also the leading scientist at their seismological department. Helen knows that SR, Inc. produces e-helpers, but she didn't know that they also deal with seismology.

"That's one fine organization. They also carry out a lot of rescue and salvage operations. That's where the name[38] comes from, actually. They are also working on certain issues that nobody knows about. All I know about them is that I'm not supposed to know about them." He giggles at the play on words. "And their boss has very good connections to the government, especially the PM. There are rumors that they are very good friends, if you know what I mean."

Helen understands and she's now sure that those contacts and those rescue operations are very "investigatable." But Helen does not understand why such a successful company would want to employ such a mediocre researcher, as he seems to be.

It was Simms' original plan to go back to work after the dinner with Helen, but it's now very late at Tony's, his regular bar, which is across the park from the university and just a few steps down from the arts museum. They have had two bottles of

---

[38] SR, Inc. stands for Salvage and Rescue Incorporated. The company is used as a front for the activities of the para group. By using their secret parabilities, the group has gained a reputation as a highly technical rescue organization. SR Inc. has also started an electronics and science department that created the e-helper and turned it into a worldwide success.

wine and the waiter, who is very familiar with Simms' habits, calls a taxi for him.

Helen goes back to the Hyatt, which she chose specifically for its proximity to the university. After this conversation, she feels that she might need some cheering up. Except for the minimal information about SR Inc., she now knows just about as much as she did two bottles of expensive wine ago. Her feeling that there is more to these earthquake predictions than the public knows has strengthened. There must be a group behind Simms that works with some kind of revolutionary method. And why are they hiding? There must be an interesting reason for that.

Helen doesn't consider herself "beautiful," and she spent the whole day in jeans, a simple shirt, casual hair, and ugly glasses in order to appear neutral. But she knows how to make herself look much more interesting and this is what she does before she goes down to the bar.

When she steps out of her hot shower, she inspects herself in the mirror from all sides. The image she sees gives her a good dose of self-confidence just when she needs it. Her long legs lead to a well-trimmed triangle and up to a flat belly, and her breasts seem to her to be exactly right; pert, but not what you'd call small. They don't need any extra support. Her shoulders are flawless. She has had two birthmarks removed but otherwise she is completely *au naturel.* As usual, she critically inspects her nose, which seems a little big to her, but a little make-up can disguise this. When a man faces her and looks into her gray-green eyes, she just has to put on her special smile to win him over. Sometimes she thinks of herself as a Barbara Streisand type...

She decides to put on her shoulder-less, gray-green outfit that complements her eyes and her mascara so well. The scent of Chanel nineteen also has something "green" about it. Her well-tanned legs don't need stockings, and high-heel shoes seem to be the perfect complement to the ensemble and to the New Zealand Summer. Before she leaves the room, she throws a wrap over her shoulders. This gives her an air of discretion, and these hotels are so often overcooled!

189

When she enters the bar, it is almost empty. Only two Japanese women, probably tourists, are there. Now she regrets having chosen the Hyatt: She remembers that the Hyatt is known for tourist groups that tend to take their schedules seriously and retire early. She sits listlessly sipping her martini. 'That Simms,' she thinks. 'What a nobody, or did he trick me? And his regular bar... Why would anyone want to go there regularly when there are dozens of special little restaurants on every corner.'

Helen notices a movement behind her and looks over her shoulder; from the door to the garage comes a good-looking man of about thirty-five or forty. With a searching look, he slowly approaches the bar. He notices Helen's look and smiles at her. "It's a shame how little care is taken around here for our charming lady tourists," he says with a soft voice and a hint of an accent, probably German.

He continues, "I'd really like to keep you company, but I'm expecting a business acquaintance. Apparently he's still getting dressed. Do you mind if I join you for a while?" He waits for her consent in the form of a nod and a pat on the stool next to her before sitting down.

Helen is surprised: No American man would ever wait for such a gesture. They would just sit.

He introduces himself. "Everyone calls me Marcus."

"My name's Helen. I'm with the *Post*, the *Washington Post*, so I'm here on business too. I'm not just a tourist. But you were going to ask that anyway, weren't you?"

Marcus smiles. "That's what a beautiful young woman gets when she sits down at a bar alone. You have to expect being approached with the same old lines. But why not continue: What are you drinking there, or rather, what have you *been* drinking, your glass seems to be empty."

"What every American woman would choose as her first drink in a bar like this: a dry martini."

"Well, would you trust me to choose your next couple of drinks?"

"What's that going to be?"

"You'll see. Dave!" he calls to the bartender, "Let's have two of the usual."

190

Helen sips the drink cautiously. "I've never had one of these before. Good stuff, though. I should've known that you'd order these."

Marcus and the bartender exchange a glance of disbelief.

"It's a different kind of vodka, and this taste, it's Kiwifruit juice, isn't it?"

The bartender applauds but Marcus is not perfectly satisfied. Marcus sneers. "Americans will never get it into their heads that these fruits are called Zespris, not Kiwifruit."

"Take it easy, Marcus." The bartender turns to Helen. "One would never expect such a rude individual makes his living saving lives." He turns back to Marcus. "Good job there yesterday. I can't believe how fast you found that buried child. It really feels safer here in Auckland since you've been around."

Helen listens up. "My neighbor just saved someone's live yesterday?"

Dave waves her off. "He does it all the time. Didn't he introduce himself? That's Marcus Waller, the boss of SR Inc. You must've heard of them."

Helen almost falls off her barstool.

"The drink wasn't *that* strong," Marcus jokes, while Dave goes to the other end of the bar.

Helen decides to proceed aggressively. "No, it's not too strong. Actually, I think I need another. You know I came all the way from Washington to write an article about Professor Simms. I met with him today and his whole institute didn't seem very genuine to me. When I asked him about that, he told me that all of their success wouldn't' have been possible without a company called SR, Inc, so I said to myself, 'You really should go and talk to that company.' And now here I am, accidentally sitting next to the boss. So excuse me if I'm flabbergasted by such a coincidence, *Schicksal*, as you'd say in Germany, wouldn't you?"

Marcus sees Helen differently now. This seems to be one clever reporter. It's good that SR Inc. is prepared to handle people like this. "A lot of people underestimate Simms, but it's true, he couldn't do such a great job without the data we provide. Whatever Simms finds out is checked again by us before it's handed over to the PM, of course."

"But what kinds of methods are you using? Why are you the only ones who can do what you do?"

"We are the world leaders in electronic data capture of earth movements and caverns. That's why we were able to help so fast yesterday in the house collapse, and this is also how we were able to do such a good job during the rescue operations after the earthquakes that Simms predicted." This is new to Helen. She knows that she will have to investigate it. "This is also how we could find new oil fields and aquifers in certain parts of the world. You may have heard about Lake Sahel, which we found in Africa. It has turned a large area of desert into a prosperous farmland."

Helen nods halfheartedly. She has heard about that, but she was not aware that SR, Inc. was behind it.

"These new methods are very precious to us and we don't want them to be used incorrectly, so we decided to keep them secret and didn't even think about patenting them. We can also classify underground explosions, so certain would-be nuclear nations are not exactly friendly towards us. So we're not shouting our name from the rooftops, and all our research we keep very well guarded. We just want to continue our good work. You'll see what I mean when you take the SR, Inc. tour tomorrow."

"But I can use what you've just said, right? That there is a connection between finding natural resources and predicting earthquakes, and that you have a monopoly on it?"

Marcus shrugs. "All of this is already listed in our brochure. You'll get one of those tomorrow too. But we don't really like to use the word 'monopoly.' It's our policy to either apply for patents, which are only good for seventeen years, or keep our inventions secret for a couple of years before we make them public. So our 'seismological monopoly,' as you call it, will run out in 2037. But you'll learn more about this on the tour tomorrow. I'm afraid you'll have to excuse me now, I just saw my business acquaintance leave the elevator."

Marcus shakes her hand and rushes towards the lobby. "Good to see you, Jan!" are the last words she hears from him.

Helen gets back to finishing her drink. The conversation with Marcus was nice but also a bit frustrating. How is that going to make a good story? There do not seem to be any big secrets. The whole thing would be suitable for a scientific magazine, but it won't make a sensational expose for the *Washington Post*. When she is about to leave the bar, she overhears one sentence from Jan, Marcus' business friend. "...you mean every single power plant?"

She can see that Marcus is a bit embarrassed because he puts his hand on Jan's arm to quiet him. But Helen's hopes for a good story have returned: 'What do they have to do with power plants?' She'll have to find out more!

"What's the weather going to be like tomorrow, hon?" Helen asks Dave, even though she knows very well that it will be pouring all day from the weather forecast.

He answers her regretfully, "Museum weather, I'm afraid. You should really check out the Auckland Domain, the Antarctica Museum, and Kelly Tarton's Aquarium. They're all worth a visit. And if that's not your cup of tea, then you could always go and win a million Eggs at the casino."

"Eggs?" she asks surprised.

"That's what we call the Euro here."

"I see. Under these circumstances, I'll go and have a long sleep. But first I'll have another of your Zespri vodkas."

As she is having another drink, several businessmen approach her. She flirts a little with them, just enough not to behave suspiciously until Marcus says good-bye to Jan. To her delight Marcus comes over to her again.

"I just wanted to give you my card in case the tour isn't enough for you. See the red dot in the upper corner? This means that everyone who has such a card will be allowed through to me. I always have a couple of minutes for those people. But now let me wish you a good night." Very much to Helen's surprise, Marcus kisses her hand. "This is how we do it where I'm from originally, Austria."

"Oh, like President Schwarzenegger! I thought your accent was a little soft for a German."

Exhilarated, Marcus walks back to his car: 'So there are still young women out there who find me attractive, even after my fortieth birthday.'

But Helen stands up and goes over to Jan. All Jan knows about her so far is that she seems to know Marcus pretty well.

"Hello, I'm a friend of Marcus. He didn't have time for me because of you," she teases, "so I think you owe me a glass of wine. They do have wine in New Zealand, don't they?"

Jan plays along and enjoys how Helen overwhelms him with her charm. She soon knows that he works for Siemens South Africa, and that they just received a substantial contract to establish certain details about all the power plants in the USA and Europe. Siemens seems to be a logical choice here, but why Siemens South Africa? Helen is not totally convinced by Jan's answer.

Jan responds, "Well, we built some of those power plants ourselves and we have the reputation of being reliable and cost effective."

Helen is sure there must be another reason.

The next day Helen decides not to take the SR, Inc. tour. She books a flight to Johannesburg instead. For some reason, she is sure she will find out more in Jan's environs.

Two days later Klaus and Marcus sit down together at the office. "You're right. We should plan the breakdown to occur on several levels," begins Klaus. "How far have you gotten?"

"I've engaged a group from Siemens South Africa, led by a friend of mine. They're putting together a detailed list of power plants and distribution points in the US and Europe. It'll include every network, computer, and safety regulation as far as possible without arousing suspicion. I picked South Africa because of my friend and their experience building power plants. Workers are also much cheaper there than in Germany, and I just thought it would be better to pick a country that won't be directly affected by the breakdown. They don't know what this whole thing is about, of course. They believe that we have some information about terror attacks against power plants and want to find measures to tighten security."

"Of course, the breakdown will happen before we can actually tighten the security, so we'll be too late. The project is slated to take place in fourteen months, but as soon as the warnings are given out for October 17th, that'll be in mid September, I'll make sure they speed up their work but there won't be enough time. We should try to protect at least a couple of plants in order to have an alibi, but they won't make a big difference, like it didn't make a difference that the power plant in Churchill Falls was still working. I'll be able to provide you with more information in a couple of weeks. But do you think it will it be possible to crash the computers controlling the power-stations?"

Klaus shakes his head uncertainly. "I wish we could apply all our means. We wouldn't have a problem to get the electricity supplies back up again. But I'm afraid we'll have to use simpler methods."

"What's that supposed to mean?"

"Well, we have our drones all over the world, right? There should be about 34,000,000 buzzing around worldwide. They do a hell of a job when it comes to avoiding terror attacks, especially since we use knowledge management systems like Hyperwave to coordinate those huge masses of data. Remember how Putin called terrorism "the plague of the twenty-first century?" Well, I think we have that plague under control now. No one knows about those drones, so the terror organizations must believe that they have traitors within their ranks. As you know, I made sure all the drones were equipped with lasers, giving off short impulses. Those lasers could easily cut all outdoor electrical wires. That would shut down the electricity network. And only some of the thicker cables are underground. But if we do that, we'd give away the existence of the drones, which we can't risk. So we'll have to do it with more traditional methods, like virus attacks."

"I understand that; that was the original plan. So what's the problem?"

"Let me explain the simpler part first. That's complicated enough, actually. If we want to reach almost every computer, then we'll have to do as the MoM did: We'll have to smuggle time-activated viruses into the software first, before it's distributed to consumers. We could actually manage that because all the big software companies are issuing versions of programs at the beginning of next year. But not only would that be very time-consuming, but as a matter of fact, a lot of users use their old programs for years. So we'll also have to attack the network itself. I let Hacker Harry in on the plan–he's the only one, actually–and he suggests doing this in two waves. First we'll import a harmless but annoying virus that can only be fought by the newest version of a particular anti-virus program. This program will contain the real virus."

Klaus pauses for a moment before continuing, "All this sounds very simple, but we will have to sneak people into all those companies, people who will not be allowed to know what we're up to. I start sweating when I think about all the lies that we have to come up with. So in addition to this wave, we would have to implant another version of the virus into the network and onto commercial DVDs the day before the breakdown. But even that will not do the trick. A lot of the network computers out there are protected by extremely effective firewalls that we will not be able to infiltrate; and some of the computers are only connected internally, and not to the world outside. So those intranets would have to be fought individually, which will make it necessary to physically get around their firewalls. That's how Barry did it in Pakistan, but we don't have Barry anymore. I'm afraid you and Cynthia will have to do something similar to what you did in Brussels. But it'll be impossible to get into all the problematic power plants and distribution points, so I found another solution that should help in most cases: users of computer systems use memory cards nowadays which contain certain elements of programs. These cards are usually kept unprotected in offices. That's good for us. It should be possible to smuggle the virus into those cards with the help of the drones. There is a chance that the secret of the drones will be discovered during this operation. Atlantis has calculated this at a probability of 91%."

"That's too high," Marcus interjects.

"I know. We'll have to implant a self-destruct mode into those drones and make sure it won't endanger any people who happen to be around. With these measures, we should be able to paralyze most computers in North America, Japan, and Europe. That's the end of the easy part."

Marcus is shocked. "If that was the simple part, then I don't even want to hear the complicated one."

"I'm afraid you'll have to. Of course the viruses will all have to be activated at the exact same time, but he computer clocks are not synchronized. Some of them have been set back in order to prolong the licenses on their software. Some of them are just imprecise and others are set ahead in order to find viruses in time. Every company that sells anti-virus software does that. This means that there is a good chance that our virus will be discovered and destroyed too early."

"So why didn't the MoM have this problem?" Marcus wonders.

"Because by 2080 all computer clocks worldwide will be synchronized by radio and it will be impossible to set your own time. That is, if today's trends continue. So Atlantis showed us that this will make the system even more vulnerable," explains Klaus.

"And did you find a solution for that?"

"Kind of. We'll make a special version for the virus protection companies that won't be effected if they put their clocks forward. Thus, we won't be able to activate the virus at those companies, but they'll distribute it for us. We think that this should solve most of our problems if we can develop the perfect virus. That's the main issue anyway. We have to create a virus that we, and only we, can kill."

"So the virus will have to have an extremely complex code. They'll find it very hard to break the code because most computers will have collapsed. So I'm glad we decided not to infect the entire world. Raianda's uncle, who owns a large software company in India, will find a way to break the code: he'll connect all uninfected computers and e-helpers in India, China, South America, Australia, and New Zealand in a way that they will divide the work of breaking the code between them. They'll soon find out that in a worst-case scenario, it could take three months to solve the problem, but that it's much more likely that it'll take between ten and twenty days. A computer in New Zealand will find the solution in two weeks. Any other questions?"

Marcus looks at Klaus in disbelief. "That'll never work, I know we have good computer specialists, but it just won't work."

Klaus smiles. "Yes it will. You can count on it. But it's now your job to convince the PM. She'll have to make sure that the governments will react to the breakdown in the way we want. And she'll have to cover our ass. So your mission might be just as difficult as mine. But unlike you, I have the mightiest ally already."

"Klaus, you're nuts. It'll never work that way. We'll have to come up with a new plan."

Klaus continues to smile. "I've never known you to be such a pessimist. You just go and do your part and stop worrying. I'll do mine. Wanna bet?"

Marcus is baffled. "This is the screwiest operation I've ever heard of. How can you be so sure?"

"A-T-L-A-N-T-I-S, get it?! You want to know the numbers? Total breakdown of electricity and network connections apart from a small number of computers and local e-helpers: 98%, return to normalcy: 99%, convincing the PM: 83%, appropriate legislation after regaining normalcy: 85%, danger that SR Inc. will be discovered as initiator: 69%. Oh, I should really tell you that you have to be more careful sometimes. The 69% was calculated today. It was still down at 40% yesterday, but apparently you had a little chat with a woman named Helen in the Hyatt three days ago. That wasn't a good idea. This very Helen is visiting a man named Jan in South Africa right now."

Marcus gasps but Klaus calms him down. "It was just bad luck that she met Jan. But we'll have to keep an eye on her from now on. And by the way, you should talk to Atlantis more often. He's really changed a lot. He seems to like our plan."

11 The Execution of the Plan

Great Barrier Island, New Zealand
December 21, 2020

Klaus Baumgartner and Marcus Waller sit with Atlantis, who has become a real ally and helper over the past days. He is obviously pleased with how the group has reacted to the simulation. They tell Atlantis how they are planning to avoid such a scenario. They also tell Atlantis about their reservations: despite their early optimism, they're still not sure how they can infect every high-security power plant and security system. There are more of those than they had originally estimated. It seems even more difficult to carry out attacks as "threats of an unknown group" without giving their identity away and killing innocent people. But such attacks seem to be necessary to guarantee the PM's credibility prior to October 15th.

Finally Atlantis reacts, "I'm afraid you've made one mistake. You shouldn't have excluded Stephan."

"But wasn't it sensible to try to keep him and his sister out of this... and how could he have helped us so much?"

Atlantis hesitates. "Stephan's parabilities alone wouldn't' have helped that much, but he would have been able to contact "THE WE"[39]. Once you have "THE WE" on your side, there won't be any problems. could have easily carried out the attacks and no one would ever have been able to find out about it. It's exactly what you need."

"Atlantis, you seem to know a lot about "THE WE". Couldn't you contact him and help?"

---

[39] "THE WE" is a miraculous creature that Stephan contacted once before. It's not clear what "THE WE" is, but apparently it must be some kind of intelligent animal because it was able to communicate with Stephan. From the experience that Stephan had with "THE WE", it is clear that it must be highly developed and ahead of the human race in many respects. It is unclear where "THE WE" is located at the moment. For more about "THE WE", see " Xperts: The Para Warriors".

"No, I must not do that. Only Stephan can. If he can convince "THE WE" to come to your aid, then I would be allowed to communicate with him. But I may not initiate contact."

"So you're saying that we should let Stephan in on the operation when he comes back before Christmas, and we should then ask him to contact "THE WE" for help?"

"Yes." Atlantis answers succinctly, "and Cynthia will then have to erase his memory again."

Marcus is not happy about this kind of zigzag course. Cynthia just erased part of the poor kid's memory and now they are supposed to bring it back, only to erase it again?

But Atlantis doesn't give in. "According to the latest information, the chances of succeeding without "THE WE" are not very good."

They eagerly await Stephan's return.

When he arrives, Marcus takes him aside right away "We need your help, but you should know that Atlantis thinks your memory of it will have to be erased by Cynthia. I know this is very unusual, and I'm not very happy about it, but please trust me. There seems to be no other way and Cynthia is sure that you won't suffer any negative aftereffects."

Stephan hesitates before he speaks. "I trust you, of course, so I guess I'll do it. But you have to promise me one thing. You have to promise to tell me what all this was about on my twenty-first birthday."

Marcus breathes a sigh of relief. "All right, I promise."

"Let's do it then," Stephan says casually.

Marcus explains the entire plan to his son, and that "THE WE" and only "THE WE" can guarantee that the breakdown won't incur a great loss of life.

"I'm not sure if "THE WE" can or even wants to help, but I can try. Stephan checks for the emergency pellet inside his e-helper. "THE WE" gave him the pellet after their first encounter. Stephan concentrates his thoughts on "THE WE". For ten minutes nothing happens.

When Stephan starts to doubt his chance of success, he suddenly hears a voice in his brain: 'Hello, Stephan, we didn't think that you would contact us so soon. Please be patient a little longer.'

"I've made contact," says Stephan, "but I'll have to wait a little."

Soon "THE WE" is back. 'Stephan, you agreed to only contact us in an extreme emergency. Please tell us what this is about.'

'Please excuse me if I bothered you, "THE WE", all this is very complicated but it's really important. It'll take me a while to explain everything.'

Stephan tells "THE WE" about Atlantis' simulation, about the conclusions they reached, the measures they want to take, and why they need "THE WE"'s help. Stephan adds that Atlantis has offered to keep communications going with "THE WE".

'I understand. This seems to be important. Give me fifteen minutes to think this over. I'll contact you again.'

All of them, including Atlantis, eagerly await "THE WE"'s answer. Fifteen minutes later, "THE WE" is back. Only Atlantis knows that "THE WE"'s difficult decision was actually made far away from this planet.

'We are not sure about Atlantis' role in the whole matter; the simulation and the advice he has given you may violate the Galactic Laws. But as for us, we are not bound to those laws and we are convinced that Atlantis is acting in the best interests of the human race. So we will help you. From now on we will communicate directly with Atlantis. Stephan, you should know that Atlantis can also hear what I'm saying to you. We wish you the best and hope that your operation will be a success. But I have to warn you again, Stephan, don't abuse your ability to contact me. I won't be able to help you much more often.'

Atlantis informs the others, ""THE WE" is on our side. You are very lucky. We should now discuss the tasks we will give "THE WE". Cynthia, please erase Stephan's memory now. His girlfriend Raianda is already wondering where he is."

Over the last ten days, the group has combined all their efforts. This year, Christmas had no chance to really take place because everything had to be done to prepare carefully for the meeting with the PM. The PM has been a good friend of Marcus' since the big earthquake in Wellington when Marcus saved the life of the Minister of Economy. She has managed to put everything else on hold for a whole day so she can carefully discuss this urgent issue.

Instead of at the Beehive, New Zealand's official government building, the PM decides to meet Marcus at her residence, which she occupies alone. It has a grand view over the harbor and the Papa Tongarewa, the biggest museum in New Zealand. But like many other houses situated on this steep slope, the PM's house can only be reached with a small private gondola. Tourists always find this transportation system a sensation, but it is also very practical: you park your car at the base, go through the garage, and enter the gondola which takes you up to your house. Sometimes it even functions as a foyer on wheels.

Marcus presents the PM with the plan. "First I'd like to explain roughly what we think would be necessary to avoid a situation like the one we saw in the simulation. As you'll see, everything sounds good, but it is also very complicated. In addition, I'll give you our report, which explains how our measures can be undertaken. I know you won't be very excited about this, but I'm afraid there is no other way."

The PM waits eagerly. "You guys have surprised me quite a lot in the past. Don't keep me in suspense."

"In order to avert a complete breakdown of the electric and computer networks, we present this proposal. I'll only go through the basics here with you and add a couple of sentences to the text. You can have a closer look at this with your people. This information is not secret at all.

Principle 1: Globalization of material goods wherever it is necessary, otherwise regionalization wherever it is possible and makes sense.

"This means: Globalization is good because it guarantees efficient production at those locations where production is good and cheap and allows easy access from every part of the world. On the other hand, globalization is bad because it leads to dependence of regions on other regions: it increases traffic, it leads to the exploitation of people (corporations produce their products in low-wage regions and it benefits them if they remain low-wage), and it endangers the existence of regional production units. Conversely, regionalization is good because it doesn't lead to dependencies on remote regions. Local groups produce for local people: this usually leads to higher consumer satisfaction. Regionalization is bad because it can be very inefficient. We need to create a balance between globalization and regionalization. Over the past few decades, the scales have been tipped too far towards globalization."

"I will discuss the gulf between rich and poor separately, but you'll see that this balance will lead to a certain level of regionalization. But that's not enough. Other measures are necessary, especially the implementation of a 'distance tax': goods that come a long way are taxed higher, making them more expensive. Apples in Europe would become less expensive than bananas again, for example. The tax will be divided between the countries according to their GNP: A poor country will export fewer goods to Austria, for example, but will reach a much higher margin."

"Similarly, Austrian mountain farmers will be competitive again because the distance tax will reduce the advantage of far away competitors, thereby also reducing the number of trucks crisscrossing Europe. This tax will also lead to more seasonal eating habits, probably a desirable feature. Here are some other examples: Beef from Argentina will become extremely expensive in New Zealand and Europe, and furniture made from tropical wood will be legal again, but an expensive commodity. It will no longer make sense to ship furniture components from one continent to the other. Furniture will either be mass-produced regionally by large companies, or by local carpenters whose hand-made products will probably be much cheaper and customer friendly. This tax shouldn't be taken too far. When bananas become too expensive, people will start producing them in greenhouses. This is not our goal. People will use cane sugar where they can grow it, and they will eat beet sugar where they can grow beets."

The PM interrupts. "All this is not very new. A fuel tax and a highway toll system have a similar purpose."

Marcus nods. "Yes and no. There should be an increase in the price of cargo transport, but it would be better if the money generated benefits the poor countries instead of just complicating their export efforts. We believe that we have to introduce a whole series of measures. Let me continue please."

The PM smiles and nods.

Marcus continues, "What I just said about material products goes similarly for immaterial ones, like energy and information. It is just wrong that x-rays of Americans are sent by satellite to India for evaluation, and the reports are done by Indian doctors, far away from the persons under examination, just because labor is cheaper in India."

"Principle 2: Globalization and concentration of information and energy networks should occur only where necessary; we should aim for regionalization as much as is sensible.

"By this we mean that it will still make sense in the future to run big power plants. Foreseeable nuclear fusion power plants will maybe be good examples of this. But there's no reason we shouldn't produce 20% of the energy needed per house with solar cells, heat pumps, and the like. This could guarantee the basic supplies even in the event that the net breaks down. It could also be possible that a regional power plant with simple and reliable distribution and transformation devices would produce an additional 20%. This would be enough to maintain a certain level of comfort without leading to a catastrophe."

"The same is true for communication networks. It is a mistake to run all services over one and the same network. This started in 2010 when phone companies, radio and, television stations started to provide their "goods" mostly over the Internet. The simulation has clearly shown that this is a dangerous concentration of media on a single technology. It gets even worse when complex networks are used where it isn't necessary, like for navigating vehicles. In our opinion, satellite navigation can be replaced by astronomical navigation run by local e-helpers. We're experimenting with this at the moment, and hope to develop a prototype soon. Once people start using such navigational devices, they become independent from a sudden breakdown of the net, as long as local computers are still functioning. We could see that the XPs in the simulation were still working. In addition, for local transportation, people should use electrical vehicles that do not require liquid fuel and can be recharged by solar cells. This would keep the traffic going for medium length trips".

Principle 3: Computers must be more secure.

"I don't want to get into detail here, let me just say two things: Certain computer components have to be designed in a way that some parts of the software and the data are indestructible or are able to regenerate. But more importantly, we need an institution that controls the quality of software and hardware as is already done for food products. Isn't it absurd that this has never been discussed?"

The PM is baffled. "And this report shows how this would be possible?"

"Yes," Marcus nods with assurance before continuing:

Principle 4: In the future devices will have to be built less monolithically again. Repairs will have to be made possible again by exchanging a few modules.

"Let me give you an example: In the old days, you could still replace a burnt-out headlight with just a new bulb. With today's Moller headlights, you have to replace a large component. There are thousands of examples: The economy supports the throwaway society. They like to keep devices un-repairable in order to sell their newest things. This has to be changed. We suggest a monolith tax. You'll find the details in the report."

Principle 5: The world can only function when the differences between rich and poor are not so great.

"Anything else is amoral and leads to instability. This principle will require a combination of different methods. The one method that will surely not work is the one where rich countries pay poorer countries off. This would be neither politically nor technically possible. You can't take the money from the rich to make the poor richer. Instead, the growth rates will have to be unevenly distributed. A growth rate producing ten times that of our present resources is possible over the next fifty to eighty years without additional eco-problems such as pollution[40]. We will have to make sure that underprivileged countries will have a production growth four times that of the rich countries. That way, the living standards of all countries will be balanced out over the next fifty to eighty years without destroying Spaceship Earth. This restructuring can only be realized if all countries are forced to respect specific human and environmental rights. In addition, dramatic shifts in currency value will have to be avoided."

"You're saying that all this could really be carried out?" the PM asks.

"The currency issue will probably be the most difficult one, but all the other conditions can be forced through by boycotting countries which don't follow them. You'll find all the details in here."

Principle 6: Additional measures are possible.

"This point summarizes all the necessary measures that don't fit with the other five principles. Here you'll find ideas about the best ways to stock goods and medicine. You'll have to skim over this."

The PM keeps asking Marcus about some of the details of the six principles. "Yes, I believe that those measures could help the world if they were carried out. They would probably help to avoid a catastrophe like the one in the simulation. By the way, does Atlantis believe so too?"

Marcus nods.

"But how can we convince the world to accept such dramatic changes?"

"I'm afraid the only way to do this is to shock the world," answers Marcus. He then begins explaining the plans for a breakdown in the USA, Europe, and Japan.

---

[40] See F. J. Radermacher: Balance or Destruction, Oekosoziales Forum (2003).

"We suggest that a report be published under your name as soon as possible and in as many languages as possible. We suggest the title *"The Path to a Stable World"*. The message of the book would actually be very similar to many things you have said in the past. We are convinced that this book will be a bestseller and will pave the way. In addition to the book, we suggest that you keep warning the world about attacks from different groups. We'll keep supplying the necessary information for avoiding such attacks and you make sure that the evildoers are put behind bars. But most of all, we want you to warn the world of a new dangerous group that plans to carry out unusual attacks without harming people and without leaving tracks. We want you to intensively warn the world about October 15th. This warning will have to be taken very seriously, because it'll be necessary to keep all traffic down on that day and to keep most people at home. This will be the day of the great breakdown, which will last two to three weeks. Once the breakdown is over, you'll have to approach the UN and force them to push through legislation assuring the six principles. This will help to avoid a catastrophe like that in the simulation."

The PM has gone pale. "Atlantis knows about this and approves of it?" Marcus nods. "And Atlantis believes that this plan will have a chance for success?"

"With you on our side, the chances are very good. However, there is a possibility that the world will find out that our group was behind all this. I think you can imagine the very unpleasant consequences for us, but we're willing to take the risk. We would leave you out of all of this, and it would be better if you forgot about this last part of our conversation. You'd only have to publish the book, give out the warnings and make sure that the principles are pushed through. You wouldn't even have to know that we're behind the breakdown. Cynthia could erase your memory right after the breakdown. Will you go along?"

"Marcus, I think this is the biggest decision of my life. Give me two days to think about this and to study the report and discuss it with my ministers."

"That's all I expected," says Marcus. "Let me give you those three envelopes. They all include information about attacks, but only the first one includes details about the specific group of terrorists. They plan to poison Dallas' water reservoir in mid-January. The second attack will be carried out on the Nimitz III, an aircraft carrier that is presently docked in Hawaii. You'll have to make sure that nobody is near that carrier on February 2nd, 2021. It'll be completely destroyed by a presently unknown group that will call itself UDG, the Unknown Dangerous Group. Two even more dramatic attacks will happen on March 14th, 2021. Simultaneously, Arsenal #45 on Guam and the US Air base Ramenstein in Germany will be destroyed by the UDG. We will give you further warnings before mid-September. That's when you'll issue the warning for October 15th, if you're on our side. At that time, the world will have great fear and respect for the UDG."

"And how do you plan to execute those attacks without exposing yourselves?"

Marcus smiles. "I know this sounds funny, but we won't even be there."

On January 9th, 2021 the PM warns the President of the USA of a terrorist attack on Dallas' water supply. Two days later, the responsible terrorist group is captured and tons of poisonous substances and detailed plans for future attacks are seized. For the first time, the media also find out that the warning came from New Zealand. Rumors about a dense secret service network based in New Zealand are strengthened.

On February 1st, the PM sends a warning to the biggest press agencies in the world, informing them that a so-far unknown group is planning to destroy the *Nimitz III* in Hawaii. She also tells them that outside a range of 200 meters, there will be no danger. Feverish activity sets in. The area around the dock is cordoned off. Tens of thousands of soldiers secure the area. Fighter jets and radar units scan the airspace. A fleet of battleships blocks the passage to Oahu Island. All flights to and from Honolulu are cancelled. Nevertheless, the Nimitz III evaporates on February 2nd, at 3 p.m. in front of thousands of eyes and video cameras. There seems to be no possible explanation. That same day several of the biggest newspapers around the world receive the same letter: "The *Nimitz III* was only the beginning. The UDG."

Analysis yield facts, which do not seem to be credible: it looks like the *Nimitz III* was attacked by thousands of lasers simultaneously.

The PM contacts Marcus over a secure e-helper connection. "Have you heard about the *Nimitz III*? Do you have an explanation for that?"

Marcus hesitates for a long time. "No, I don't really know what happened there," he lies. He thinks it is better that the PM knows as little as possible. But in fact, he really doesn't know any details, either. All he knows is that "THE WE" is behind this. For hours, the paragroup has puzzled over explanations for the destruction.

Raianda and Stephan are the only ones who guess what happened. They witnessed themselves how one of "THE WE"'s robots, the size of a finger, destroyed a huge Kauri tree with a thin laser beam. But they promised to remain silent about this. Now they both wonder about "THE WE"'s rationale for the destruction of the aircraft carrier.

In March, the arsenal in Guam is destroyed simultaneously with the military base in Germany. Weeks later, an arsenal in Russia, another in Great Britain, and a shutdown nuclear power plant in Japan are similarly annihilated. All this happened despite warnings and heavy precautions. The respect and fear of the UDG is growing. Apparently, they are completely convinced of their invincibility; they write the letters announcing the attacks even before they carry them out! The military is clueless.

Stephan does not dare to tell his father what he knows. He still doesn't understand the reasons for the attacks. He feels desperate and tries to contact "THE WE", but to no avail. Marcus tells Stephan that he knows something about those attacks, something that nobody else knows, or is allowed to know. He finds it hard to convince Stephan that there is no reason to worry about the situation. The only reason Stephan trusts his father is because people are never hurt during the attacks and poor countries are excluded from the attacks.

Conspiracy theories develop in some circles. Is it a third-world country that has developed a super weapon and is now using it to exact revenge on richer countries?

While the UDG's respect continues to grow, parts of the computer systems are being systematically bugged. So far, nobody has noticed that 93% of all computer systems have been infected with viruses. Harry has programmed them so skillfully that they will all activate on October 15th, 2021. After the virus is activated, the computers will only be able to carry out one activity: trying to solve a complex cryptographic problem, the decoding of the virus.

The only serious problems remaining are the intranet at large power plants, distribution points, banks, and large companies.

Helen Milton arrives in Johannesburg on December 19th, 2020. By now, Jan and her have become good friends, but the activities going on around Jan and his coworkers seem very strange to her. For months and months, they are looking for security gaps in all the power plants and control centers in Europe, Japan, and North America. Their alleged goal is to warn those units. However, all the information seems to be going only to SR Inc. in New Zealand, and Helen cannot detect any kinds of measures being put into place to solve the problems. The information includes physical problems down to the smallest openings, as well as information about "risky employees."

Jan does not notice when Helen starts making copies of the security gap information. Finally she finds a report about a power plant in Richmond, Virginia, only 150 km south of Washington, DC, where her parents live. The report includes information about all security gaps, one of which is that visitors are not checked very strictly there. Helen decides to return to the USA and have a closer look at the power plant.

She doesn't find it hard to sign up for a tour. It's a large group and nobody counts the exact number of visitors. This enables Helen to hide and stay behind alone in one of the computer rooms. She waits several hours. The room is only minimally lit by the emergency light. Helen doesn't even know what she's waiting for.

Suddenly she can see how a little bird flies in through one of the openings that were listed in the security report. The bird seems to be looking for something. It flies around in the room and finally dives down to a small memory card, like the ones in digital cameras. The bird takes the card, hides it in its feathers, but then takes it out again. But this one looks different.

Helen is paralyzed at first, but soon decides to cover the opening with her hands. But the bird tries to get out again and flies against Helen's hands several times. It hurts. This bird feels unusually hard. Finally she manages to catch it. 'Is it a bird? No this thing is made of metal. A flying robot!' Helen almost panics when the bird gets hotter and hotter inside her hand. She has to let it go and watches as it slowly evaporates.

'What the hell?' Will she be able to talk about this with anyone? But who would believe her? And who would know anything about this. 'No, I'll have to keep researching.'

Helen tries to find out if it would be possible to keep such a robot from dissolving in the event she finds another one. She asks several of her friends about ways to shut down household robots, which have become common by now, in case they go crazy.

"That kind of thing doesn't happen too often," says one, "but a strong electrical current, an electroshock I guess, would do it."

"But how would you do that?"

"The best thing would be to buy a stun stick. It's actually a pretty good weapon, too."

From now on, Helen spends more and more nights in different power plants, armed with a stun stick. She hopes that what she saw in Richmond will happen again. She doesn't know how unlikely it is that she will be present again when one of the robots happens to infect a power plant.

Weeks and weeks pass without success. The UDG keeps carrying out their attacks, but Helen never even thinks about connecting her research with those attacks. The more she learns about SR Inc., and how they have saved so many lives, the more ridiculous her suspicions it could be an evil organization seem. On September 20th, she decides to visit Jan in Johannesburg again. Two days earlier, the world was warned about the threat of

211

a worldwide attack on October 15th. The warning suggests that all traffic should come to a halt that day. It is likely that there will be massive electricity outages. It also suggests that people stay inside their houses and stock food and other goods for several weeks. This warning will be repeated so many times that people will start to be allergic to it, like they do to Christmas Carols before Christmas.

Jan and Helen react in different ways: Jan is shocked. SR Inc.'s security measures will come too late! But Helen is turning into a mistrustful journalist again. 'Could SR Inc. be behind those power outages? But then they would have to be connected with the UDG. But that's unthinkable...'

Helen copies the latest report. It's about a power plant near Gander, Newfoundland, and a huge hydroelectric plant in Churchill Falls in a remote part of Labrador. The description of Gander is: "A little power plant, sparse security, many ventilation openings."

The one for Churchill Falls reads: "Probably the safest power plant in the world. No additional security measures needed."

The two power plants are located less than 1000 km away from each other, so Helen decides to visit both of them.

Churchill Falls is classified so safe that Marcus and Cynthia decide to infect the plant themselves. Gander is on the way, so they will bug that plant "manually" too. Afterwards, they plan to fly from Gander to Goose Bay and take the road to Churchill Falls. They are expecting many déjà vu's there as a result of having seen the simulation.

So, accidentally, Helen spots the e-hummingbird, steered by Marcus from his hotel. She manages to shock the robot before it can self-destruct or exchange the memory cards. Satisfied, she puts it and the memory card into her bag.

Marcus notices that something is definitely wrong. But it is already October 10th and the hummingbirds are designed in a way that they will not be traceable to their inventors. So Marcus expects little danger of being discovered. By sheer coincidence, Helen, Marcus, and Cynthia do not meet. Helen flies to Labrador City while the other two fly to Goose Bay. Coming from different directions, both parties rent cars to drive to the only motel in Churchill Falls.

Helen gets there first and can't believe her eyes when she sees Marcus and a woman check into the motel. That cannot be an accident. Somehow, they must be involved with the whole thing. Her heart beats fast. She is sure she is on the trail of a sensation. She has observed them closely and under no circumstances can she allow herself to be discovered.

Marcus and Cynthia sign up for a tour of the power plant. He claims to be a computer specialist and asks if it is possible to talk to some of the IT staff at the plant. This time Marcus has taken a special virus-program with him, which should be able to deal with the plant's special security software. It takes a lot of cash to bribe one of the senior computer specialists, and the special virus is barely ready in time.

Marcus knows about the security precautions that await them, but they are pretty sure that their parabilities will help them through this. At the gate, both their identity data and their biometric readings are taken. With his telekinetic powers, Marcus forces the security personnel to write in their own data instead of his and Cynthia's and to exchange their IDs. Cynthia makes sure that they will not remember any of this.

When they reach the entrance to the plant itself, they face their first difficulty. They present the faked IDs and their biometric data (cornea scans and fingerprints) is counterattacked with the data on the IDs. Of course the computer notices the differences and sets off the alarm. The security guard jumps up only to find a small piece of paper saying "Stop the alarm or I'll press you harder." At the same time, the guard can feel an invisible hand– Marcus' telekinetic pseudohand–start to strangle him. That scares him enough to shut the alarm off.

Headquarters calls immediately. "What are you doing?"

"Sorry pal, hit the wrong button," the guard answers, feeling the pseudohand around his throat again. The door opens and the three of them drive inside. The guard won't remember anything unusual.

213

Cynthia and Marcus have used similar techniques before[41]. The only new thing for them is the video surveillance that sees everything in the plant. It will need to be erased when they are finished. But that shouldn't be very difficult because the people in charge will do everything to disguise their own mistake. So after all, Churchill Falls is infected as well, unlike in the simulation.

Later, Helen tries hard to reconstruct everything that Marcus and Cynthia did. She repeatedly doubts her own senses. She saw with her own eyes how they talked with the security personnel and went inside with the guide. But those employees do not admit to that. When she shows the guide a picture of him and the two visitors, the man becomes angry. "Who do you think you are, showing me such an obvious fake? I swear to God and the Calgary Flames that I've never seen those two before."

The security personnel react similarly. They consider her a troublemaker and don't even let her take the tour.

But still, whatever it may be, she is on the trail of a huge conspiracy, and at least she has the electronic bird. She decides to fly to Auckland and confront Marcus with the bird and many questions.

Marcus and Cynthia take a night flight on Air New Zealand and arrive in Auckland before Helen. They fly directly to the property on Great Barrier Island. Helen arrives soon afterwards and decides to stay again at the Hyatt.

It's 8:00 a.m. New Zealand time, on October 15th. Helen arrives at 6:00 a.m. on the last flight that would land that day. For the next twenty-four hours, there will be no more air traffic.

When Helen enters the bar, BBC goes off. The bartender switches to CNN, but it's down too. The local station interrupts its usual program. "We've just received information that all computer networks and all power plants in Japan, Europe, and North America have broken down. As of now, we can find no cause for this except we are fairly sure that the UDG is behind it. Even high security power plants like Churchill Falls in Canada

---

[41] See "Xperts: The Para Warriors".

214

have broken down. We have no further details at the moment, but we'll keep you informed."

'Churchill Falls,' thinks Helen. 'Marcus was just there. He must have something to do with the breakdown, but why?'

12 A Changed World

Great Barrier Island, New Zealand
October 20, 2021

The group sits together in the winter garden of the big house on Great Barrier Island. From there they can look down on the high waves rolling in. But despite the unfriendly weather, the flowers are already in bloom, heralding the beginning of spring.

Stephan is living with Raianda's family in India helping her father out at the Clinic. His sister Linda is visiting her grandparents in Graz, Austria. So the adults are among themselves. It has also become common for Atlantis to partake in such meetings. The situation has developed as they had planned: all of Europe, North America, and Japan are paralyzed, but the side effects are nowhere near as bad as they were in the 2080 simulation. The warnings made most people stock goods. Local traffic is still functioning minimally and the radios, which most Mollers have, still provide a modicum of information.

Everybody is positive that life will be back to normal again in two or three weeks. People have had to cut back on their material comfort. It was a shock for everyone. The economy incurs a deficit of hundreds of billions of Dollars, Euros, and Yen per day. However, there are no serious riots or similar problems. All hospitals are equipped with emergency power systems. Nobody is freezing to death, despite a viscous early cold snap in northeastern Canada. But the people in and around Goose Bay and Churchill Falls gather in one of the many homes and holiday houses with open fireplaces, and some of the large convention centers are still equipped with oil or coal heating, taking care of the rest of the population.

In order to stop the crisis, the computer virus, which has infected almost every kind of computerized system, will have to be removed. This can only be done by decoding a difficult cryptographic problem apparently developed by some kind of loony, sadistic genius. According to initial estimates, even the fastest computer would need twenty-eight years to solve the problem.

But an Indian software company soon finds a way to divide the task up into many smaller ones. Soon, millions of computers all over the world that haven't been hit are working hard to solve their own little part of the problem. It's almost like a contest among the countries that didn't receive the brunt of the attack. All in all, the world is showing an enormous helpfulness towards the infected countries. There are a lot of surprising and moving details: Mexicans, for example, who have not been treated very well by the US over the last decades, suddenly begin donating all sorts of goods to Texas, New Mexico, Arizona, and California. The Russians cross the Bering Straight in order to help people in Alaska. The Chinese help their old archenemies, the Japanese. Turkey, which still has not been allowed membership to the EU, does not hesitate to help Greece. Even countries like Libya and Algeria, whose refugees have been treated like animals by the European Union, are sending an almost embarrassing amount of material aid to Spain and Italy. The helpfulness seems to know no end and despite a few tragic incidents, no casualties arise.

"Whoa, who would have thought that there would be such a level of solidarity among our species?" Maria exclaims for them all. "Atlantis, I tried to find out how close you were to the truth in your simulation. Well, it was all true: all the details about Greece and the route from Graz to Konitsa are accurate. And I even think you exceeded your competencies a couple of times. The simulation included information that isn't even known yet, like the cave southeast of Nacodoches, Texas. We were able to buy the land and have already started researching the great cave. The same is true for a third cave system in Carlsbad, New Mexico. Only two have been "discovered" so far. And that goes for Bragg Creek and the farm called "Wildonstufe" near Graz. How could you know all this?"

Sounding almost as though he is smiling, Atlantis answers, "You continue to underestimate the technology of the Ancient Ones, and don't forget, there are many more supercomputers out there that you haven't encountered yet. You've completely ignored the second one in your possession, but she is not insulted. We work as a team, you know. But as I said before, there are many more of us, and we can do a lot of things that you may not even be aware of.

"Stupid Galactic Laws", mumbles Klaus.

But Atlantis heard this. "Maybe the day will come when you realize how important those laws are when it comes to protecting human and other emerging civilizations. Then you'll change your point of view."

Marcus gets an unexpected call from SR Inc.'s offices. "We have a problem here. The cruise ship *Maui*, hosting a convention of 2000 doctors on their way from Hawaii to the Marquesas Islands has departed despite all warnings. Of course, their satellite navigation system has crashed, and now they're in the middle of a storm. They're in great danger of running aground on a reef. What shall we do?"

"We'll be right there. Get the Moller 800 with the astronomical navigation system ready. Load it up with emergency supplies and don't forget inflatable motorboats, the ones that can be closed up completely with the steel skin. And don't forget some hollow buoys, the ones with the signal lights. They are big enough to support people in an emergency. But leave enough room for Maria, Herb, Klaus, Cynthia, me (Aroha shakes her head), and for another four people. I'll need an experienced sea rescue team." He then turns to Atlantis. "You want to come along too?"

"Thanks for the invitation. I haven't traveled in a long time."

Marcus takes the five by four centimeter box that contains Atlantis. It has an in-built microphone and a loudspeaker, but it is still unknown how Atlantis can see and use his other senses. Then they get in the Moller to fly to Auckland.

When they arrive there, they immediately board their newest Moller 800 and depart in the direction of Marquesas. Five valuable hours pass before they get there. Ninety minutes ago, the radio aboard the ship was able to broadcast a relatively precise position, but since then there has been no contact. There are signs that the ship could sink at any moment. They can only hope that the Maui had enough lifeboats on board and that they haven't hit the reef yet.

When they are only 500 km away from the position of the ship, Maria switches her para-eyes to telescope mode and starts to scan the possible locations of the ship. She gasps. "Almost all of the thirty lifeboats are already in the water. They're packed. And some people are in the water wearing only life vests. They're all drifting towards the reef. Further south, where the reef opens up into the lagoon, there is a small island with a sandy beach, but I have no idea how we could get all of them there. We just don't have enough time to rescue every individual group, and now they've drifted pretty far apart."

Atlantis notes calmly, "Since I'm already here, please allow me to take over the coordination. Every boat has a number. That should help with communication. Klaus, fly to *Maui's* Lifeboat (LB) 27 first. It's in the most immediate danger. We'll have to secure it first by towing it back out into the open sea. We'll take care of those "secured" boats later on. When we tow a boat into the lagoon, I'll refer to it as "saved." Maria will guide you to LB 27 and then to the other boats. Please be prepared to follow these commands: when I say "buoy," drop a buoy; when I say "boat," drop a boat, and one of you must jump into it. Klaus, this will require you to fly very low and at a maximum of fifty km/h. Our boats will then approach the individual lifeboats from the *Maui* and tie them on. Our motors are strong enough to tow the lifeboats away from the reef to the south. At first, we won't have enough time to tow them into the lagoon right away. We'll have to "secure" them first. Once we have dropped our three boats and our six buoys, Cynthia and Marcus are to activate the net underneath the Moller. Marcus will then lift the swimmers and the people by the buoys into it with his pseudo-hands. Cynthia will erase their memories. I have a difficult job for you, Herb. You'll have to defend the swimmers from shark attacks by para-slowing them. We'll improvise the rest. We'll be within reach momentarily."

Almost blindly, Klaus steers the Moller through the storm. Only Maria's eyes, the Moller's altimeter, and Atlantis' navigational devices can peer through the impenetrable curtain of tropical rain.

Calmly but loudly, Atlantis commands, "Buoy 1.......Buoy 2.......Boat 1: Secure LB 14 and LB 16........Save LB 22.......Secure LB 15 and LB 17.......Save LB 24.......Buoy 3: Four sharks for Herb, they've already attacked one swimmer.......Boat 2: Secure LB54, LB 5 and LB 8 in that order.......Secure LB 11.......then secure LB 9 and LB 1.......Save LB 2.......Attention! We are now at LB 27, lower a cable and hook, secure LB 27 and tow it towards LB 28, Maria.......Buoy 4.......Buoy 5.....Boat 3: secure LB 19 and LB 21.......Save 26.......Secure LB 28.......Secure LB 3 and LB 6. Faster, puny humans!"

This is the first time that they ever heard Atlantis get excited, and he's never referred to them as "puny humans" before.

"Buoy 6.......Release LB 27.......Maria, set course for LB 13. It must be secured immediately, drop the net. Marcus, lift two swimmers beneath you into the net."

Marcus does so easily. Before they reach LB 13, it capsizes. Seventy people fall into the churning water. Not all of them are wearing life vests and a group of sharks homes in on them. "Marcus, save those people who don't have life vests first. Herb, slow down those sharks, especially those ahead of us."

One by one, Marcus lifts the swimmers into the net. "The net's full. We have to fly to the lagoon to let them out!" shouts Klaus.

"Herb, jump into the water and, as far as possible, keep the sharks at bay until we get back. We shouldn't be too long."

Herb doesn't hesitate for a second. His friends admire his courage.

"Klaus, memorize this position. Full speed to the island!"

Soon afterwards, forty disoriented people tumble out of the net into the pouring rain. "Straight back!" roars Atlantis. "Go 300 meters reef-ward of our last position. They should have drifted there by now". Atlantis is right. Marcus lifts the rest of the swimmers into the net. He's exhausted. It's back to the island again...

"Maria, set course to LB 12, we'll save it and get LB 10 on the way."

The complicated maneuver works: When they reach the island with RB 10 and RB 12, RB 22, 24, 11 and 16 are already there.

LB 10, 20, 23, and 29 are still out there in the wild sea, but they're far enough away from the reef to not be facing immediate danger. However, there is absolutely no sign of LB 12, 29, and 30.

"Maria, where are those three boats?" asks Atlantis desperately.

"Who's the super-computer around here anyway? I guess they sunk," answers an exhausted Maria. "There's absolutely no sign of them."

"Set a course to Buoy 1," orders Atlantis. "That's where we saw the first people. That's where the *Maui* must have sunk."

Eight uniformed people are holding on to the buoy. "All of you get into the net!" orders Atlantis.

Marcus groans with the great telekinetic strain that Atlantis forces on him.

Maria shouts reproachfully, "Atlantis, that's just too much for Marcus."

"He'll be all right. That'll be his last difficult task."

As soon as the men are in the net, Atlantis says over the external speaker. "Is the captain among you?"

One of the men lifts his hand.

"Let's get him inside here."

Atlantis immediately asks the captain, "How many lifeboats did you lower?"

"All the thirty we had. But three of them sank: 12, 25, and 30." On the way to the island with LB 9 and 14, Atlantis commands them to drop buoy 1 one more time because he has detected more swimmers.

After they land on the island, Atlantis orders them to unload the Moller: Weatherproof tents, cots, dry clothes, blankets, medicine, hot drinks, and emergency food cans which heat up automatically upon opening. That should be all they need at first. Atlantis cedes command back to the captain who doesn't even know who is talking to him. He doesn't know, of course, that he is talking to a tiny supercomputer from the distant past. Atlantis reacts angrily. "It doesn't matter who I am. Please take care of the people whose lives you endangered by leaving the harbor on October 15th. We'll get the other lifeboats and try to find more survivors. When we return, we expect you to have erected the tents and have figured out how many people are still missing."

The majority of the lifeboats are still out in the stormy sea. They are full of cold, exhausted, and dazed men and women. But they are well off compared to those who are still holding onto the buoys. But they all know that they would have died out there if the huge Moller hadn't miraculously shown up, dropping buoys, and boats, and towing them away from the reef.

In the end, all but four passengers are safe and warming up in the tents. Two passengers were seriously injured in shark attacks. It is a miracle that not more passengers were attacked or killed by the beasts. After Cynthia is finished with her para-job, the rescued people are even more confused. They all seem to have strange gaps in their memories. Marcus says good-bye to the higher-ranking officers and the organizers of the medical convention. "We'll make sure that you get more goods, but I'm afraid you'll have to wait another couple of weeks before you're picked up. So I guess you'll have plenty of time to finish your convention," he says a little sarcastically.

Half a day later, the friends are back on Great Barrier Island. The situation hasn't changed much: rescue troops, who were organized before, continue to work here and there, but the sinking of the *Maui* remains the biggest incident. The breakdown of the infrastructure had unpleasant effects for the civilians of the affected countries; however, the media reports show that the breakdown is already causing some other new and serious considerations.

Even those parts of the world that have not been directly "attacked" now face dramatic difficulties. Tourism has effectively stopped completely, imported goods are becoming scarce and factories are forced to slow production because exporting is not feasible and because no bank transactions can be carried out.

The PM's book, *The Way to a More Stable World*, was already a bestseller before October 15th, but now she is seen as a foremost expert on social issues. There are rumors that many important people have suggested her as a nominee for the Nobel Prize.

Auckland, New Zealand
October 22-31, 2021

By now Helen has become a great fan of Auckland and its environs. She enjoys the many hikes through deserted areas, the sailing trips she is invited on, and the nice and friendly atmosphere everywhere. She visits the old government house across the street from her hotel where the university professors meet, the pubs, coffee shops, and ethnic restaurants downtown where the young people gather, cultural centers like the Aotea Center, and the casino, with its interesting clientele. But she has not forgotten about her main goal here: To find out in what way SR Inc. is responsible for the present chaos, which is already casting its shadow over New Zealand.

It becomes one of Helen's habits to lunch near SR Inc.'s offices because many employees prefer to eat out instead of going to the cafeteria. She soon gets to know a group of SR Inc.'s programmers. She is fairly certain that they must know something about the breakdown if SR Inc. is involved. A young man named Harry seems to be the big shot among them. Apparently, his technical knowledge outweighs all of the others.

Helen still has the robot bird from Gander and the memory card it had with it. She puts the memory card into her little computer and starts it. The card is ejected immediately and the computer announces what she has already heard hundreds of times on TV. "You can only erase me if you find the private RSA key that belongs to the following public key...." This is followed by a series of 500 numbers.

She whistles in surprise. If she hadn't stopped this "bird," it would've infected Gander's computer system with a virus. 'If you want to infect all those power plants, then you have to find out how to get such a "bird" inside through a vent.' That's exactly the kind of information that Jan was sending to Marcus from Johannesburg!

Now she has a plan: she knows that Harry always leaves his office late and then walks through he park.

The next evening Helen takes a spot on a park bench with her laptop open. When she sees Harry coming, she starts to curse at it and smack it angrily. Of course, Harry notices the young, attractive woman seemingly abusing her computer. Helen is dressed simply but seductively. Harry does not fail to notice her cleavage inside her open-neck blouse.

"What's the matter?" he asks.

"I must've picked up a virus," she says, looking up to him.

"Let me take care of this", he says calmly. "I always carry the newest antivirus program with me. I guess you could say that viruses are my specialty," he laughs. Helen finds him cute in a way.

He sits down next to Helen, who gives him a slightly better view down her blouse when she hands him her computer. Helen notices how Harry pales when he reads the virus' message on the screen.

He stutters, "But...that's not possible! That's the virus that infected all of North America and Europe, but not here, we don't have this here!"

Harry is confused. After all, it was he who made it impossible for the virus to reach New Zealand over IP addresses. 'How the hell did it get on her computer? She must've gotten it from a bugged DVD. But those are zone-specific, so that's not possible either.'

"When did you first notice this virus?" Harry asks, penetrating Helen with his eyes.

Helen makes sure that he finds her attractive in every possible way. She answers, "I worked just fine until I put this memory card in."

Harry takes the card and notes the serial number, thinking, 'This is one of the cards that we equipped the self-destructing e-dragonflies with. How did this woman get this?'

"This is the exact virus that has half the world paralyzed now. Millions of computers are trying to break its code. I'm afraid you'll have to wait until someone does so. However..."

Harry steps on the brakes just in time. Of course he could help her; he knows the solution. But that would be completely irresponsible and could endanger the whole plan.

Helen notices Harry's "however." She is more certain than ever that she is on the right track. Now it is time to gamble a

225

little. "Anyway, thanks for your help. I think I'll have to see a virus specialist tomorrow. But now it's time for dinner. Thanks for your help. Bye!" She gets up, making sure to show her long, beautiful legs, and turns to walk away.

But Harry stops her "Wait a second. I forgot your name... I'm on my way to see some friends who've invited me to dinner. One of them is a virus specialist. Maybe he'll be able to help you. Just come along."

Helen smiles. "I never told you my name. I'm Helen, from Washington; the district, not the state. I'm stranded here, for obvious reasons, but you Kiwis[42] are really friendly. If it's not a problem then I'll come with you. What's your name?"

"Harry," he says, glowing. This one will really impress his friends.

And indeed his friends are impressed. Helen soon finds out that, as expected, Harry was too modest: he is really the virus specialist. Helen pretends to drink a lot, but in reality, she pours her wine into the rubber tree when she's sure that no one is watching (it will always remain a riddle for the host why the tree suddenly started growing faster). At some point she decides that this will do for now. "I think I'd better go now," she slurs.

Harry immediately assures her that he will accompany her.

Helen thanks him with a kiss. "You're a darling, as usual."

Harry does not understand the "as usual" part, but it definitely earns him the respect of his friends; for the whole evening, Helen has played a super-sexy role and now has them all wrapped around her finger. It was not so difficult with a bunch of sex-starved computer freaks.

When they leave, Helen holds onto Harry's arm, pretending to be having some difficulty walking. Harry lives nearby.

"A cup of coffee will do you good," Harry suggests.

After they have coffee, Helen seems to sober up a little. She embraces him and kisses him, and when Harry gets a little more

---

[42] A friendly nickname for New Zealanders, also the name of New Zealand's national bird which cannot fly. However, the Kiwifruit is called "Zespri" in New Zealand.

courageous, she lets him cop a feel or two. "It's already so hot here in the spring. I think I need a shower. Don't you too?"

Harry cannot believe his luck. Soon he is running his eyes over Helen's beautiful body. Helen also likes what she sees, but when she plays drunk again, Harry suggests, "You shouldn't walk anywhere tonight. Why don't you stay here? You can have my bed. I'll sleep in the living room."

Helen is almost moved by that. After the way she has acted, he should have been sure he was getting her into bed, and he has turned her offer down. But she doesn't want him to go without her! When they have almost reached the peak of pleasure, Helen stops him for a moment and looks him in the eye. Suddenly, Harry notices that she is not just a drunk pick up. He returns her look, and says a bit insecurely, "You played with me. You're completely sober, aren't you?"

Helen sees her success in danger, but somehow, she doesn't want to lie to Harry any longer. "Maybe I'm even more sober than you, but I'd really love you to continue. Please promise to give me an honest answer to a simple question. Please trust me. I won't use it against you."

Harry nods, eagerly awaiting the question.

"Is it true that you are the one person on this planet who knows the most about this virus?"

Harry inhales deeply. He knows that he is about to break his promise to Marcus, a man he respects deeply. But somehow he trusts this woman, and should he fail, he'll have to live with the consequences."

"Yes," he says.

"Thank you, Harry. I was pretty sure you were. But now I'm 100% sure that I want to make love to you. Please show me the way."

The next days are like a dream for the two of them. They can share so much. They spend half of the nights in Irish pubs and the other half in bed. They spend most of their days by the sea and have so much to talk about. Helen shows Harry the bird and tells him about her research. Harry tells her about the virus and the reasons that he thinks Marcus has for unleashing it. Helen realizes that Harry trusts Marcus completely and that he is

227

willing to take full responsibility for telling her about the virus. Helen believes that Marcus has only good intentions, but she's not convinced that such measures should be taken in order to reach any goal, however noble.

On October 30th, fifteen days after the breakdown, the virus is decoded by a computer in New Zealand. Slowly, the worldwide situation is improving.

By now Helen has read the PM's book and appreciates most of her views. She is happy to see that the UN makes resolutions concerning all her principles. For reasons of domestic politics perhaps, every country eagerly ratifies the resolutions. But Helen still cannot approve of the methods that SR Inc. used to pave the way for the PM's success, even though it is beneficial for the entire human race. 'The end doesn't justify the means' is still her motto. She is convinced that it is necessary to write and expose for the Washington Post.

"Please talk about this with my boss," begs Harry.

"He won't even give me an appointment."

"I promise you, if you call his secretary and tell her that your name is Helen, that you work for the *Washington Post,* and that you know everything about the virus, you'll get an appointment in a New York minute. If you don't get an appointment in the next three days, then go ahead and do whatever you want. But if you do get an appointment, then please meet with him... and let me come along too."

Helen agrees. Two hours later, she gets her appointment. A Moller picks her up in Auckland and takes her to Great Barrier Island.

Marcus is waiting for her in a comfortable room overlooking the ocean. He welcomes Helen and Harry. "Our computer genius and a great guy." They are served tea, coffee, and apple strudel. Maria stops by to hug Harry and tells him how happy she is about his new girlfriend.

Helen is not willing to play along. She doesn't want to be lulled, and she notices that Harry trusts Marcus more than anyone should ever trust another person.

Marcus begins, "Thanks for coming. But let me say two things first. No one can be trusted completely. That's a pity, but that's the way it is. I know Harry trusts me completely and when he leaves here today, he'll understand that that was a mistake. Anyone can make a mistake, no matter how many good things he's done. The end never justifies the means. Second, you should believe in and love others. I believe in Harry and I love him like I love most of my long-time colleagues, even though I know that he broke his promise. But I believe in him and I know that he must have had good reasons. You are the reason, Helen. You're very pretty, but trust me, I know that Harry can see more deeply."

Helen is obviously disconcerted, but Marcus doesn't let her go. "I know that I surprised you with this, Helen. Let me be frank with you. I know a lot about you. I know that you made friends with Jan in order to get a peek at our plans. I also know that you were in Gander and captured one of our drones, which would normally have self-destructed. But you don't know that we have a supercomputer that can do even more than Harry, and that even Harry knows it. This computer showed us a simulation about how the world in the years 2080 to 2084 would look if nobody interfered. I want you to see the simulation and how we proceeded afterwards. Then we can talk."

They watch the whole simulation; only the details about "THE WE" are omitted.

After four hours Marcus comes back into the room. "Helen, do you understand now why we did what we did?"

Helen nods half-heartedly. "Wasn't it an Austrian poet who wrote, 'Justice can never becomes injustice and injustice is never right?' Whatever you did, shows that you don't believe these words. You seem to believe that injustice is sometimes justified, namely when it averts catastrophe."

Marcus responds more sharply than Helen expected. "There are a lot of beautiful words that sound like absolute truth, but sometimes you have to adapt them to the circumstances. Words are weaker than deeds. Do you really want to talk about literature now or what? I know you're a Catholic; how many of the Ten Commandments have you really followed lately? I don't want you to confess here, but be honest with yourself and admit that you've broken a lot of those wonderful, hollow words."

For a long time they all remain silent. Almost simultaneously, Helen and Harry begin to speak. "We understand, Marcus; we're on your side. But why did you show us all this? Isn't that a bit dangerous for you?"

Marcus waves them off. "I need you both. We've just avoided a catastrophe, but we're running directly into a new one. Just let me show you something." Marcus reaches into his vest pocket and takes out three dried out mosquitoes. Harry and Helen look at them, more than a bit confused.

Marcus continues, "Those aren't real mosquitoes; they're flying robots. We don't know who produced them or why. The drones we've developed are already scary, but someone seems to be much further along than we are. I'm afraid all this is not a game, but close to what you see in James Bond movies: a grasp for world power. Just like in those science fiction books and movies, just like the MoM in the simulation, and he got pretty close. We have to find out who or what's behind this. We could really use you on our team. Are you in?"

Helen remembers her first evening with Harry and says, "Yes, we're in."

Harry nods.

"But we're only in on one condition," she continues. "You have to answer one simple question."

Marcus curiously lowers his head.

"What would you do if we said no?"

Marcus laughs. "Cynthia has heard everything, so in such a case, she would make you forget everything you just heard and your entire knowledge about the virus. Sorry."

Helen jumps up. "I knew it! But I like working with honest people. Now I'm really on your side, like Harry always was and always will be. You can trust us."

Marcus smiles. "Well, we've already agreed that you shouldn't trust anyone completely, but let's make the best of it.

Information on Books in the XPERTS Collection

All books are available in German from Freya Pub.Co., see www.freya.at and can be ordered via all good bookstores, but most easily via www.iicm.edu/Xperts . All English versions can be ordered through www.booklocker.com . However, due to the high shipping costs, international customers outside the US and within the European Union can order "The Paradoppelganger" and "The Paranet" at lower cost through www.iicm.edu/Xperts . Within the US, Booklocker is the best source. Outside the US readers are encouraged to either neglect the high postage ☺ or to buy the e-book versions from www.booklocker.com : No delay, no postage, lower price, and you just download the file, and print it out locally.

Here is a summary of the books in the Xperts Series currently or soon available. The series is growing rapidly. All books, where no author is mentioned I have written myself. For the others I have written a 'script' and edited the resulting book. If you have any questions, suggestions, or are interested in becoming one of the authors of a book in the Xperts Series, contact me at hmaurer@iicm.edu . If you want to find out more about me than you ever cared to read, consult www.iicm.edu/maurer . I will answer all emails (nothing worse than being ignored) except if I am really down ☺ .

Note that although there is a thread through the books (some persons appear in each book) the novels are completely self-contained and can be read independently of each other in any order. Those marked bold are available as of 2004. I have arranged the book in more or less chronological order (according when they take place), so this might be an obvious order to read them. But, feel free to start with anyone that tickles you!

"Xperts: The Telekinetic": In a way, this is the first book in the collection. The student of physics, Marcus, discovers that he has telekinetic and timewarping powers, and uses them to seduce girls, to make money, and to help people. He is also very much aware how dangerous this 'parability' can be for him. He is eventually captured by a para-militrary group of the European Union with dubious motives, and manages to escape only with the help of his girl friend Maria, who will be his big love for life. They flee to New Zealand to start a new existence. Marcus and Maria (and other persons) are the thread that holds the Xperts Series together....

"Xperts: The Paradoppelganger": This is another novel involving Marcus and Maria. Their daughter Lena discovers a strange para-gifted person. In the process of trying to make him join the group the reader visits Brazil and Europe, and is drawn into historic mysteries, extending back in history even to the Egyptian pyramids. This novel also gives a glance at what future PCs and the Net might look like... a tribute to the fact that the Editor (and author of this book) is a computer science professor. However, don't get turned off: this is a novel not a scientific book!

"Xperts: The Paracommunicator" (by Jennifer Lennon): Aroha, a young Maori woman, finds half of an ancient device in the hills near Auckland, New Zealand. Herb, also of Maori origin, independently finds the other half. Their function, and that of the mysterious black 'stones', cannot be fully understood. However, on a dangerous mission in Africa (Namibia), given to them by Marcus, it is clear that neither Aroha nor Herb would have survived without the help of the strange artifact.

"Xperts: The Parashield" (by Sam Osborne): The West-Australian Ryan finds out, as he grows up, that he can shield himself and other persons nearby, by creating through mental powers an impenetrable shield of energy. If not for his girlfriend Hannah who has some awesome 'parabilities' his enemies would eliminate him before the team of Marcus can intervene. This novel is written with a South-Western Australian background and the suspense and complexity increases as it develops.

"Xperts: E-Smog!" (by Ann Backhaus): An Australian researcher, Mandi, discovers by a fluke the dangerous side-effect of elector magnetic fields, as emitted by just about any electric device. With the background of an authentic description of the Australian West, of Malysia and Singapore, Mandi tries to put up an impossible fight against huge international companies, and succeeds to some extent, due to Marcus' group and her brilliant negotiating skills (release planned for 2005)

"Xperts: The Parawarriors": We are in the year 2019. A nuclear war between Pakistan and India seems to be unavoidable. Marcus and his team try to avoid the worst, at horrific costs. All efforts seem to be in vain. Yet, after interludes in India, Bali and La Reunion some form of normality returns, only to be disturbed (or helped?) by super-computers from an ancient civilization millions of years ago, and a strange intelligent animal "The They" that remains a mystery for a long time.

"Xperts: The Param@ils" (by Peter Lechner): This novel gives a different twist to the Xperts Series: the economy is all that matters! A story of intrigues, human emotion and some strange emails capture the attention of the readers, with Marcus' group again playing a pivotal role in solving a complex scheme. (In preparation)

"Xperts: The Paranet": In 2080 the then existing network of computers breaks down completely, throwing the world into total chaos. This novel shows how dependent we are going to be on computers and computer networks, and how civilization will virtually cease to exist if such a total breakdown ever happens at a stage when mankind is

'Sufficiently networked'. Billions of people are about to die, is there any hope for them? Yes, by mounting a terrorist attack in the past!

"Xperts: Supervision": Big brother with cameras, flying cameras, intelligent databanks and total security is catching up on us. This is a chilling novel, with a bright line of hope shown on the horizon, if we just decide to act NOW. (In preparation)

Check the Website www.iicm.edu/Xperts to stay up-to-date on all developments concerning books in the XPERTS Collection.

A Preview of...
XPERTS: The Parawarriors

1.   The Second Nuclear War?

December 2019

For seventy-four years, mankind has restrained itself from using nuclear weapons. The devastating effects they had on Hiroshima and Nagasaki weighed heavily on our minds. This restraint is now coming to an end.

In May 2019, the civil war in the Indian province of Jammu and Kashmir has once again reached critical mass. Of India's twenty-eight provinces, Jammu and Kashmir is the only one with a strong Muslim majority; almost two thirds of its population practice Islam, while Hindus dominate in all the other provinces. Contrary to the Indian law, Hindu fundamentalists have been trying to win a direct influence on the legislature for almost twenty years. Because of the growing number of Muslim fundamentalists, the situation in Jammu and Kashmir has been becoming increasingly tense.

There is no doubt that Pakistan supports the Muslim agitators. The border between India and Pakistan has been closed since June 2019, diplomatic relations between the two countries are frozen, and another war is in the air. Pakistan seems to be just waiting for the Islamic rebels gain control of most of Kashmir, and despite massive military efforts on the part of the Indian government, their success can no longer be ruled out.

December 8, 2019, 8:00 Delhi Time

Tired and dejected, Indian Prime Minister Arun Vajassa enters his office in Delhi. Several worrying phone calls interrupted his sleep. The reports he finds on his desk confirm his worst fears: his government is losing control over Jammu and Kashmir.

There is no longer much room left for reasonable solutions. Over the past few weeks, Vajassa has tried to persuade the UN and the superpowers to act as a mediator between his country and Pakistan. Unfortunately, his efforts failed because this 'civil war' is considered an internal Indian issue, unlike the earlier open wars over Kashmir. Vajassa cannot help thinking back to the last international effort to try to resolve the conflict at Kashmir Conference two years ago. Vajassa still remembers what General Ibn Muhammed Yussin, who still governs Pakistan, said in a private conversation there: "Six wars over Kashmir have not won us the province, but, should our Islamic brothers ever come to power there, and should they ask us for help, we'll be there for them. And we will make sure that there is no resistance from your side: our nuclear weapons will be aimed at every large Indian city."

For the last two years, and despite international protest, the number of Indian and Pakistani nuclear arms has sharply increased. Would General Yussin really carry out his threat? After all, Pakistan has held the nuclear first strike doctrine since 1988.

Suddenly, Vajassa's thoughts are interrupted by a knock on his door. His secretary tells him that the General Staff has been waiting for quite a while now. Vajassa looks at his watch. It's already 9:20. He has been brooding over the situation for more than an hour, and has already kept his generals waiting for twenty minutes.

He rushes to the conference room. It is clear that the meeting will be unusually tense. The air force general in charge of the nuclear arsenal summarizes the situation:

"Unfortunately, I have mostly bad news. Let me start with the worst. Pakistan has moved an unexpectedly large number of nuclear weapons from Dalbandin, their test area in northern Baluchistan, to the missile silos close to Dalbandin and southwest of Islamabad. We have to face the fact that this would allow Pakistan to wipe out all large Indian cities. A first strike could kill two hundred million of our people. The radioactive contamination and the breakdown of any infrastructure would probably spell the end of our country."

Vajassa remains composed. "This news does not come unexpectedly, but we seem to have reached a new level now. How about the situation in Kashmir?"

"Terrible. We've lost control of most of Jammu and Kashmir. Massive Pakistani forces have gathered at the Line of Control. They have 2000 tanks and 280,000 men there. We don't have much to counter that, but we do have thirty percent of our entire armed forces at the southern border of the province. If we were to go in, we'd be sure to face huge resistance. We know that the rebels have long been preparing to blow up bridges and other strategic targets in such a case. We have reports that almost 800,000 Hindus have been arrested over the past several days in order to guarantee that the majority of the population supports the rebellion. The rebels have taken over the radio station in Srinagar. They keep calling for more support and are now officially asking Pakistan for assistance. And Pakistan seems to be preparing to acquiesce."

Vajassa pales: the words of the Pakistani general still echo in his head. So they will march in! Indian forces will not be able to stop them. Should we just give them Jammu and Kashmir without a fight? No! That is unthinkable. They would kill all the Hindus there. And who knows what the Hindus in "the rest of India" would do to those one hundred million Muslims living in India in retaliation! That could even force Iran and other Islamic powers into the conflict.

Jammu and Kashmir must be defended: India has no option but victory, and after all, India's army is, as a whole, superior to Pakistan's. Shouldn't that guarantee success? Pakistan has desperately tried to match India's military strength, but they realized that they could never keep up with an opponent who is economically five times stronger. That is why General Yussin threatened to take India's cities as nuclear 'hostages'.

The members of the General Staff wait for Vajassa's reaction. They know that he has to make a difficult decision. Following an ancient Indian ritual, he breathes deeply seven times. Then he speaks:

"We have no choice. The very existence of our country is in danger. We must eliminate the nuclear weapons in Pakistan." The generals gasp. They know what this means.

The Prime Minister Continues, "We will arm the missiles we have in Chandipur[43] with nuclear warheads and destroy the two bases in Pakistan. How quickly can we do that?"

Without hesitation, General R. Rao answers: "It will take about three hours before we can launch the rockets from Chandipur–2 p.m. would be realistic. Our base in the Thar desert could be ready even faster."

The Prime Minister shakes his head. "The Thar base is too dangerous. Pakistan could already be trying to neutralize it at this very moment. They would find it much harder to deal with our base on the East Coast; they have only a few inaccurate medium-range missiles there and cannot deliver the warheads to more distant targets."

They all nod. This argument has been discussed very often.

Vajassa continues, "Begin preparing for the destruction of the bases. Use impact detonators to minimize the radioactive contamination in the area. Don't forget, we don't want to destroy Pakistan; we only want to get rid of their nuclear weapons. At a little after 2 p.m. General Rao and I will activate the nuclear weapons via a high security connection. Even though we're in a hurry, we have to make sure that Pakistan has no idea that our first strike on its way; otherwise, the first strike could be on us."

In spite of this last warning, Vajassa knows that Pakistan and other countries, will soon know about their preparations: it will be a race against time. If Yussin carries out his threat and rains nuclear bombs over India before they can stop him, it could spell the end of the subcontinent. The nuclear fallout could also mean the end of the world.

---

[43] Chandipur nuclear base on the coast of Orissa province

December 8, 2019, 11:00 a.m. Islamabad time.

In a bombproof bunker in Islamabad, General Ibn Muhammed Yussin, President of Pakistan, discusses his plans for an invasion of Kashmir with his general staff.

Suddenly, General Massuda bursts into the room. "The Indians are opening their silos on the East Coast! They're getting ready to attack!"

"Are you certain? Are those the only silos they're preparing?"

But the agents's reports all agree: whatever the Indians are planning, it is not merely a major attack, but a nuclear assault on Pakistan's nuclear arsenal.

Yussin is horrified. He had always thought that threatening Vajassa two years ago was enough to keep him from having to take any extreme actions. He had hoped that this would force Vajassa to accept the Pakistani annexation of Kashmir. He was wrong. He knows exactly what the Indians have in mind: they "only" want to eliminate his nuclear weapons and then lead a conventional war in defense of Jammu and Kashmir. India's military strength would guarantee success in this case.

Not even for a second does Yussin consider giving in. He could still prevent an Indian nuclear assault by halting the invasion of Kashmir, contacting Vajassa and agreeing to the nuclear disarmament treaty that has long been on the table. But wouldn't he lose face that way? Without hesitation, Yussin decides to set the course for the greatest catastrophe in the history of mankind:

"There is no way we can prevent the nuclear attack but our enemies will have to pay the price. I order you to aim all available nuclear missiles at targets in India, including all their large cities. Make sure to set the bombs to explode at the optimal altitude to guarantee maximum destruction. When can we launch them?"

"We are already prepared. The first missiles can be in the air by 1330 hours, but...won't the Indians retaliate with all their might?"

"Not if we destroy them immediately and completely. Our attack will hit them so fast that they will no longer be able to

239

launch their missiles. They are the same kind of weaklings as the USA. They made sure that they need two authorities to activate their nuclear weapons."

They interrupt the meeting of the general staff to initiate the attack. The generals cannot keep from shuddering: even if Yussin's plan is successful, they'll still murder hundreds of millions of civilians. The radioactive fallout will contaminate their own land, and rest of the whole world.

India's preparations are noticed in other countries too. However, everyone underestimates the seriousness of the situation. What they don't know is that both sides will launch their missiles at the same time: 1330 in Islamabad is the same time as 1400 in Delhi.

The superpowers have so far considered this confrontation to be just like all the others in the region's long history of conflict. Now, they are slowly beginning to realize the weight of the situation. The lines of communication run hot. There is enormous pressure on India and Pakistan. Soon it is clear that Pakistan will not withdraw. Under these circumstances, some governments even empathize with India's decision to launch a preemptive strike.

Even New Zealand gets into the matter. The Prime Minister contacts her man in Pakistan: "We're in a state of Emergency. The Indians are activating Chandipur; the Pakistanis are activating both their big nuclear bases. Have all precautions been taken yet?"

She gets a hasty response: "Yes, besides the usual uncertainties. We also know that the missiles will be launched at exactly 2 p.m. Delhi time. Let's hope for the best."

The PM thanks her "communications agency" on Great Barrier Island[44] for putting together the secure connection. It's late in the evening in New Zealand and the PM knows that a long

---

[44] An island just of the coast of Auckland

night is yet to come. Difficult telephone calls to the USA, Russia, and China lie ahead of her. The governments of these countries will be stunned by her optimism.

December 8, 2019, 14:00, Delhi

General R. Rao reports to the Indian Prime Minister Arun Vajassa: "Everything is ready in Chandipur. We can now initiate the launch sequence." …

Continued in XPERTS: The Parawarriors

Printed in the United States
25560LVS00004B/1-60

9 781591 135296